P9-BYR-920

VANISHED

SHEELA CHARI

DISNEY • HYPERION BOOKS
NEW YORK

First Edition
1 3 5 7 9 10 8 6 4 2

V567-9638-5-11152

Printed in the United States of America

Designed by Joann Hill

Library of Congress Cataloging-in-Publication Data
Chari, Sheela.
Vanished / Sheela Chari. — 1st ed.
p. cm.
Summary: Eleven-year-old Neela must solve the mystery when her beautiful, but cursed, veena, a classical Indian musical instrument, goes missing.
Includes bibliographical references (p.).
ISBN-13: 978-1-4231-3163-2
ISBN-10: 1-4231-3163-0
[1. Veena—Fiction. 2. Lost and found possessions—Fiction. 3. Blessing and cursing—Fiction. 4. East Indian Americans—Fiction. 5. Mystery and detective stories.] I. Title.
PZ7.C37368Van 2011
[Fic]—dc22 2010019660

Reinforced binding

Visit www.disneyhyperionbooks.com

THIS LABEL APPLIES TO TEXT STOCK

For my mother

PROLOGUE

It was close to midnight when the last train left the station. On board sat an American woman in a fluttery shirt, a famous musician on her way to the biggest music festival in Chennai. But the festival wasn't the reason she was in India after so many years. If she could go back to the store, the shopkeeper might have the answer she was looking for.

Outside the air grew damp and foggy as the train rumbled through the darkness. The woman closed her eyes and fell asleep next to her husband, but not before wrapping her arm tightly around the instrument case on the other side of her.

At dawn the fog thickened, creating a beautiful mist over the countryside. The fog was also nature's way of covering up dusty village streets, roaming animals, and makeshift huts, brown with filth.

And then the unthinkable happened.

Several hundred feet ahead of the moving train, a large wispy mist, which wasn't mist after all but something more solid, crept across the tracks. The engineer slammed the emergency brakes, but that didn't stop the train from striking the cow, or from derailing and plunging into a ditch.

Rescue workers arrived on the scene, pulling out survivors from the wreckage. At the end of the day, one of the workers made a strange discovery.

Everyone gathered around as he unzipped the torn cover of what seemed to be an instrument case. "Not a crack, not a dent," he said in surprise.

The others stared at the stringed instrument and the figure on the peg box, which was different from anything they had ever seen. The case had been found in a car where none of the passengers survived. It seemed like a miracle, but no one was sure if it was an act of God or something sinister.

"Could it be?" wondered someone.

"Rubbish," said his supervisor, who didn't believe in curses.

But when the man came later to add a tag, the case was gone. Exhausted, he looked around the shadowy field as best as he could, then gave up and went home. It would be easier to search in the morning hours when there was light.

The next day came, but no more thought was given to the missing instrument, and it was soon forgotten, having never been officially recorded anywhere. Instead, its journey continued, passing through many hands, sounding lovely for those who could hang on to it.

CHAPTER 1

There was no place in Ms. Reese's sixth-grade class to form a circle. So when their teacher announced that they needed to make room, everyone pushed back their desks and chairs with a great clatter, curious to know what required so much space. Neela, who saw an ocean of blue carpeting open around her, wondered if she had made a big mistake.

"Dude, is that a harp?" Matt asked.

A harp! Hardly. Neela glanced at her friend Penny, who shrugged.

"A harp's flat, stupid," Amanda said. "That thing looks big and lumpy."

"Amanda," Ms. Reese reproached gently.

Neela unsnapped the case and pulled out her instrument. The class leaned in to have a look.

"This is my veena." She was going to add that it belonged to her grandmother until six months ago, when it literally arrived on her doorstep from India. But her knees began to shake, so she sat down and crossed her legs lotus-style, hoping no one would notice.

"So tell us more." Ms. Reese flashed her smile where the skin crinkled around her eyes. It was the smile she reserved for students who were about to humiliate themselves.

Neela looked through her note cards. Would anyone want to know about Guru, the veena maker who put his initials on the neck of every instrument he made, and that she might even have a "Guru original"? She decided to stick with the first card. "A veena is a stringed instrument from India," she read, "dating back to the eleventh century. It's made from jackwood, and played by plucking the strings."

"What's on the top where the strings are connected?" Matt asked. "It looks like a ninja."

"It's a dragon." In spite of her shaky knees, Neela fingered the peg box proudly. "All veenas have some kind of animal decoration. It's for luck."

"Would you like to play something for us?" Ms. Reese asked. There was that smile again.

Actually, that was the last thing Neela wanted to do. She had heard about how some musicians got stage fright, but she was sure that what she had was far worse. At home she could play all the notes, and sometimes when she closed her eyes, she imagined herself in a concert hall with hundreds, even thousands of people watching her. But if there was a real, live person in the room other than her parents or her little brother, something happened, as if her notes stuck together and became an out-of-tune, out-of-rhythm mess. Something happened to her, too—shaky knees, a dry throat, and once or twice, she saw spots.

Sudha Auntie said the best cure was to keep playing in front of people. "It will teach you," she said, "to forget your nerves."

Neela wasn't sure about Sudha Auntie's theory. Just this summer, she was on the stage at the temple before her family, friends, and what seemed like the entire Indian community of Boston. She was performing for the first time on her grandmother's veena, when halfway through, a string suddenly snapped, nearly whacking her in the face. Her teacher hissed from backstage, *Keep going*. But Neela could *not* keep going; she could only look helplessly at the tittering audience. Did people laugh at an eleven-year-old mortified onstage? Yes, they did.

With that performance fresh in her mind, Neela didn't understand how she could end up bringing her veena to school. Last week when Ms. Reese announced the Instruments Around the World unit, a bunch of kids raised their hand to bring instruments no one had seen before: a Chinese dulcimer, a Brazilian *berimbau*, even a set of Caribbean steel drums. In the midst of all that hand-raising, Lynne, the new girl, turned to Neela and said, "Don't you have that really big Indian instrument? I heard you telling Penny about it." Then, before Neela knew it, she had volunteered to bring her four-foot veena to school. So here she was, with her veena, her nerves, and the whole of Ms. Reese's class watching her. Neela took a deep breath and began.

She was aware of everyone in the classroom. Penny was in the front, sitting with her feet tucked under her, as she always did. Amanda was in the back, whispering something hateful to the girl next to her. Matt was already starting to fidget. He was rocking slightly, tossing back that strange hair of his, bleached to a startling shade of orange. Then there was Lynne, the girl who had joined their class this year—was she really taking pictures? Next to them all, Ms. Reese was poised to shush, poke, prod, threaten, and restrain—whatever it took to force the class to listen to Neela until she was done.

The song was a short one Neela had learned last year about the goddess Lakshmi. There was that run of notes in the beginning and the slide all the way down to *sa* that she loved because it was like falling fast, sudden, and landing with both feet on the ground. The next notes, the high *ga-ma-pa*, were always impossible to hit. And then as she continued, she noticed the sound of her grandmother's veena, which was normally so rich and woody, became twangy—maybe the room was too cold? The more she listened, the more distracted she became by the twanginess, so that her fingers forgot what they were doing. Every time she made a mistake, her face heated up until she was sure her cheeks were as pink as Amanda's painted fingernails.

"Thank you," Ms. Reese said to the beet-faced Neela when it was over. "What a treat."

"Good job, Neela," Penny said, flashing a smile full of braces at her. But that was because, nice as Penny was, she didn't know a thing about how Neela felt after playing in public.

Neela tried to ignore the disappointment that filled her. It was as if there were two Neelas—the imagined one that played before hundreds of people, beautifully and effortlessly, who could hit the high ga-ma-pa every time. And the real one. With the shaky knees. The one who skipped notes, whose string snapped in public.

At least she didn't snap a string this time. She began to put away her veena, then stopped in surprise when she saw a small group around her.

Matt was the first person who asked to try her veena. He strummed a few notes, then pretended to do a rock-star riff. "You should get this wired and plug it into an amp. An electric veena—that'd be awesome."

"Yeah," Neela said, though it was the weirdest suggestion she had ever heard.

Penny was next. "How do you even lift the whole thing?" she asked.

"It's big, but it isn't heavy. It's mostly hollow. See?" Neela showed Penny by raising the veena up with one hand.

"Can I try playing?" Amanda asked.

Neela was surprised. Amanda, the girl who changed her nail color every day, who still called Neela "Salad Head" because she wore coconut oil in her hair maybe once in third grade? Interested in her veena?

"Um, sure," Neela said. She felt a cloud of fruity perfume envelop her as Amanda bent down, plucking each string with a single, nail-polished finger.

"What's this mark?" Amanda asked.

"It looks like a scratch," Penny said.

"Oh, that. It's the veena maker's initials. My teacher says the veena is a Guru original." Neela couldn't help flushing with pride.

Amanda nodded, not all that interested. "I was talking to my mom," she said, "and I might have a—" Before she could finish, she yelped, pulling her hand back from the floor.

Behind her stood the last person waiting for a turn. Lynne had knelt down with her camera, not noticing she had stepped on Amanda's hand. "Your veena is cool. I love the dragon," she gushed to Neela. She took a few shots from different angles.

Amanda stood up, glaring.

"Nice, uh, camera," Neela said.

Lynne sniffed. "It's junk. What I really want is an SLR with a telephoto and zoom lens."

Neela blinked.

"Someone needs to wear thicker glasses," Amanda announced loudly to Penny, while rubbing her hand. Penny glanced at Lynne to see what she'd say.

Lynne's eyes flashed behind her tortoiseshell frames. "Someone needs to wear less hairspray," she retorted.

Before Amanda could answer, Ms. Reese asked everyone

to move their desks back. “Amanda, Penny—that means you. Lynne, time to put away the camera.”

Penny returned to her desk. So did Amanda, but not before glaring at Lynne, who stuck out her tongue at her.

“I guess you must really like your veena,” Lynne said as Neela put the veena away.

“Um, sure. It’s my grandmother’s. She gave it to me.”

“So you’ll play on it for a while and sell it afterward, huh?”

Neela sat back on her heels. “Why would I sell it? It’s my grandmother’s!”

“Oh yeah, right.”

Neela watched as Lynne returned to her desk, brushing an explosion of curls from her face. From her desk she pulled out a notebook and wrote something down.

Strange, Neela thought. But Lynne was a strange person in general. She didn’t talk much to anyone, although sometimes she would smile and say a few words to Neela. Most of the time she was writing stuff in her notebook or doodling on the back cover. At recess she would take photos of dandelions or cracks in the pavement or anything else that most people didn’t bother looking at.

Neela sat down at her desk, thinking again about her performance. Whenever she felt depressed about her playing, she tried to remember Lalitha Patti, her grandmother, who had mysteriously mailed the veena to her a few months ago.

Lalitha Patti was the other musician in the family and

the reason Neela chose to learn the veena three years ago. Her grandmother wasn't a professional and hadn't given a public performance in her life. But she loved the veena and owned several, which she kept on stands in a separate room in her house. When Lalitha Patti played, the world seemed to stop. So intense and focused was her playing that she hardly seemed to know anyone else was in the room.

Once her grandmother stared in amazement as Neela tried to explain stage fright to her. "Why do you have to play in front of anyone at all?" Lalitha Patti exclaimed.

"But I thought . . ." Neela's voice trailed off because she didn't know what she thought.

"Shut yourself off in your room," Lalitha Patti said. "Learn to play for yourself first, and the rest will come. You'll see."

Play for yourself. Neela remembered those words now as she sat at her desk. What Lalitha Patti said made sense. Still, what was the point of having a beautiful veena if you were too scared to play in front of anyone?

Outside, the October sky turned dark as Neela started home, the wheels on her veena case squeaking against the pavement. The case, designed by her father's friend, was a hard plastic shell covered with thick canvas, but the wheels made it easy to drag. Some days she walked with Penny, but most of the time she walked by herself because Penny got a ride with her mother. But Neela didn't mind. It gave her a chance to reflect over the day before she got home.

As she walked today, she thought about the way the veena had first come into her life. It was a Saturday morning in April. The tulips were in bloom, with splashes of yellow and pink along the walkway behind the mailman who came to deliver the package. He brought it inside, and after her mother signed for it, the whole family crowded around, wondering what on earth it could be.

The box was large and padded, bigger and taller than Neela, with *Fragile* and words in Hindi stamped across several places in purple ink, smudged but official-looking. The package was addressed to her from Lalitha Patti, care of Chennai Music Palace.

When Neela opened it, the whiff of India assailed her nose—that mysterious combination of laundry detergent and mothballs and coconut oil. After digging through layers of Bubble Wrap and foam, her parents helped her pull out a veena and set it on the wooden floor of their living room. On the ground, it rocked slightly from side to side, as if impatient to begin its new life in Arlington.

"Chennai Music Palace?" Mrs. Krishnan said, amazed. "Your mother bought Neela a new veena?"

But Neela had recognized the instrument right away. "Not a new veena!" she exclaimed. "It's one of hers."

Mr. Krishnan looked at the veena and then inside the box to see if there was a note, but except for the packaging, the box was empty. "She didn't *tell* me she was mailing anything," he said, baffled.

"Maybe it has something to do with what happened last month," Mrs. Krishnan said.

In March, someone broke into Lalitha Patti's house in India and stole one of her veenas—her most expensive one with inlaid rubies, coral, and emeralds.

"I'm calling my parents," Mr. Krishnan said. As he dialed, Neela knelt beside the veena, fingering the long neck and sweeping curve of the dragon peg box. Out of all the veenas her grandmother owned, this one was Neela's favorite. It wasn't nearly as fancy as the veena with the jewels, and its wood was dark and more faded than all the others in Lalitha Patti's collection. But it was quite old, with intricate carving along the neck and face, and the frets were made from bronze instead of the customary brass. Most of all, Neela loved the peg-box dragon. Unlike most other veenas that had only a dragon's head, this one had a complete body with wings folded down and a pair of legs and tail painted along the sides. With its slanting eyes, pointy face, and curling tongue, the dragon was the fiercest-looking one in Lalitha Patti's collection. It didn't even seem Indian, but like a creature from the time of King Arthur and the knights of the Round Table.

Neela could hear her father talking behind her. "But why?" he asked. "She's only been playing for a few years. It's too fancy for her." There was a silence as he disappeared into the kitchen, his voice becoming a murmur. Several minutes later he came back to the living room.

"Is it from Chennai Music Palace?" Mrs. Krishnan asked.

"No. She's friends with someone there who helped her ship it, that's all."

Mrs. Krishnan looked at him with more questions in her eyes, but he shook his head. "Here," he said to Neela. "She wants to speak to you."

Neela took the phone from him and couldn't stop talking. "It's beautiful, my favorite, thank you, how could you know . . . What made you? Why?"

All to which her grandmother said, "Enjoy, Neela. Just take very good care of it." For a moment Neela thought she heard something else in her grandmother's voice, a note of caution. But then Lalitha Patti only said, "And keep up your practicing."

Practicing! She could hardly wait.

At Neela's next lesson, Sudha Auntie's face scrunched up as if she were savoring a piece of rich chocolate in her mouth.

"What?" Mrs. Krishnan asked. "Something bad?"

Neela's teacher smiled in delight. "Look at the initials on the neck. It's a Guru original."

"A what?" Mrs. Krishnan asked.

"Guru—he made this veena. Didn't your mother mention it to you?" Sudha Auntie asked.

Mr. Krishnan shook her head. "Not exactly. Actually, she—*oomph.*" Mrs. Krishnan had stepped on his foot. He looked at her and fell quiet.

"Sorry," Mrs. Krishnan said.

"I'm surprised, when getting a Guru original is such a

catch." Sudha Auntie peered at the dragon. "And I've never seen a peg box like this—you've got a whole dragon here! But I guess Guru did things his own way."

"Does it play well?" Mrs. Krishnan said. "That's all that matters."

"What's so great about Guru?" Neela asked.

"Why, he was a legend," Sudha Auntie sputtered. "He did everything by hand, and he knew how to pick the right wood. It's even said that he had a special carving tool from God that he found in the Kaveri River one day after meditating."

Mr. Krishnan grinned. "At least it didn't need batteries."

"So Guru was famous," Neela said, ignoring her dad. It would be cool to own a veena made by a famous person.

"Famous? Yes, though not in the way you'd imagine," her teacher said gravely.

She was about to say more when Mrs. Krishnan spoke up. "What Sudha Auntie is trying to say is that you should consider yourself very lucky," she said.

"It's not every day a kid gets such an instrument," her teacher said. "You'll have to be responsible." She said this in an extra-stern way, as if she thought Neela spent most of her time being the opposite.

But Neela was used to Sudha Auntie's remarks, so she just nodded, which was the easiest way to ignore her teacher. And that was how after three years of practicing on Sudha Auntie's student veena, Neela suddenly came to have a veena of her own. Not any veena, but an old, lovely one, made by a legendary craftsman, and a gift from her grandmother. Now if she could only play on it without humiliating herself.

Neela reached Winthrop Street and pulled a bag of chips out of her backpack. She continued walking, enjoying the sharp, salty taste of fried potato melting in her mouth. Around her the autumn leaves swirled along the pavement, and the wind whipped the tree branches back and forth. She was watching the waving branches when she thought she heard something behind her like the sound of a twig breaking. She turned around. But no one was there, only a weeping willow fluttering wildly against the wind.

Then, just as she passed the stone church where she had her art class, it started. One by one the drops fell, then another and another, until the splashes felt bigger and bigger against her skin. Suddenly there was a clap of thunder, and the rain came down like a great avalanche of water.

Neela had never seen so much rain in her life. She ran, dragging the veena behind her until she spotted an archway over the front doors of the stone church. Under the narrow overhang she escaped the pounding rain and was able to catch her breath.

Now she understood the expression to "look like a drowned rat." In just a few minutes her ponytail had come undone, with most of her hair plastered to her face in wet, heavy locks. Outside the arch, the rain continued as street gutters swelled, and puddles collected along the sidewalk like ponds. She leaned against the big wooden door and wiped her face with her sleeve, which did little, since her sleeve was just as drenched as the rest of her.

How long would it rain? As she wondered this, the front door opened. Surprised, Neela turned around and found a silver-haired man standing in the doorway. He was remarkably lean and tall, wearing a hunter-green argyle vest; neat, dark wool pants; and a cream-colored linen shirt with a crisp collar. His vest, pants, and even his shirtsleeves were wet, along with the rest of him.

"So, you're here," he said. And then he revealed another strange thing about himself. Instead of having a beautiful voice to match his elegant clothing—Neela would have guessed something European—she was taken aback to hear a thick, throaty Boston accent: *Ya heya.*

Neela shivered. "I was just waiting for the rain to stop," she said. I should go home, she thought. She was only two streets away. But it was still raining hard. What if the rain leaked into her veena case by the time she got home?

The man cleared his throat. "I saw you from inside. Why don't you come in before you turn to soup?"

The image of herself turning to soup was so odd she laughed. The man laughed too, the lines softening around his mouth in a friendly way. He seemed nice. It would be so good to get out of the cold for a few minutes. She could feel water squishing between her toes.

Still, she hesitated. She had always been told never to go

anywhere with a stranger. She looked at the rain again. It was coming down just as heavily, as she saw pinecones, leaves, and even someone's notebook wash along the sidewalk.

"It could be a long time before the rain lets up," the man said mildly. "And the church certainly doesn't mind."

"I guess I could come in for a while," she said. She reached for her case.

"What's that?"

"My instrument. I can't leave it outside."

He opened the door wider and she stepped in, engulfed by warm air and the scent of something sweet like dried herbs. Curious, she looked around. She had entered a vestibule that connected the chapel to the rest of the building. She'd never been here before, always using the basement entrance for her art class. The ceiling was high, and from it hung a single domed chandelier. Except for the chandelier, the only other light came from the chapel.

The man pointed to a coatrack. "Hang your jacket there. You can store your instrument next to it." Neela took off her coat, glad to be rid of the dripping thing.

"I'm making hot cocoa in the kitchen," he continued. "Would you like some?"

"I love cocoa," she admitted. She wheeled her veena behind her.

The man stopped. "For heaven's sake, you can leave your instrument right there. It's so big, I wonder if it will even fit through the kitchen door."

Neela hesitated. "I'd rather not."

"Nothing will happen. You're in a church." When he saw she hadn't changed her mind, he said, "Would you rather leave it in the closet?" He led her to a coat closet farther down the hall. "This is where I hang my things. You can put it next to my coat."

Neela made sure that her veena fit neatly inside the closet. "Thank you," she said, relieved. "It's just that I don't normally go outside with it." She felt much better about coming in from the rain.

The old man smiled. "I completely understand. But don't worry," he said to her as she followed him inside. "Your veena will be safe. You have my word."

CHAPTER 2

The old man's shoes left watery prints as Neela followed him down the hall to the kitchen. She wondered again why he was wet. If he had things hanging in the closet, then maybe he worked in the church. But then shouldn't he have been indoors before the rain started?

"You're sure it's okay?" she asked.

"Have a seat," he said as if he hadn't heard her. "What a day. Got caught in the rain, too. Not that I mind. I'm used to far worse."

Neela listened, fascinated by the sound of his words: *I'm yusta faa waas.* The plumber who came to fix the garbage disposal last week talked the same way. She tried to remember the way this man spoke so she could imitate him for her best friend, Pavi, later. The trick was to drop the r's.

"You want a towel for your hair?" he asked. "You've got so much of it there."

Neela patted her hair self-consciously, realizing she was a mess. "Um, no, thank you, I'm fine," she said. She redid her ponytail, gathering the stray ends.

He reached for a teakettle that was on a shelf built into the wall next to the burners. The kettle was made from bronze and seemed old, with a black, curving handle and a spout in the shape of a strange creature. She looked more closely.

"Is that a dragon?"

The man nodded, filling the kettle with water and setting it on the stove top. Then he said something she didn't understand. "It's a wyvern." Before she could ask what he meant, he asked, "So, do you have a name?"

"It's Neela."

"Hmm. Is that an Indian name?"

Neela sat down at the counter. "How did you know?"

He looked amused. "You don't need to be Sherlock to figure it out."

Neela flushed. She knew she had what her father called classic Indian features: an oval face with high cheekbones, large eyes, and long jet-black hair. Still, it always surprised her to know that others saw this part of her first, the part she couldn't see unless she looked in a mirror.

She waited a moment and then said, "And your name, sir?"

He scooped cocoa powder into two mugs. "You can

call me Hal," he said. As they waited for the water to boil, Neela noticed a strange sound, like air being deflated out of a tire. *Phsst phsst.* Puzzled, she glanced behind her. It was coming from outside the kitchen door. *Phsst phsst.*

"Do you hear that?" she asked.

Hal looked at her. "Hear what?"

The sound stopped. At that moment, the teakettle started whistling.

"That's just the kettle," he said.

Neela frowned. It was definitely not the teakettle. In fact, she could hear it again faintly, as if it were retreating from the kitchen door. And then it was gone, and Neela almost wondered if she hadn't imagined the whole thing.

By now, Hal had poured the hot water into the mugs and finished them off with a dollop of cream from the refrigerator. As soon as Neela took a mug from him, she forgot about the sound, lacing her fingers around the hot ceramic. It felt so good to hold it in her hands, as if its warmth were seeping into her skin and spreading out to the farthest tips of her body. She looked around surreptitiously, wondering if there might be a bag of potato chips, but decided she was pushing her luck.

He sat next to her at the counter. "You're a musician?"

Neela nodded. "That's my veena I have with me. I've been playing for three years. I used to play the piano, and I've done a little voice, but it's the veena I love."

"Love?" Hal repeated. "How can a kid like you know anything about that?"

Neela felt the skin prickle along her neck the way it did when one of her parents said something completely annoying. "All the great musicians started when they were kids."

"Whooee. I can see I pushed the wrong button. Don't mind me, then." He leaned on the counter with both elbows, rubbing his temple with his fingers. "So how do you get an instrument like this? Is there a veena store in Arlington?"

"Of course not!" she said. "My grandmother sent it from India. Before that, I borrowed my teacher's veena for three years, and hers wasn't very good. I mean, it was nice she lent it to me, but I love my grandmother's veena so much more."

"Yes, love," Hal said.

Neela observed the fine arch of his eyebrows, which were the same silver gray as his hair, and the sharp slope of his strong nose. Something about him nagged at her. Somewhere, someplace, she had seen this man before. "Are you a minister here?" she asked.

Hal glanced at her in surprise. "No, I gave that all up a long time ago. I'm damn lucky I did, if I can say that in a church."

Neela tried to shrug casually, even though she felt a twinge of excitement that an adult had sworn in front of her. She was still trying to figure out where she had seen him. If he wasn't a minister, then maybe she had seen him somewhere else. His face seemed so familiar.

She looked around the kitchen. "It's a nice church. I like coming here for art class."

Hal nodded as if he knew about the class. They talked about it for a while, and Neela told him how most of the time there weren't any rules, and that was what made the class fun. "We don't get much done," she said, "but I guess it doesn't really matter."

Hal had a far-off look on his face, as if he were trying to levitate an object in a distant place. His fine eyebrows were drawn together intensely. Was he a relative of someone in her art class?

Before she could ask, he suddenly jumped up from his stool, as if the object in his mind had sprouted wings, and he was off to catch it. "I have to go," he said.

Neela looked at the clock and was astonished to see it was almost four. She was late for home by almost an hour. "Me too," she exclaimed. "Thanks for the hot cocoa. It was nice to—"

Hal cut off her compliment midsentence. "You have to wash your own mug. Use that sponge and the soap. Make sure you clean it really well. I mean, *really* well."

Then before Neela could say anything, Hal walked out a door in the back without even a glance. Neela was left staring at his departing figure and the banging-shut door. After a moment, she collected her wits. What was all *that*? And not even a good-bye?

She stood at the sink, fuming. At first she thought she'd leave her mug unwashed on the counter. But she had been raised to listen to elders, even rude ones, and her upbringing eventually won out. She turned the faucet on and looked out the window, seeing that the rain had pretty much stopped, though there was water still pouring noisily overhead from the gutters.

As she scrubbed and rinsed the soap from the mug, her annoyance at Hal slowly dribbled away. She wondered again why he seemed so familiar. It had something to do with his eyes and that expression of concentration on his face. Maybe it wasn't him she had seen before, she decided. It was that *look*.

A few minutes later, Neela was done with the mug and was about to leave when the teakettle caught her eye again. Hal had replaced it on the shelf while she drank her cocoa. What had he called it? A *why*? A why-something. It was hard to tell, with his accent. She looked at it more carefully. The dragon was made out of cast iron, with outstretched wings and scaly legs. Its face was sharp and triangular, with eyes set back high in two slits. Without thinking, Neela reached out with one finger. The dragon felt cold and smooth, except for the mouth, which was very sharp, despite its miniature size.

She slowly retraced her steps out of the kitchen to the vestibule. She wondered what she would tell her mother, who would be worried about her by now. At the coat closet, she opened the wooden folding door, still thinking of what to say at home, when she stopped. At first she thought she was mistaken. But the closet was so small, the truth was plain and simple. An awful feeling crept over her. She stared at the coat still hanging in the closet, a dark vinyl jacket that Hal had said was his, and the gaping space next to it where her veena should have been.

She searched the vestibule and then went as far as the doors of the chapel. Inside, the chapel was dark and empty, the somber-colored sky barely shining through the multicolored stained glass behind the altar. She felt a tightness in her throat as she entered, looking around the nearest pews, afraid that someone would ask her what she was doing, but looking nevertheless, wishing desperately that the veena had been moved to the chapel or else stored somewhere close by. But no matter where she looked, she found nothing.

At last she went back to the kitchen. Maybe Hal was still around; maybe he had put the veena away someplace else; maybe he had done something so explainable and obvious that the whole disaster she imagined unfolding before her would disappear instantly.

She walked back through the vestibule, continuing down the hallway to the kitchen, and opened the door through which he had left, thinking it led to another part of the church. But when she opened the door, she was dismayed to see an alley instead. There was no one there, only a long walkway with puddles of water on the ground.

"Hal?" she called out. Her voice sounded feeble to her ears, like a small pebble thrown inside an empty cavern. Beyond the alley lay the great, yawning expanse of the parking lot, with no sign of Hal or her missing veena.

CHAPTER 3

It had stopped raining when Neela trudged home. *Just take very good care of it*—her grandmother's words came echoing back to her. And now, somewhere out there, her grandmother's veena was traveling farther and farther away. Neela choked up, imagining it thrown carelessly into the back of a car, rolling around along the bumpy roads of Arlington. Her grandmother would never forgive her.

Maybe Hal had planned the whole thing, from the time he opened the door and found her, a drowned rat in the pouring rain. And yet, something didn't seem right. Sure, Hal could have tricked her, but how could he know it would rain, and how could he know she would stop at the church because of it?

Unless he was following her already. She remembered

the sound she heard walking home, like someone stepping on a twig behind her. Was that Hal? But why would he follow her? And if he did, it didn't explain how he could be in the church before her and how he seemed to know his way around. It also didn't explain why he wanted her veena.

When she climbed up the front steps of her house, the door flew open. "I was so worried!" Mrs. Krishnan hugged her hard as Neela inhaled the scent of her mother, a mixture of cardamom, flour, and Lysol.

Normally Neela would have cried at this moment, but she was distracted by the sight of her mother. "What are you wearing?" she asked.

Mrs. Krishnan had on a neon green *salwar kameez* from India, the top in a checkered pattern with sequins and gold lamé, the pant bottoms puffing out like balloons. "I'm doing laundry. It was the only clean thing I had. But who cares about me? Go put on something dry."

After Neela changed, she found her mother in the living room holding a mug of cocoa. "What?" her mother asked, seeing Neela's face. "I thought you liked cocoa." She was looking around the room. "And where did you put the veena?"

Neela had been dreading this moment. She sat on the couch and began to recount the awful story.

Before she finished, her mother interrupted. "You followed a stranger to have cocoa?" She set down the mug as if it were poison.

"Wait," Neela said. "It gets worse."

When she was done, Mrs. Krishnan had her hands up to her mouth in disbelief.

"I should have known," she said. "I should have known." Neela wondered how her mother could have known, unless she was a mind reader. But she kept quiet because then her mother said, "It's bad luck. I should have *known*."

Like strep throat or the chicken pox, or the Great Plague, which Neela had read about in social studies, bad luck was one of those things her mother tried at great lengths to avoid. She was training to be a pharmacist, and it was her belief that all human experience was the result of chemistry and luck, good and bad. But mostly bad. Neela's father, who worked in a research lab at MIT, would always exclaim, *That's so unscientific.* But there was no changing her mother's opinion. Bad luck was an impenetrable force working against them all. Worse, it was contagious.

Just then the back door jiggled as Mr. Krishnan came in. "Hello, mateys," he called, using his standard greeting. He bit into a muffin he picked up from the kitchen.

"You're home early," Mrs. Krishnan said.

"Meeting got cancelled," he said, chewing. He looked at her curiously. "Why the clown outfit?"

"Can't a person do laundry here? And we've got bigger things to worry about."

When he heard Neela's story, Mr. Krishnan stopped chewing. She wondered what happened to the piece of muffin in his mouth, whether he had swallowed it or it had spontaneously disappeared. "I don't believe it," he said. "In a *church*?"

"She shouldn't have done it," Mrs. Krishnan said.

"She didn't have a choice," he said.

"But she *did*."

"I'm sorry," Neela said miserably. It was so much worse when her parents were talking about her in the third person, as if she wasn't there.

"Are you going to tell your mother, then?" Neela's mother asked.

Mr. Krishnan shook his head. "I don't know."

Neela stared at the floor, wishing it would open up and swallow her. But the floor did no such thing. She was on her own.

Dinner consisted of *dosas*, thin crepes made from rice and lentils, accompanied by *sambar*, a thick, spicy soup. Over their dosas and sambar, Neela and her parents discussed the missing veena.

Mr. Krishnan tried to be hopeful. "Maybe it's still there at the church."

"Or maybe it vanished," Mrs. Krishnan said pointedly.

Mr. Krishnan gave her a look. "Who would steal a veena in a church?" he continued. "No one would even know what it is."

"Wait a minute." Neela thought of something. "When Hal showed me the closet where I could store the veena, he said, 'Your veena will be safe. You have my word.'"

"So?" Mrs. Krishnan said, dipping a piece of dosa in sambar.

"Don't you see? He said *veena*. But that was before we started talking about it in the kitchen. How could he know what was inside the case when it was closed?"

"Maybe he's seen one before," Mrs. Krishnan said.

"No—it's a custom-made case. *Nobody* would know what was inside."

"Where is Neela's veena?" asked four-year-old Sree.

"It's taking a nap," their mother said. "Just like you did before dinner." She pushed back a lock of his lanky, black hair that had fallen over his eyes. He was perpetually in need of a haircut because he was scared of the barber, and it was impossible for Mrs. Krishnan to cut his hair unless she had a whole bag of lollipops to bribe him with.

"Veenas don't sleep," he said.

Neela remembered something else. "And there was that teakettle."

"What teakettle?" Mr. Krishnan asked.

"The teakettle with a dragon on it. Hal used it to make my cocoa."

Sree stared at his plate and bowl. "There's a fly in my sambar."

Their mother sighed. "No there isn't, Sree."

"Don't you see?" Neela said impatiently. "The teakettle had a dragon on it . . . My veena has a dragon, too."

"Somebody stepped on the veena," Sree tried again.

"But maybe Hal didn't take your veena," Mr. Krishnan countered. "Maybe the janitor stored it somewhere."

"Neela stepped on it," Sree persisted.

"Nobody stepped on the veena," Mr. Krishnan said. "Eat your sambar, Sree."

"I'm done," Neela announced. Why didn't she see the connection before? She jumped from the table.

"You didn't finish your plate," her mother called after her.

But Neela was already halfway to the study, her thoughts leaping ahead. A dragon teakettle. A dragon veena. Maybe she could find something that connected the teakettle with the veena if she searched the Internet. And what had Hal called the dragon? A why-something.

Twenty minutes went by, and while she found pictures of veenas with dragons and dragons on teakettles, nowhere could she find anything that linked the two together. She stared at the computer screen. She had reached a dead end.

Her mother called her from the kitchen. When Neela got there, her mother held a small brass plate with a tiny piece of camphor on it. Sree was standing next to her, watching. Neela groaned. "Oh, Mom. Not that."

Sree widened his eyes. "What? What?"

"It won't hurt anyone," Mrs. Krishnan said. She said it lightly, but there was a frown on her face as if there was something else on her mind.

Sree jumped up and down. "What?"

Mrs. Krishnan lit the camphor and it burst immediately

into bright bluish-orange flames. A sweet, acrid smell filled the room. *"Drishti,"* she said.

In front of Neela, Mrs. Krishnan moved the plate with the dancing camphor flames in two circles, one clockwise and one counterclockwise.

"What's drishti?" Sree asked.

"When you drop dead because somebody wishes it," Neela said.

"Who's dead?" he wailed.

Neela's mother glared at her. "No one, Sree. *Drishti* is a word for bad luck. I just performed an *aarti* on Neela, in case someone wished her bad luck today."

Neela watched her mother. "How is that supposed to bring my veena back?" she asked skeptically.

By now the camphor had burned out, leaving a black, sooty residue on the plate. With an index finger, Mrs. Krishnan smeared a dot of the inky soot on Neela's forehead, and then Sree's. "When I was growing up, we always did this if we needed to ward off the evil eye."

"Why does somebody wish bad luck on Neela?" Sree asked.

Good question, Neela thought. Because it felt like a ton of bad luck had been dumped on her.

Mrs. Krishnan pushed the hair out of his eyes. "Sometimes we want what others have. We want them not to succeed. But I do think you can change bad luck and hope for the best."

Sree still didn't understand. "Why?"

"Maybe you can ask Lalitha Patti if we visit her in December."

"Are we going to India?" he asked.

"Are we?" Neela asked. She felt a glimmer of hope despite herself. Her best friend, Pavi, also had family in Chennai and always went there in December. Maybe Neela would get to see her if they went at the same time. Which would be good since Neela wasn't sure how Lalitha Patti would react to being around the grandchild who had lost her veena.

"I'd rather go in June," Mrs. Krishnan said, "but I may need to finish up my classes in the summer."

"So you can help people take their medicine?" Sree asked. This was his rough understanding of what pharmacy was all about.

"Yes, Sree."

As Mrs. Krishnan cleaned off the brass plate, Neela thought of all the people who could wish her bad luck. Amanda? Hal? Or was it someone else she didn't know?

That night, Neela had a hard time falling asleep. She kept thinking of Hal and the missing veena, and what her grandmother would say when she found out the awful truth. She remembered that on her visits to India, Lalitha Patti would take the veena out only on certain days, as if it was too special to use daily. And when she did, she would practice on it for hours and talk to no one. Why her grandmother would then send such a special instrument to Neela, it was hard to say. But she had, and now Neela felt that in the biggest and most terrible way, she had let her grandmother down. Was it bad luck, as her mother said? Neela wasn't sure. But her only hope was to find the veena before her grandmother heard what happened.

Neela got up from bed. The floor was cold under her feet as she made her way quietly down the hall. She would ask her mother if they could go back to the stone church tomorrow after school. They could have another look around. Maybe Neela had missed something the first time.

As she got closer to her parents' bedroom, she heard voices inside. She was about to knock on the door, when she heard her father speaking in Tamil. From the way he kept starting and stopping, she could tell he was on the phone.

He's talking to Lalitha Patti. Neela's stomach dropped in dismay. She had thought he would wait at least until tomorrow.

"Please don't worry, *Amma*," Mr. Krishnan said, using the name for mother in Tamil. He repeated this many times. At last he said, "We'll find the veena. I'm sure of it."

How he could be sure, Neela didn't know. He was just trying to make her grandmother feel better. Maybe she was really upset on the other side. Even crying. Neela felt tears rise in her own throat.

Mr. Krishnan gave a sigh that was so loud, even Neela could hear it through the door. "That's just a story, Amma. It couldn't possibly be true."

Neela swallowed her tears. What was he talking about? She heard her mother murmur something, but Neela couldn't make it out.

Then, as if he'd heard enough, Mr. Krishnan said, "All right, all right. Let me call you tomorrow. Maybe we'll find the veena by then, and you can forget about all of that."

All of what? Neela waited for her father to hang up. Maybe he and her mother would say something more afterward.

She was right. When the phone call was over, her mother was the one who started.

"I still can't believe she would send that veena to Neela," she said.

"She got spooked."

"Then she should have sold it, that's what."

"You can't sell a veena like that," Mr. Krishnan said. "It's too lovely. It's the kind of veena you hand down in the family."

"She has four other veenas!"

"But this one has the loveliest sound. You've heard my mother play on it. Maybe it's the wood, or the way it was carved. There's something special about that veena."

"There's something special, all right," Mrs. Krishnan said. "It's *cursed*."

Neela stood stock-still. Did she hear right? Did her mother say "cursed"?

"Now you're sounding like my mother," Mr. Krishnan said.

"Well, the veena did disappear. Isn't that what the curse says?"

Neela's heart started beating. She strained harder to hear them.

"There has to be some other explanation," Mr. Krishnan said.

"Even so," Mrs. Krishnan said. "Maybe it's better the veena is gone."

"What do you mean?"

"Just think. Do you really want Neela playing on a veena with a history like that?" she asked. "It's . . . bad luck. Maybe we *shouldn't* look for the veena anymore."

Neela panicked. What kind of history? Would her parents stop looking for the veena because of this curse? She almost opened the door on them, but then she heard her father.

"Lakshmi, you can't mean that. Think how much Neela loves the instrument, too."

Her mother was silent. "All right," she said at last. "We'll search the church tomorrow. After that . . . I can't promise anything."

As Neela heard her parents turn off their lights to sleep, she tiptoed quietly back to bed. Her ears were ringing with what she had just heard. The veena had a curse. And *that's* why it was gone. Neela remembered the looks her parents exchanged over dinner, the conversation between them when her father first found out: *She shouldn't have done it . . . She didn't have a choice.*

They weren't talking about her! They were talking about Lalitha Patti, about whether *she* should have sent the veena or not. All of a sudden, everything that had happened in the past twelve hours took on a new meaning. Was it Hal, or was it a mysterious curse that had made her grandmother's veena disappear from the church? Either way, would Neela ever find the veena again? She lay on her back, staring up at the ceiling. So many things to figure out, so many things to remember. It would be harder than ever to get to sleep.

CHAPTER 4

The next morning, Neela slept through her alarm and woke up groggy. And late.

Of course, this was nothing new. She was always late. Time was something mysterious and unstoppable in the Krishnan household. It was as if her whole family were in a crazy race, all of them trying to catch up, but always just missing the finish line.

"Remember, I'm picking you up after school so we can go to the church," Mrs. Krishnan called out from the car window as Neela raced inside the school yard. Neela was running so fast, all she could do was nod.

In class, she slid into her seat exactly three minutes late, her hair still tangled at the ends of her ponytail. Everyone else was already at their desks, except for Matt. He was always late, too, usually later than she was, though sometimes they both pulled up to the curb at the same time in their respective minivans.

Ms. Reese, who kept track of late minutes, raised an eyebrow at Neela. It was her teacher's rule that anyone whose late minutes added up to thirty had to stay after school to make up the "lost" minutes. By Neela's count, she was already up to twenty-five.

As their teacher handed back yesterday's spelling quizzes, Neela thought again about her parents' conversation from last night. She glanced back at Penny, who sat behind her, and wondered if she should tell her friend about it. But Neela wasn't yet sure what *she* thought of the whole thing herself. So she decided to wait.

At first the idea of a curse on her veena seemed thrilling. Was it one of those ancient curses that affected anyone who came in contact with the instrument? Maybe she was cursed now, too. But that's when she began to feel annoyed. Why didn't anyone tell *her* about this curse? Even after the veena was stolen?

Just then, Amanda turned around from the row in front, her auburn hair hanging gracefully down her back. Self-consciously, Neela ran her fingers through her own hair. She could feel the knots that were still there, and hoped she'd washed out all the toothpaste that got in the ends when she was brushing her teeth this morning.

"Hey, Neela," Amanda said, "are you bringing your instrument to school again?"

Neela wondered why Amanda cared. "It's too heavy to carry," she said warily.

"I wanted to tell you yesterday, but couldn't because of Miss Photo Freak"—Amanda glanced at Lynne—"that my mom heard about your veena and wants to borrow it."

"Borrow it?" Neela didn't understand. Who would want to borrow a veena?

"For her job. They need to do a photo shoot with Indian instruments." Amanda's mother was a photographer for a magazine in Boston. "They're doing some article about rooms from all around the world."

So that was it. Keep your mouth shut, Neela told herself. The last thing she wanted was to talk about her missing veena with Amanda.

Ms. Reese came by. "Nice work." She handed Neela her test, facedown. Neela turned it over to see a perfect score, and flushed with pleasure. She let herself momentarily bask in the glow of a good mark.

"So?" Amanda asked.

Neela turned to her. "I'll have to ask my mom." Good! Hopefully that would keep Amanda from asking more about the veena.

Amanda handed something to Neela. "That's my mom's business card. You can talk to her yourself at her work."

Neela looked at the card: ELIZABETH BONES, SENIOR PHOTOGRAPHER, *BOSTON LIVING* MAGAZINE. It looked so professional, complete with a Boston address. No one had ever given her a business card before. "I'll have to get back to you," she said miserably, "because we kind of don't know where the veena is right now."

"You don't know where your veena is?" Amanda's voice rose an octave. But before she could say anything more, Matt, who just sat down next to Neela, had overheard the whole thing.

"Dude! You *lost* it?" he said.

"But it was so big, Neela!" Penny said.

"Did it break?" someone else asked.

"Did your parents bust you?"

All of a sudden, everyone around her buzzed with questions. At first she was embarrassed, but as she began to answer more questions, she found herself privately enjoying the attention.

As she described what had happened at the church, she left Hal mostly out of the story except as someone who let her inside. She couldn't say why, but something made her keep quiet about him. And she definitely didn't mention what her parents had said about the veena or about her grandmother. "We're going back this afternoon to see if it's still there," she finished.

"That's awful," Penny said. "I hope you find it."

Matt shook his orange hair back. "Filched in a church. That's intense."

By now, Ms. Reese had noticed the chatter around Neela's desk. "Class, keep it down. Neela, Matt, save your conversation for recess."

Neela reddened and turned to face the front. Most of

the time Matt drew bizarre pictures of space aliens or read thick books that had creepy-sounding names in the title. Also, after bleaching his hair to a wild orange color, he had started wearing old, ratty T-shirts with the names of rock bands she'd never heard of before. So even though they sat next to each other, she rarely talked to him. Certainly they had never been shushed by Ms. Reese. And now everyone in class knew about her lost veena, thanks to her big mouth.

Neela looked up to see Lynne staring at her, as if she was about to say something, but at that moment Ms. Reese told everyone to be quiet, and Lynne looked quickly away.

"By the way, congratulations to Neela and Lynne for their perfect scores," Ms. Reese said.

"Spelling maestros," Matt hooted.

"Geeks," Amanda said. Then, as if she remembered she still needed something from Neela, she smiled at her to show it was a joke. She ignored Lynne.

Neela squirmed. It was one thing to get a good score on her quiz, but another to have Ms. Reese tell the whole class. She glanced at Lynne to see how she felt about it. If Lynne cared, it didn't show on her face.

After homeroom, Neela was about to leave for the class next door when she noticed the business card Amanda had given her was missing.

Penny, who was waiting for her, said, "Aren't you coming?"

"Did you see that card Amanda gave me?" Neela asked.

Penny shook her head. She got on her knees and helped

search around the desk. “Are you going to talk to Amanda’s mom?” she asked.

Neela shrugged. “Not unless my missing veena suddenly turns up.” Saying that made her feel bad all over again. It sounded so improbable when she heard the words out loud.

“Well, the card isn’t here,” Penny said.

“It’s so strange.” Neela remembered placing the card on top of her desk next to her folder. The folder was there, but the card was gone.

“Maybe Amanda took the card back?”

“Yeah, I wouldn’t be surprised,” Neela said. *Just to mess with me.* But she didn’t say that last part out loud, because she knew Penny and Amanda were friends.

The two girls hurried off to their next class. Neela had better things to think about than Mrs. Bones’s photo shoot. And being late once today was already enough.

CHAPTER 5

"Sree, stay with Neela and me," Mrs. Krishnan said. "Don't run off; the church people won't like it." She said this to Sree every time they went somewhere, but it didn't make any difference since he always ran off anyway.

Neela watched her mother as they walked up the steps to the church. She was remembering what her mother had said last night, about how she didn't want to look for the veena anymore after they searched the church. For a moment Neela was tempted to say, *Mom, I know about the curse*. But she decided to wait. Now they were here, she wanted to first see what they might find. Besides, she had been eavesdropping, and she knew that was something her mother hated.

"Let me do the talking," Mrs. Krishnan said to Neela when they got inside.

"But I'm the one who saw Hal," Neela said. "Unless there's something more *you* know about him or my missing veena." She couldn't help adding that last part, wondering what her mother would say.

Mrs. Krishnan glanced wearily at Neela. "I didn't mean that. Just, you tend to . . ."

"What?"

"Nothing." She sighed. "Adults just talk better to each other. You can watch Sree."

Neela frowned. At least I don't keep secrets, she thought. Maybe that was what her mother meant, that adults were better at keeping things from each other.

When they reached the office, they found two women sitting at L-shaped desks, illuminated by the glow of their table lamps. One had mousy hair, and both sides of her desk were piled high with things: papers, books, several boxes of candy, even a half-opened garbage bag filled with clothes. The other woman was plump, with salt-and-pepper hair and a shirt that was very ironed and very white. On one side of her desk a nameplate read MARY GOODWIN, CHURCH SEXTON. Neela looked, but she didn't find a nameplate for the mousy-haired lady. It was probably lost somewhere under the mound of things on her desk.

"Can I help you?" Mary Goodwin asked.

"We seem to have misplaced my daughter's instrument." Mrs. Krishnan said.

"We think maybe somebody here took it," Neela added.

Mrs. Krishnan gave Neela a withering look. "She means the church is the last place it was seen," she said quickly.

She described what had happened yesterday.

Neela bit her lip. Fine, maybe it was better her mother talked. At least it gave her a chance to look around the office. Not that it was the most exciting place, with two vinyl chairs the color of seaweed, and a melamine coffee table that had seen better days. Behind Mary Goodwin's desk, a poster of a big sunflower read "Jesus Loves You!"

"I'm sorry," Mary said, "but we haven't seen anything like that at all. In fact, I left early yesterday, so I wasn't here."

"And I can't think of anyone named Hal working at the church," said the lady behind the pile of clutter.

Mary nodded. "Julia's right." Her gaze fell from Mrs. Krishnan's face to Sree, who was holding his mother's hand, his hair, as usual, over his face. "Aren't you cute?" she said expressionlessly. Sree didn't say anything. It was as if he could tell she didn't mean it.

"Sree," Mrs. Krishnan murmured, pushing his hair back. "He's shy," she said to Mary.

"But there was a man named Hal," Neela insisted. She couldn't believe it. Someone here had to know who he was. "He was tall, kind of old, well-dressed, and he made me hot cocoa. He used this teakettle with a dragon on it."

"Oh, the teakettle," Julia said.

Mary stopped. "Why, yes, we do have that. But no one ever *uses* it—it's an antique."

"Mary's nuts about that teakettle," Julia said. "Wasn't it made by a monk?"

A flush crept into Mary's face. "It comes from a turn-of-the-century monastery in England, handmade by a Benedictine monk." Her voice trailed off. "Excuse me, dear?"

"Neela," Mrs. Krishnan said.

Neela had spotted something on Mary's desk, on the other side of the computer. She held it up, a piece of embroidery stretched inside a pewter frame. "It's a dragon," she said.

Mary leaned forward and took the frame from her. "I'm sorry, dear, but this has been in the family for a long time. Delicate, you know." She opened a drawer and stored it inside. "Now, what was I talking about? Oh, the teakettle."

"Maybe it was an intruder," Julia offered.

"Oh, yes," Mary said, fixing a firm look on Neela. "An intruder."

Neela was amazed by the way Mary had snatched the frame from her. The embroidery looked fairly new—not at all like a family heirloom—with a stitching of a dragon that was like the one on the teakettle. The dragon seemed to be part of something that looked like a shield from the middle ages, bordered by ornate patterns and a pair of swords crossed at the top.

"An intruder?" Mrs. Krishnan repeated.

Julia made a little clucking sound. "That's awful. And he used your teakettle, too, Mary."

"Well, it's not my teakettle," Mary corrected. "But you're right. It is awful."

"We haven't had an intruder in years," Julia said.

Sree tugged on his mother's hand, bored. "Just a minute, Sree," his mother said.

"Hal wasn't an intruder," Neela said. "He knew where everything was. He acted like he belonged here."

"Ah, well, he was a *smart* intruder," Mary said.

Neela was about to say more when she felt her mom's hand press her shoulder, so she kept quiet. She was sure they were wrong about Hal. Besides, Mary was hiding something. What was there in that embroidery she didn't want Neela to see? Was it the dragon?

Mrs. Krishnan handed a piece of paper to Julia. "That's our contact information. Please let us know if you see or hear anything about the veena."

Julia smiled and took the sheet from her. "Veena," she repeated, looking at the word on the paper. "I've never even heard of such an instrument before. Have you, Mary?"

If Mary heard Julia, she pretended to ignore her. Instead she began to rearrange the three loose papers on her immaculate desk into a new stack. Meanwhile, Julia dropped the contact sheet on the top of her mountain of papers. Neela wondered if it was the last time anyone would ever see it.

"Would you mind if we have another look around?" she asked glumly. She was beginning to think she had reached a dead end.

Mary rose from her desk to show them to the door. "Of course not, dear," she said. As she crossed the floor, Neela heard it: *phsst phsst.*

Neela stopped and stared at Mary Goodwin's feet.

"Mary, your shoes squeak something awful," Julia said. She had noticed Neela staring. "I've been telling her to get them changed. I can hear her a mile away."

"Oh, well, I've had these for so long," Mary said, waving her hand as if to shoo Julia.

Neela looked up at Mary. "And you weren't here yesterday, were you?" she asked.

Mary paused. "That's what I said, dear. You ought to pay attention so that others don't have to repeat themselves to you." She pointed out the door. "The kitchen is that way. Best of luck finding what you're looking for." She said the last sentence with a sense of finality. Everyone could tell she was really saying good-bye.

"She was so unhelpful," Mrs. Krishnan said, after they were in the hall.

Neela glanced behind her. "Be careful what you say," she said in a low voice. "This place echoes like a cave."

Just then, without any warning, Sree ran down the hall into to the vestibule.

"Sree, come back!" Mrs. Krishnan called out. "Now what?" she said to Neela, exasperated.

They had stopped in front of the kitchen. "I'll be in here looking," Neela said.

Mrs. Krishnan nodded. "All right, I'll get Sree. Don't go anywhere else. I don't want to search for you afterward." She disappeared into the vestibule.

As Neela entered the kitchen, she thought again of

Mary. So that funny sound yesterday was Mary Goodwin's shoes. Which meant Mary had been standing outside the kitchen door. Had she looked in? Had she seen Hal? What if Mary was the one who had taken her veena? Maybe she had peeked in the kitchen, saw Neela having cocoa, and then took the veena from the closet and ran off with it.

Neela sighed. But that explanation sounded so . . . ridiculous. How on earth could Mary have planned that, when Neela's coming to the church was purely an accident? It made no sense. At any rate, Mary had lied when she said she wasn't in the church yesterday afternoon. And she had snatched away the embroidery because there was something in it she didn't want Neela to see.

Was Mary's behavior a clue? Neela wasn't sure. But as she looked around the kitchen, she began to feel another wave of despair. Not only had the office failed to provide any real information about Hal or her veena, but the kitchen was swept clean, the counters spotless. What could she possibly find there?

The only thing in sight was the dragon teakettle, which was up on the shelf. She walked over to the other side of the kitchen and carefully lifted it down. The weight of the kettle made her swing it momentarily before setting it on the table. It was heavier than she imagined. She looked again at the kettle, at its webbed wings and the handle, which she now saw was a tail with a point at the end. This time she also noticed that the dragon had only two legs with claws at the ends of its feet, and that its face looked like a bird's.

Come to think of it, didn't the dragon on her own veena look the same way, with the same bird face and wings? Or maybe all dragons looked like that. She had no idea. She tried to think back to Mary's embroidery. It seemed as though that dragon had looked like a bird, too.

Down the hall she heard her mother's voice, then footsteps coming closer. Neela picked up the kettle quickly to return it to the shelf, and in her haste, banged it against the side of the counter. The next thing she heard was the sound of metal hitting the kitchen floor. She looked down. The dragon head had broken off! Horrified, she picked it up, knowing any minute she was about to get caught. Then it was too late because the footsteps had arrived at the doorway, and she glanced up miserably, expecting to see her mother.

But it was not Mrs. Krishnan. To her surprise, standing in the doorway was Lynne, from school.

"It was an accident," Neela sputtered. She felt as if she had been caught with her pants down.

Then something strange happened. "Slide it back on top of the teakettle," Lynne said. When Neela could only stare at her, Lynne walked over and took the kettle and dragon head from her. She inserted the head along a tiny groove until the girls both heard something click into place. "It's supposed to come off," she explained. "You just loosened it." She reached up and set the kettle back on its shelf.

Neela was still staring agape at Lynne. Before she could speak, they heard Mrs. Krishnan's voice, this time closer, until she appeared in the kitchen. "So, did you find anything?" she asked Neela, Sree in tow.

"No, nothing here." Neela flashed an uncertain look at Lynne.

"There wasn't a rabbit," Sree announced, as if that had been weighing on everyone's thoughts.

Mrs. Krishnan glanced at Lynne curiously. "Are you a friend of Neela's?"

Lynne pushed up her glasses and nodded. "We're in school together. I'm Lynne."

"Is this your church?" Mrs. Krishnan asked.

Lynne shook her head. "I'm just taking an after-school class here."

"Me too," Neela piped up. "Except mine meets on Tuesdays."

"Mine meets today. Photography."

"Watercolors."

After that, there wasn't much left to say. Neela stared at Lynne's face, which was half covered by her mass of dark curls. She was still trying to figure out why Lynne had come to the kitchen in the first place. "Well," Mrs. Krishnan said at last. "Nice to meet you."

As they left the kitchen, Neela couldn't help glancing back at the teakettle on the shelf. There was something important about it. Maybe something Mary didn't want her to know. And now Lynne was connected to the teakettle, too.

CHAPTER 6

That evening, a bunch of things happened. First, Neela's father filed a police report.

"A what?" asked the clerk at the police station when Mr. Krishnan explained what had been stolen. Neela, who went with him, listened as he patiently spelled out the word.

Mr. Krishnan was given a form to fill out, and a case number when he was done.

"We'll call you if we find anything," the clerk said, without looking up.

Her father didn't have much hope. When they returned home, he said, "I don't know what they'll do about it."

Then the family had a conversation about "What to Do Next."

"Let's play Transformers," Sree said. He held a toy up

in his hand as if he was ready to pound it into someone.

"We can search the church again," Neela said. "We can also put an ad in the paper."

Neela saw her mother purse her lips but say nothing.

"Those are all good ideas," Mr. Krishnan said. He sighed as if he didn't have any good ideas of his own.

Neela thought this was the moment to tell them that she had heard what they said the night before. Her parents would be annoyed for a minute or so, but then they would have to tell her about the curse. And she was dying to know. But just as Neela was about to speak, the phone rang.

Mr. Krishnan went to answer it. "Hi, Amma," he said.

Neela gulped. She listened as her father talked to Lalitha Patti. He said pretty much what he had the night before, except with the added bad news that the church hadn't turned up anything. "I'm sure we'll find it," he said again and again. But it sounded even less reassuring today, especially when he kept repeating "I'm sorry" in between.

Neela stole a look at her mother. Was she still planning not to look for the veena anymore? Mrs. Krishnan's face was tight, even a little angry, but as soon as she saw Neela watching her, she relaxed her expression and began straightening the items on the coffee table. "Sree, don't throw your Transformer around," she said, a little too sharply.

"Neela, here," Mr. Krishnan said. He held the phone out to her.

Neela looked beseechingly at him. Was there some way out of it? In her father's eyes she saw that the answer was no.

She wiped her hands on her pants and took the phone. "Hi, Patti," she said. She tensed, waiting to hear a sobbing person on the other side.

But surprisingly, her grandmother's voice was calm. "Neela, how are you? You're safe? Nothing happened to you?"

"Uh, no," Neela said, startled.

"Good," Lalitha Patti said. "I don't want you to feel bad about this. I know you probably think it's all your fault."

"But it *is* all my fault," Neela said. "I'm the one who lost it."

"It isn't so simple. You might have left the veena alone in the church. But maybe you were destined to do it."

"I was?" Neela blinked. She glanced at her parents, who were sitting on the couch with Sree. What did Lalitha Patti mean? Was she talking about the curse? "Are you saying it's okay the veena is gone?"

Lalitha Patti sighed. "What's done is done."

"But what if there were some way to get the veena back?"

Lalitha Patti paused. "Do you know who took it?" There was a faint hope in her voice.

Neela looked again at her parents. "Not exactly."

"Forget about the veena." Her grandmother lowered her voice a notch. "Unless you can't."

"But—" Neela was about to say more, when her father interrupted.

"I have one more thing to ask her," he said.

Wordlessly, Neela gave him the phone.

"June or December," she heard him say. "We're still deciding."

Neela went to the living room and frowned at the empty spot where her grandmother's veena used to be. Her conversation with Lalitha Patti had unsettled her. Even more puzzling were her last words: *Forget about the veena. Unless you can't.* Was this her grandmother's secret way of telling her to keep looking?

Saturday evening, Pavi's family came over for dinner. Neela opened the front door to find her best friend in corduroys and an apple-green sweater, wearing a small, glittery sticker on her forehead.

"What's with the *bindi*?" she asked.

"My mom's been on my case about it," Pavi said. Behind her, her brother, Bharat, ran upstairs to play with Sree, while the parents sat down in the living room.

"My mom gets on my case, too," Neela said, "but that doesn't mean I'll wear one."

Both their mothers wore bindis, the traditional dots that adorned women's foreheads in India.

"Yeah, but I changed my mind. They're kind of cool. Gwen Stefani wears one."

Neela considered Pavi's bindi. It was a pretty light green, bordered with glitter, and Pavi wore it low, just above her eyebrows, as was the fashion these days.

Still, Neela didn't like to wear one in public. Once in

first grade she wore a bindi to school, and Amanda and Michelle Manser had run around screaming, *Neela has chicken pox cooties!* The worst part was that until then, she and Amanda had been friends. In fact, Amanda, Penny, and she used to sit next to each other at snack time, play on the swings together, and share their crayons at the drawing table. But then the chicken pox cooties thing happened. After that, Neela never wore a bindi to school again. She figured that just a small dot on your forehead made you eligible for embarrassment. And she wasn't sure, but somewhere around that time, even though Penny would still do things with both of them, Neela and Amanda stopped being friends. It was gradual, one of those things she didn't notice, like the sun setting, until it was gone.

But Neela didn't mention any of this now to Pavi. "It is pretty," she said instead, trying to be agreeable. "I guess it isn't a big deal."

Pavi's eyes flashed. "Not a big deal?"

Neela sighed. Pavi could be so touchy. "I just meant, it's cool, that's all."

"People treat you different when you wear a bindi."

"Then why do you wear it?"

Pavi grinned and answered in typical Pavi style, "Maybe I *want* to be different."

~

After dinner, the conversation turned to the missing veena and what to do next.

"Well, there's the insurance," Mr. Sunder said. "You would get some money back."

"Are you going to buy another veena for Neela?" Mrs. Sunder asked.

Neela's mother shrugged. "She was doing fine on Sudha Auntie's student veena. Maybe she can go back to playing on that."

"Sudha Auntie's veena?" Neela repeated. Her heart dropped. She had not considered this yet. Her teacher's squeaky, oversized veena suddenly seemed like a punishment after being spoiled for half a year on Lalitha Patti's gorgeous-sounding one.

"Sure," Mrs. Krishnan said. "It was good enough before."

Neela felt herself on the verge of tears. "But it's so . . . squeaky," she faltered.

"You can play out of tune on it just like you did with Patti's veena," Mr. Krishnan joked. "Maybe we won't even be able to tell the difference."

Neela stood up and glared at her father. "I don't play out of tune."

"What? I was kidding. Besides, you're not playing *any* instrument right now."

"Fine. Maybe I should play on Sudha Auntie's veena for the rest of my life."

She ran up to her bedroom. Upstairs, she nearly tripped on Sree and Bharat, who were playing in the hall.

"Neela, you want to push the red engine?" Sree asked, when he saw her.

But Neela was in no mood. "Find somewhere else to play with your stupid trains," she said angrily, stomping past them.

"She's mad because she's a loser," Sree said to Bharat.

"I'm not a loser!" she yelled behind her. She knew it was Sree's four-year-old way of explaining what had happened. Still, she didn't want to be called a loser—even if it was true.

Neela closed her door and lay down on her bed. She wasn't sure what she was angrier about—the idea of going back to Sudha Auntie's veena, or her father saying she played out of tune in front of Pavi and her family. As long as Neela could remember, Pavi was better at everything than Neela was—a better swimmer, a better student, a better veena player. Pavi would never lose her veena in a church. The worst part was that the veena wasn't even something Pavi really wanted to play in the first place. It was her parents' idea, which they got from seeing Neela, and Pavi had simply gone along with it. Pavi's parents had bought a veena over the Web for cheap. It wasn't a great veena, but it was adequate. Then, on this adequate veena, Pavi breezed through the early exercises with little effort. Of course she never had a problem with playing in front of people. *Picture everyone in their underwear*, she would say.

And now Pavi would have all her exercises memorized, and Sudha Auntie would lavish her with praise. At the same lesson, Sudha Auntie would yell at Neela for losing her veena.

The door opened. "It's not as bad as you think." Pavi flopped onto the bed next to her.

"Easy for you to say," Neela mumbled.

"You just need Sree to screw up big so your parents can forget about you. Maybe he can set the rug on fire? Or leave the water running in the tub?"

Neela smiled in spite of herself. So many times she wished Pavi lived in Arlington and went to school with her. She had known her for more than six years, from the time they met at a swimming class, and Pavi was the only one who could really make her laugh. She could do impressions of just about anyone, including her whole family, the swimming instructor, and even the priest who presided at the temple their families both visited. This was all, of course, before last summer, when they stopped taking swimming lessons together, after Pavi suddenly became really good.

Neela turned over. "You want to hear the weird stuff that happened at the church?"

Pavi looked interested. She nodded.

Neela described Mary's embroidery of the dragon, and the way she hid it away, and how her shoes squeaked just like the sound outside the door the day the veena was taken. When Neela got to the part about the kitchen and the metal dragon head falling on the ground, Pavi shivered with a mixture of horror and delight. "Did you get busted?" she asked.

Neela shook her head. "That's the weird part." She explained how Lynne appeared in the kitchen and fixed the dragon. "So it's like having three suspects."

"Three?" Pavi asked.

"Hal is number one. Mary with the shoes is number two. And Lynne."

Pavi looked doubtful. "There's nothing that links Lynne to the veena."

"But isn't it strange she showed up in the kitchen at the same time as me?"

"She had a photography class."

"Or she was following me."

"But what does your veena have to do with that coffeepot?"

"Teakettle."

"Whatever."

Pavi's point was valid. Neela didn't know the connection either.

She debated. There was still one other thing she hadn't yet told her friend about. But she knew Pavi would say she had lost her mind. A mysterious curse? A veena disappearing because of a spooky past? And if Hal or Mary or Lynne were involved, it seemed impossible they could have anything to do with Lalitha Patti's secret story all the way back in India. Neela decided to keep quiet. Meanwhile, she needed to talk to Lalitha Patti again.

From downstairs, Pavi's parents called for her and Bharat to get ready to go home.

Pavi jumped up. "See you at Sudha Auntie's." She and Neela got to see each other every week at their veena lesson.

"Aren't you going on Sunday?" Neela asked. Her family was going to a veena concert that afternoon near Harvard.

"Oh, yeah, right. See you there."

Downstairs, Pavi said to Neela's parents, "So, back to the student veena?"

Neela gave Pavi a *Don't* look. She didn't want to bring up the subject again so soon.

"Well, yes, but we came up with another idea, too," Mr. Krishnan said.

Neela sighed. "Oh?"

"We decided to go to India in December instead of June," Mrs. Krishnan said.

"That's when we're going," Pavi said excitedly. "We can get our tickets together."

Mrs. Krishnan nodded. "We can travel at the same time. In fact, Neela's cousin is getting married around then, too. Maybe we can make it to the wedding."

"What does all of this have to do with the student veena?" Neela asked.

"We haven't decided for sure, but maybe while we're in India, we can think about buying you a veena."

Neela stared at her parents. "But what about Lalitha Patti's veena?"

"We're not happy about it being lost," her mother said. "But we'll claim the lost veena with our insurance and use the money to buy another one. That's the best we can do."

"But . . . but we can't give up looking for the other veena." Neela tried to keep the despair out of her voice, conscious of Pavi's parents watching. "What if we looked just a little more? Like putting an ad in the paper and—"

"We could do all of that," Neela's mother said, "but the point is, that veena is gone. And we have to face the fact that we won't get it back."

Neela stared at her mother's face, which had that I've-made-up-my-mind look on it. She remembered her words from the other night, how it was better if they didn't find the veena. All because of a curse. A curse no one would tell Neela about.

"Think," Neela's father said. "A new veena." He forced a smile, as if trying to convince her what a great idea it was, but Neela could hear the sadness in his voice, too.

A year ago, Neela would have been ecstatic at the prospect of getting a veena of her own. But that was then. And now . . .

Pavi, who didn't notice the change in Neela's expression, was hopping around with excitement. "Neela, hey, what about the trip? We'll have so much fun!"

Behind her, Sree and Bharat were cheering, and even the adults had to smile. Neela tried to show the same excitement as everyone, but inside, she felt a wave of despair. Was she the only one dismayed by this latest development? Because a new veena did mean she could graduate from Sudha Auntie's student veena. But it also meant her grandmother's veena was gone . . . for good.

CHAPTER 7

Sunday afternoon, Sree's wailing could be heard all over the house and even in the driveway, where Neela was looking for a lost headband in the backseat of the minivan. She didn't find it, but she did find an unopened bag of potato chips that had fallen down in the back. She leaned against the side of the car, eating them.

Her mom's voice came through a half-open window. "Sree, I'll be gentle."

"You'll cut my brain."

"I won't. Here, have a lollipop."

"I don't want a lollipop," he cried.

"Take it," Mrs. Krishnan said angrily.

Neela sighed. Aside from the fact that it was embarrassing to hear her family yelling through the window, she didn't get why her mom didn't take Sree's butt to the barber and have him yell and scream there instead.

She ate the last of the crumbs off her fingers, thinking about the afternoon concert. Alfred Tannenbaum, an American, was performing on the veena. Sudha Auntie was friends with him, and she had mentioned he was a professor at Tufts. When Neela asked if he taught veena, Sudha Auntie answered in her usual snide tone: *Well, he doesn't teach yodeling!* Neela's parents, whose friends had raved to them about Tannenbaum's live performances, had been looking forward to the concert all week. For once, her dad took the time to match his socks, and her mother wore a fancy sari, as she did when they went to the temple.

It always surprised Neela that the two of them cared so much about music, when neither of them could carry a tune. "Why didn't you ever learn the veena?" she asked her dad once. "I mean, Lalitha Patti is so good, why didn't she teach you?"

"What makes you think she didn't try?" he asked. "We had so many lessons, and most of the time she screamed at me, until she finally gave up. Because I'd rather play outside with my friends. I guess all the music genes in our family skipped me. So I had to settle for these denim ones instead," he said, pointing down at his pants. He made jokes, but Neela knew that when he thought no one was listening, he sang to himself.

Mr. Krishnan poked his head out of a living room window. "What are you doing?"

Neela crumpled the bag of potato chips in her hand. "Getting ready," she said.

He stared at her for a moment. "I see. You're getting ready for a concert by standing in the driveway next to the minivan."

"Fine," she said. She came back in, stuffing the empty chip bag into her pocket.

Inside, Sree was lying on the floor of the bathroom, tears streaked across his face, unopened lollipops strewn everywhere. Mrs. Krishnan stood over him, shimmering in a Mysore silk sari bordered by gold thread, with a pair of scissors in her hand. She looked at Mr. Krishnan and Neela. "I'm getting nowhere. His hair looks like an overgrown forest."

Next to her feet, Sree continued to whimper.

"You're cutting his hair," Mr. Krishnan asked, "in your sari?" He looked at her as if she were insane.

"I wasn't planning to. Then I saw his hair, and I couldn't stand it anymore."

Mr. Krishnan sighed. "Why didn't you do it yesterday?"

"Saturday," she said.

Neela rolled her eyes. It was her mother's belief, from the time she was a child, that it was bad luck to cut hair on a Saturday. Sometimes Neela wondered how anyone got anything done with her mother around.

Mrs. Krishnan looked at her watch. "I guess we should get going. I don't suppose we'll be on time."

Mr. Krishnan said, "Are you kidding?"

Miraculously, Neela's family pulled into the last parking spot on Amherst Street. The miracle continued as a delay in setting up the sound equipment gave them time to find seats inside. Neela sat down next to her dad and surveyed the audience. She spotted Pavi and her family, sitting near the front. They were always early, well-dressed, and groomed. Neela pushed back her flyaway hair and brushed away a few potato chip crumbs that were still on her shirt. At least no one could see what she looked like in the dark.

When the musicians came onto the stage, their instruments were already there waiting for them, so they just had to tune. Professor Tannenbaum wore an orange-colored kurta and khaki pants, and had a wave of gray hair poofing out around his face. Neela thought he looked exactly like an owl. An old, poofy-haired owl.

The concert began. Professor Tannenbaum started with an invocation. Neela knew what it was because her parents had explained it to her before. It was how all South Indian concerts started, with a musical prayer to the Lord Ganesha, the remover of obstacles. For good luck, her mother had explained. Neela knew all about luck in performances, though she personally never seemed to have any.

"When is it over?" Sree whined. "I'm bored."

"Sshh," their mother said. "It just started."

Sree squirmed in his seat. "Next time you can cut my brain out," he said.

"Dork," Neela said.

Following the invocation, Professor Tannenbaum started with the first song from the Pancha Ratnas or "Five Gems," as they were known. Lalitha Patti played it during every visit, and hearing it now made Neela's stomach knot up, remembering all over again how she had lost her grandmother's veena. To make herself feel better, she tried to picture herself all grown up and on the stage, playing the song instead, with accompanists and an audience and flowers in her hair, wearing a gold-colored sari or a flowing kurta shirt or whatever musicians would be wearing by the time she was grown up. And, of course, without being terrified to death. The image of her in the future helped, but only partly, because when she closed her eyes, she still saw herself playing on her grandmother's old veena.

During the break, Sudha Auntie materialized out of nowhere. For someone well over seventy, Neela's teacher moved with an uncanny quietness and speed. Neela first heard her voice, then felt a claw hand on her shoulder, and when Neela turned around, her teacher was standing before her. How did she do that? It was almost creepy.

Before Neela could say anything, Sudha Auntie said to Mr. and Mrs. Krishnan, "You don't mind, but I'm borrowing Neela for a moment." Then, with surprising deftness, Sudha Auntie extracted Neela from her seat and brought her down the aisle. She had Pavi already in tow on the other side of her. "Girls, you must meet him," Sudha Auntie declared.

Neela and Pavi exchanged looks. "Alfred, Alfred!" their

teacher called to the man onstage. Professor Tannenbaum was already swarmed by a bunch of people from the audience, but this didn't seem to stop Sudha Auntie. "Some students I want you to meet." And with that, she thrust Neela and Pavi right into the middle of the swarm. Everyone stared stonily at the two girls for cutting the line. Neela inwardly cursed her teacher.

"Talk," Sudha Auntie prodded. "Tell him you're veena students."

Pavi mumbled something of this sort to the professor.

Neela hated it when a grown-up told her what to say. She mumbled hello and was about to turn around, when Professor Tannenbaum said, "I remember you!"

Neela stopped. "You do?" She had never seen Professor Tannenbaum before.

His face broke into a delighted smile. "You're the girl whose string snapped at the temple last summer."

The swarm stopped to look at Neela more closely. Yes, their faces seemed to say, this was the very same girl. Some of them even smiled.

Neela felt her face go hot. Would she never be able to forget about that stupid string? "Lucky me," she muttered, and stepped back. Like a curtain, the crowd closed back around Professor Tannenbaum, surrounding him again.

Sudha Auntie came bounding after her, with her superhuman agility. "Hey," she demanded. "*What was that?*"

Neela kept walking. "He remembered my string snapping."

"But he still remembered you," she said. "It was a compliment."

Neela didn't say anything. It hadn't sounded like a compliment to her.

Sudha Auntie waited a moment, then said, "All right, suit yourself." She turned back in the direction of the stage. She probably had more important things to talk about with the professor, such as her star student, Pavi.

Neela stepped out into the lobby. It was quiet and cool out there—a good place to hide herself away from everyone. If only she could hide herself away from her mistakes—but they seemed to follow her everywhere. It didn't help that the most embarrassing one had been witnessed by Professor Tannenbaum, and that he had mentioned it in front of all those people, who seemingly had all been to the same dreadful performance. If there was a contest for bad weeks, this one would get the grand prize.

Neela felt inside her pocket and found the crumpled-up bag of potato chips. But they were gone, and there was nothing else to eat. As she went to toss the empty bag in a nearby trash can, she accidentally bumped into an Indian man who was also throwing something away.

"Sorry," she said automatically.

"Sorry," he said, too, stepping back. He was neatly dressed with a trimmed haircut and starched collar. "You are fast, I did not see you." He had an accent like her grandparents, and now that she had a better look, she saw he was young. He might be the same age as her cousin, Arun, who had just finished college in India and was getting married. Neela also noticed the flash of a ruby-and-gold ring on the young man's finger where the light hit it. She had never seen anyone his age wear jewelry like that before.

"You too," Neela said, without thinking. Then she stopped. Why did she say that? It didn't even make any sense.

"You are enjoying the concert?" he asked. "Or getting bored?"

"No, I wasn't bored," Neela said. "I play the veena, too."

"Really?"

Neela nodded, feeling suddenly important, when only a minute ago she had wanted to put a brown paper bag over her head.

"Good. Very good. Because, like it or not," the guy went on, "the veena is dying."

"What?" Neela hadn't expected this.

"Dying away. Not many people are playing it anymore."

"But that's not true," she said. "I know so many. Professor Tannenbaum, my teacher, my friend, and . . ."

The guy smiled. "Trust me, veenas are hard to sell nowadays. The magic is all gone. Even if the veena has the loveliest, sweetest sound of all Indian music."

Then, before she could respond, he walked away. Who was he? She watched him sift through the crowd and back through the doors of the auditorium. He was slender, with long thin legs, and he walked comfortably through the lobby, as if he had been to the recital hall before. And yet his accent was so strong, he had to be from India, not here. She wondered again who he was. He didn't act anything like her cousin Arun.

Curious, she followed him back in. The lights were blinking, which meant the concert was about to start again. Inside, she spotted him at the front, talking to Professor Tannenbaum. Standing a few feet away was a woman dressed in black, with straw-colored hair cut to her chin. She was photographing them with a huge camera, the kind where the lens stuck out and looked complicated and professional. Neela wondered if she was from the newspaper.

Neela crept closer to the young man with the ruby ring so she could hear what he was saying to Professor Tannenbaum. She stood behind a few people so she didn't look too obvious.

"It is not a problem," he said, flashing the same delicate smile Neela had seen a few minutes ago. "Some sealant will do the trick."

Tannenbaum said, "I knew I could count on you. But the crack is fairly large." He directed the young man to his veena to show a long crack that ran along the length of the bottom. "I don't know how it happened. I don't remember banging it against anything."

The young man looked carefully at the instrument. "This isn't that kind of crack. It was caused by heat. Maybe a hot summer followed by a rainy fall?"

"Why, yes," Tannenbaum said thoughtfully. "That must have been it."

The young man gave Tannenbaum a business card.

"This number will work until the end of the week. Call me. I can have it fixed for you."

"Is this your last stop?" Tannenbaum asked. "I thought you came to Boston last month. Surprised to see you still here."

"I had some unexpected business. Then it is home for me."

Tannenbaum smiled. "I can't believe you're all grown up. I still remember when you came as a small boy with your father, and he was the one doing the repairs."

The young man smiled back. "Sometimes I think I know Boston like the back of my hand."

He said something more, but by now the people in front of Neela were jostling her, trying to get back to their seats. She leaned in further to catch the last of his words, and bumped into the photographer by mistake.

"Watch it, kid," the woman said. She was pretty, but her face was sharp and unsmiling.

"Excuse me, we're supposed to sit down," Neela said coolly. She hated being called "kid."

The woman ignored her but stepped to the side to let Neela pass. By now, the young man had finished his conversation, and Tannenbaum returned to his place onstage. The lights flickered again, and everyone took their seats. As Neela sat down, she looked for the young man with the ruby ring, and the blond photographer, but they had disappeared into the shadows of the audience.

After the concert, on their way back to the car, Neela's parents talked about Professor Tannenbaum. They said he was just as good as any player from India.

"Even his pronunciations were excellent," Mr. Krishnan observed.

Behind them, around the corner, Neela heard a woman's voice.

"I think these photos are enough . . . Why didn't I think of Tannenbaum before?"

"No . . ." came a man's voice. "You have to . . ." muffled words, then, ". . . a Guru original."

Neela turned around. Before her appeared the Indian man with the ruby ring, and the mean woman with the camera. They walked past Neela without even looking at her, and went inside a coffee shop. Neela stared at them through the window of the shop. They were in line at the counter, still talking. The woman waved her arms as she spoke, and the man twirled his ring around and around his finger. Had he really said "Guru original"? Like what Sudha Auntie had said about the missing veena?

"Neela!" their mother called from the car. "What are you doing?"

Neela stood rooted to the ground. She desperately wished to hear what they were saying. How often did you hear someone on the street talking about a Guru original? She glanced at her mother. "I'm getting a drink of water," she yelled, and went into the coffee shop before her mother could stop her.

By now, the man and woman had bought their coffee and were sitting at a table near the counter with the condiments and napkins. Neela pretended to get a napkin, and stood nearby trying to hear what they were saying.

"I wasn't sure my e-mail would reach you before you went back to India," the woman said. "My friend said you're only here for a short while. So I guess I lucked out."

"I'm happy to be at your service," the man said.

"I have to admit, you're a lot younger than I expected. What are you, fifteen?"

He smiled. "I finished college last year. But I've learned a lot over the years working with my father."

"Well, let's get down to the nitty-gritty." She glanced through some notes. "Like I asked in my e-mail, can you tell me again what a Guru original is?"

The young man took a gulp of his coffee. "It is a term our customers came up with, named after one of our most beloved artisans, Guru. His veenas are called Guru originals, as opposed to instruments made by other veena makers that try to imitate his workmanship."

She fixed an intent look on his face. "So, then, they're valuable. Like a Stradivarius?"

He laughed. "The famous violins of Italy. I hear people have tried for years to figure out the secret behind the beautiful sound. Unsuccessfully, I might add."

The woman waited. "You haven't answered my question."

He stopped smiling. "I do not know if I can. The wood

Guru used to make his instruments came from a very special area in South India, near the district of Thanjavur. Ordinarily, veenas lose their quality of sound over time as the wood ages. But in the case of Guru, something different happened, maybe because of the particular weather patterns at the time, which allowed the wood to season in a slow and unusual way. What he ended up with finally was a rich, dense wood, and with a sound that is superior even today. Combine that with his meticulous design, and you have a veena with a sound matched by no other. Stradivarius? No. But for many, valuable nevertheless."

"How many Guru originals are out there today?"

"Hard to say. No more than a dozen, I believe."

"Fascinating," the woman said, writing what he said down. "So if someone were to have one, all the way here in Boston, that would really be something."

He stared at her. "Well, yes."

Just then the door to the café swung open.

"Neela!" Mrs. Krishnan gestured from the front.

The couple at the table stopped talking at the sound of Mrs. Krishnan's voice. At that moment, the young man's eyes met Neela's. His look of recognition was immediate. But he neither smiled nor acknowledged her in any way. Instead he looked on curiously as she slinked over to her mother.

"Where's your 'drink of water'?" her mom asked evenly.

"I guess I didn't have any change on me," Neela said, her ears burning. Her mother had come at the worst moment. Neela could feel the guy's eyes on her. Did he think she had been following him? Or just that she was some silly young girl getting chewed out by her mother?

As her family drove down Amherst Street a few minutes later, Neela peered through the window to catch a last glimpse of the man and woman before the car turned the corner.

Customers, the guy had said. He had some kind of business that involved Guru originals. He knew about them; maybe he sold them. At any rate, he was an expert, because the woman with the camera was asking him questions as if she were interviewing him.

But why was she so interested in them? Neela couldn't help noticing the look in the woman's eyes when she said: *So if someone were to have one, all the way here in Boston, that would really be something.*

She must have got a hold of one, Neela thought suddenly. That was the only explanation. She thought of the marks on her grandmother's veena, the initials Sudha Auntie said were Guru's. Was it possible there were *two* Guru originals in Boston? Or could this woman know something about her grandmother's veena?

Neela shivered. "A Guru original," she repeated to herself.

"What?" Mr. Krishnan said.

"Nothing," she said. She couldn't explain it, but the incident had caused a small thrill in her, as if the trail to the missing veena, which had been icy cold until now, had suddenly thawed.

CHAPTER 8

The only nice thing about being late to school was that there was no one to collide with when running down an empty hall. At 8:35 a.m. Monday morning, Neela barreled into class while Ms. Reese was doing announcements. Behind her, Matt ambled in leisurely. Nothing ever seemed to faze him, not even Ms. Reese's late minutes.

"How do you spell 'tardy'?" he whispered. He was wearing a T-shirt with a photo of a bunch of shaggy-haired rockers and the word QUEEN written above them in big lettering. The shirt smelled musty, as if it had been inside a suitcase for the last twenty years.

Neela ignored him. She had too much on her mind, like the blond photographer and the guy with the ruby ring. And now that Neela was in school, it was back to thinking about Lynne and their encounter at the church. With all these strange happenings, overheard conversations, and coincidences, Neela couldn't forget that Lynne was part of the puzzle as well.

Neela glanced at Lynne now and noticed she was wearing a tie-dyed wraparound skirt with a shirt that had—Neela looked again—purple feathers along the cuffs and hemline.

Matt must have noticed, because he whispered, "What's with the feathers?"

Neela shrugged. She wasn't sure of anything when it came to Lynne.

Matt made tiny squawking sounds as he sketched an electric guitar in his notebook.

"Stop," Neela whispered. She had to bite her lip to keep from laughing.

Matt shaded an area with his pen. "She draws wicked dragons, though."

"Matt," Ms. Reese said.

Neela blinked. "What did you say?"

"Dragons," he repeated. "Check out the back of her notebook."

"Matthew and Neela." Ms. Reese's voice rose.

Neela reddened after hearing her name, but she was too intrigued to care. First her veena, then the teakettle, and then Mary's embroidery. Now Lynne's notebook had dragons, too?

In Art, they were making papier-mâché puppets. This was Mrs. Averil's favorite project, so they did it twice a year.

Neela picked up her puppet from the back and looked for a seat next to Penny, but Amanda was already sitting next to her.

"No one's sitting in that chair," Amanda said when she saw Neela. But the chair she was talking about was on the other side of her, and Neela really didn't want to sit next to Amanda. Instead, she took the chair across, even if it meant having to sit next to Matt again.

Today in class they were painting their puppets. Neela had started out with a duck, but as she added more papier-mâché, it ended up looking like a frog. She painted the eyes, starting with white and then adding a layer of blue and green. When she was done, she surveyed the results. "Great. My frog looks like he got beat up."

"Put bandages on him," Matt said. He was making a space alien.

"Put sunglasses," Penny suggested.

"It doesn't even look like a frog," Amanda said. She was painting something white and lumpy-looking.

"What are you making?" Matt asked her. "A turnip?"

Amanda bristled. "It's a sheep. Can't you tell? It's white."

"I think it looks *bah-h-d*," Matt bleated.

Penny giggled.

Amanda reached across with her paintbrush and dabbed a big blotch of white on Matt's forehead.

"Hey," he exclaimed. "Why did you do that?"

Amanda laughed. "You're Indian. I just made you Indian."

Matt didn't understand. "I'm Indian because I've got paint on my face?"

"It's a dot. You know those dots they wear."

Matt gave her a long look. "You're a strange person, Amanda Bones." He wiped his forehead with a paper towel, making the paint smear across his forehead.

"That wasn't funny," Lynne said. She was seated at the next table, making a dragon with wings. At the moment, though, she had put down the dragon to glare at Amanda.

"It was a joke," Amanda said.

"It was a stupid joke," Lynne said.

"I was totally joking," Amanda said crossly. "Right, Penny? Even Neela thought it was funny."

Neela flushed, but kept quiet. She wondered if Penny would say anything, but Penny went on painting as if she hadn't heard a thing that Amanda had said.

"And they're called bindis, not dots," Lynne said.

"Whatever." Amanda rolled her eyes. "And why are you wearing chicken feathers? This isn't a farm, you know."

"They're ostrich," Lynne said coolly. "It's a designer shirt."

Amanda sniffed. "I'm allergic to feathers."

"Then stay away from me," Lynne muttered.

After that, Matt got a hall pass and went to wash his forehead in the bathroom. Neela glumly continued painting. She remembered Pavi's comment about how bindis made people treat you differently. Neela wasn't even wearing one, and yet she felt like she'd been singled out unfairly. It was like first grade all over again, when Neela didn't have the guts to speak up, and Penny kept quiet the entire time.

Only this time Lynne was there to defend her. How Lynne even knew about bindis was another story. But that didn't matter. What mattered was that Neela had said nothing while Lynne had stood up to Amanda, even though *she* was the one with the feather shirt and funny glasses and . . .

Neela noticed then that Lynne's chair was empty. She looked up just in time to see Lynne slip quietly out the door of the classroom. No one was allowed to leave without a hall pass. But apparently no one, including Mrs. Averil, had noticed Lynne slip out. And there at her table next to the unfinished papier-mâché dragon, Lynne had left her notebook behind.

Neela leaned forward to get a better look. Just as Matt had said, the back of Lynne's notebook was covered with dragons, each drawn in varying levels of detail. The largest one was remarkably good, with raised wings and scaled legs. And each dragon had a pointy tail, a beaky face, and two legs, just like the dragon on her veena and the one on the teakettle in the church.

When she was sure no one was watching, Neela reached for the notebook. Her conscience jabbed at her as she flipped through the pages under the table. Yes, she was going through Lynne's private things, but maybe there was something important about the dragons.

As she looked through, a magazine clipping fell out of the notebook and fluttered to the floor. She picked it up and saw it was an ad for cameras on sale at a local camera shop. One was circled in thick black ink: *Amazing images! Outstanding performance! State of the art SLR!* A lot of exclamation marks, Neela thought. She remembered the photographer at yesterday's concert. The fancy camera in the ad looked like something she would use. Neela stuck the clipping back into the notebook.

By now, Matt had returned, his forehead washed off. "Mission—terminate all animal forms," he said, and pretended to swoop his space alien over Neela's frog puppet.

"Stop it," she said, turning away to shield the notebook on her lap. She didn't care about the frog, but she didn't want Matt to see what she was doing.

"Must seek others," he said. Behind her, Neela could hear Penny and Amanda squealing in annoyance at him.

Neela continued flipping through the pages, seeing mostly homework assignments and notes from class that Lynne had scribbled. But then she came to a page with a drawing that made her stop. It wasn't a dragon. It was a veena.

Lynne had drawn it very carefully, including the frets, a resonator, all seven strings, and a dragon peg box. Next to it was a date, and a list:

In very good condition

Initials still visible, though faded

Approximately four feet in length

Not a single mark or scratch except for the neck

The date at the top of the page was from last week, the same day Neela had brought her veena to class. This was a drawing and description of *her* veena. Even the peg box was identical, with a full dragon body, tail, and wings. Then Neela remembered all the photos Lynne took of her veena in class. It was as if Lynne was keeping track of her veena because she knew something Neela didn't. And now Lynne had disappeared in the middle of class. Before Neela could change her mind, she made her way to the front of the classroom. She looked back once at her teacher before ducking out the door, Lynne's notebook tucked under her arm.

CHAPTER 9

The library was just outside the art room. It was also Neela's favorite place in school. Except for kindergarten, all the other classrooms, including the art room, opened to it, with the library at the center like a hub. Even though the library wasn't enclosed, the air felt different there. Maybe it was the scent of books that made it so special. At any rate, Neela didn't mind sneaking out of Art if it meant going to the library, especially when she saw Lynne on a computer at the information center, busy copying something down onto a piece of paper.

The book aisles were arranged in a semicircle around the information center, which made it easy for Neela to creep unseen along an aisle behind Lynne. What exactly Neela wanted to do, she didn't know yet.

Just then, Lynne rose from her chair, rubbing the blunt end of her pencil. Apparently her lead had broken. Neela, who happened to know that the pencil sharpener was all the way on the other side of the library, decided this was her chance to see what Lynne was doing on the computer. As soon as Lynne had walked off, Neela sprang from the aisle to get a closer look at the screen.

Veronica Wyvern veena player

That was what Lynne had entered in the search field. The results had returned several pages of information. On a piece of scrap paper, Lynne had written: *Missing in accident?* But Neela had no time to think, ducking behind the bookcase again before Lynne saw her.

Neela leaned against the shelf. Veronica Wyvern, veena player, missing in accident? They seemed like three completely unrelated things. Neela was so caught up in her own thoughts that she didn't notice someone come up from behind her.

"Neela!"

She jumped.

"What are you doing out here?" asked Mrs. Averil. "And you too, Lynne."

Neela saw that Lynne was wondering the same thing.

"Amanda told me she saw you both leave class without a hall pass."

Neela cleared her throat. "I was bringing Lynne her

notebook that she forgot." She held it up for them to see.

Lynne took the notebook, surprised. "I was returning a book. I didn't know about a hall pass."

"Everyone knows about hall passes." Mrs. Averil frowned. "I'd like the two of you to come in over the lunch hour and help clean up the art room. That will probably help you remember better next time."

Neela was about to make a face in protest. That was so unnecessary! But she controlled herself. Who knows? If she complained, maybe Mrs. Averil would keep them after school as well.

"Come along, girls," Mrs. Averil said. "Art class is over."

Their teacher couldn't have planned it better if she had arranged for a tidal wave to hit the art room. There were gobs of papier-mâché everywhere, on tables, chairs, and even the floor. Soggy paintbrushes with paint still on them dripped color onto paper towels, and scraps of paper littered the ground like confetti.

Mrs. Averil must have been dying to catch us in the hall, Neela thought. Maybe that was why someone was always getting into trouble in art class, so Mrs. Averil could have somebody around to clean up afterward. Neela watched as her art teacher ate a sandwich leisurely while reading a newspaper at her desk. "Girls, don't forget under the tables," she said.

Neela's thoughts returned to Veronica Wyvern and the veena. But now she was starting to have second thoughts. Maybe Lynne's Web search in the library had nothing to do with Neela's missing veena. Maybe Lynne was interested in veenas, and she was just researching them for fun. It didn't seem like something most kids in their class might do, but then again, Lynne wasn't your average person. She happened to like dragons and photography and feathery shirts. Why not add large Indian stringed instruments to that list?

Maybe the first thing to focus on was the teakettle. That was where the whole mystery had started. If Lynne knew how to fix the teakettle, she might also know who Hal was and how to find him.

So as they picked up construction paper from the floor, Neela said, "I'm sorry for getting you caught in the library." She wasn't actually sorry, because Lynne would have been caught anyway, but she figured it was a good way to begin.

Lynne shrugged. "It's not your fault that Amanda the weasel told on us."

"Oh, her," Neela said. "Yeah, she's always like that."

"You mean thoughtless and dumb?"

Neela thought for a moment. "I guess Amanda has perfected herself over the years."

Lynne grinned. She picked up some more paper from the ground and said, "So were you spying on me?"

"No," Neela lied, "I was returning your notebook." It was strange for Lynne to accuse her of spying—after all, hadn't Lynne been spying on *her* at the church?

"I knew I'd left it here. I was coming back for it."

Neela decided that there was no other way but to be direct. "How did you know how to fix the teakettle at the church?"

When Lynne didn't answer, Neela went on. "I saw an old man use that teakettle, even though it's an antique and no one is supposed to touch it. I think he's the same person who stole my veena."

"Girls, lunch hour is almost over," Mrs. Averil called. "Maybe less chatting and you'll finish in time. I need the area near the sinks cleaned, too."

Neela sighed. Just as she was getting close to an answer from Lynne, their teacher had to butt in. While she and Lynne were at the sinks, sponging the sides, Neela tried again. "So, have you used that teakettle before? Do you know the old man who was using it?"

Lynne looked uncomfortable. "I don't know anything about that teakettle."

"You have to. Otherwise you wouldn't know how to fix the dragon."

Lynne stopped sponging. "One day before art class, I was messing around in the kitchen, and the dragon head came off the kettle, just like it did for you. But I figured out it was removable, and I slid it back on. That's all there is to it."

The bell for the end of the period rang. From outside the hall, they could hear the main school door opening and students returning inside from recess. Their voices echoed along the corridor, with the sounds of lockers opening and slamming shut.

Neela looked at Lynne skeptically. "What about Hal? Do you know him or Mary Goodwin?"

Lynne narrowed her eyes. "Hal? I don't know any Hal."

"What about Mary Goodwin?" Neela pressed.

Lynne hesitated. "She works in the church office."

"You're a chatty little duo, aren't you?" Mrs. Averil called out. She had finished both her lunch and her newspaper, which she tossed in the wastepaper basket. "The period's over. You're free to go. Next time, try not to leave class like that. You're big girls now and you know better."

Big girls! Neela felt Lynne writhe next to her as they left the room.

Their next class was right across the hall. Neela started to feel desperate. So far, Lynne had answered none of her questions, except the one about Mary, and even then, Neela could tell that Lynne was dodging the truth somehow. Now class was beginning, and it would be too late to bring up the subject again. She had to think of something else, and fast.

"Wait," she said. "Who is Veronica Wy . . ." She had no idea how to pronounce it.

Lynne froze. "You *were* spying on me!"

"I saw you writing at the computer," Neela said in a rush. "And I wanted to know, because if she's a veena player, and I lost my veena, then—"

"Then what? That I took your veena? Or I know where

it is? Why do you think I have something to do with your missing veena? And I don't know anything more about that stupid teakettle or Veronica Wyvern!" Lynne stormed off.

Neela stood frozen in place. Behind her, Penny and Amanda came back in from recess.

"Mrs. Averil's such a pain," Penny said.

"Sorry you got stuck with Lynne," Amanda said, though she didn't sound sorry at all.

"She doesn't even talk," Penny added.

"Yeah," Neela said, but she was barely listening. She was thinking how clearly Lynne had said the veena player's name: Veronica Wyvern. As soon as she said it, Neela remembered where she had heard it before. Hal!

It's a wyvern. That's what Hal had said about the teakettle in the church. And it was the same name Lynne had written down in the library. Neela walked with her friends to their desks in a daze. She could hardly wait to talk to Pavi.

CHAPTER 10

Every Wednesday after school, Neela and Pavi carpooled forty minutes away to their veena lessons. Sudha Auntie's husband had passed away some years ago, and she now lived alone with two Pomeranian dogs that she kept in the backyard during lessons. She taught all her lessons in the parlor of her old Victorian house.

When Neela first heard about the parlor, she pictured a room with a roaring fire, lacy-looking lamps with tassels, and rocking chairs on which they might sit, having tea and cookies. Instead, Sudha Auntie's parlor contained one futon sofa and a brown vinyl recliner with rows of tufted buttons that looked like teeth. Around the room were several handicrafts from India (the exact term Neela's mother used was "junk"), in various states of disrepair. The fireplace, which had never seen a single fire during Sudha Auntie's time, roaring or otherwise, was used as a storehouse for books. In front of this makeshift bookcase, Sudha Auntie had laid down several rugs and rested her two student veenas, which her pupils used at their lesson so they wouldn't have to carry their instruments from home.

"So what did you girls think of Tannenbaum?" Sudha Auntie asked when they were settled.

Pavi shrugged. "He was good, I guess. The concert went too long, though."

Sudha Auntie turned to Neela. "And you? Did you like Professor Tannenbaum?"

Neela frowned. From past experience, she knew this was a trick question. If she said yes, her teacher would hound her for reasons why. If she said no, her teacher would give her one of those disappointed looks, along with a lecture. "Yes," Neela said carefully. "I liked his opening song."

"Why didn't you talk to him, then?" Sudha Auntie persisted. "Why didn't you tell him that, instead of running off?"

Neela stared at her fingers. She didn't want to have to bring up the whole snapping string incident again. Why didn't her teacher ever bug Pavi? It didn't seem fair.

"He seemed to have plenty of other people to talk with," she said. She thought of the young man with the ruby ring and the woman photographer.

"Never turn down an opportunity to learn from a master," her teacher said. When neither Pavi nor Neela responded to this piece of unsolicited advice, she sighed. "All right, Neela, why don't you start first? Hopefully you practiced before this whole disaster struck."

Reluctantly, Neela sat down in front of the student veena that she had, until six months ago, borrowed for three years. It was hard to believe she was back to this instrument, which now seemed so ugly, after playing for so many months on her grandmother's sleek veena. As she readied the instrument, Neela felt something scratch her leg. She peered at the underside of the veena and was surprised to find duct tape stuck to the bottom of the neck. Great. So it was a damaged veena now, too.

She began carefully, but her opening was poor, and she screwed up at least seven notes, conscious of the duct tape rubbing against her leg. Sudha Auntie made *tsk tsk* sounds the whole time, as if the wrong notes were driving her up the wall. Halfway through, she finally yelled, "You skipped an entire line! Memorization—it's not something you pick and choose."

"Sorry," Neela said meekly. Tears came to her eyes as she continued.

Pavi shifted uncomfortably. Neela was sure her tears would spill, but she blinked furiously and kept playing. In her mind she tried to imagine the way she was at home, the way it had been with her grandmother's veena all these months. But all she felt inside her was a resounding guilt. Her grandmother's veena gone, and *this* was her punishment for it.

Sudha Auntie continued *tsk*ing until Neela reached the end. "Practice is essential," she chided.

But I do practice! Neela thought the words silently to herself.

"Uh, it's kind of hard to practice without a veena," Pavi said.

"She had three whole days before it happened," Sudha Auntie pointed out unsympathetically.

"And I think she's worried about who took it," Pavi added.

Neela watched them talking to each other. It's like I'm not even here, she thought.

"Such a beautiful instrument," Sudha Auntie remarked. "It was too fancy for her, anyway." She saw Neela's expression. "What? I can't think of anyone your age playing on a Guru original." She looked off into space. "Though it's odd your veena disappeared like that. Because there's a story about one of Guru's veenas that kept vanishing."

Behind Sudha Auntie, Pavi made the sign for crazy by spinning her finger in a circle next to her ear.

But Neela sat up instantly. "There's a story about a veena that vanishes?"

"Oh, yes. Everyone knew about it in Thanjavur, where I grew up. But I really heard it much later, after I married and moved to Chennai."

Pavi was making the crazy sign more furiously, but Neela ignored her. Maybe this was the story of the curse her parents had brought up the other night. Of course Sudha

Auntie would know about it. Why didn't Neela think of that before?

"How would the veena vanish?" she asked, hoping that would give Sudha Auntie all the material she needed. Usually Sudha Auntie didn't need much to launch into a story.

Pavi made a face and pretended to strangle herself.

"Well, since you asked." Sudha Auntie settled down on the futon. "The story goes that Guru married a young woman named Parvati, who was very beautiful and an accomplished veena player. But with his profession and her background, they didn't have much money to spare. After they married, Guru made a beautiful veena for her, different from anything else that had been done. It's said he even used jewels Parvati wore at their wedding to decorate it. There were many things said about this veena—how splendid and grand it was, that it gave a rich, wonderful sound."

"So what happened?" Neela asked. "Did it vanish in the middle of the night?"

"Goodness, no," Sudha Auntie said. "That comes later. So as you might guess, for a veena maker in Thanjavur, times were tough. The money wasn't exactly rolling in. Eventually they ended up having to sell away many of their things, including that veena."

"They sold the veena?" Neela exclaimed. "How could they?"

"Hey, you have to eat." Pavi had been listening with interest despite herself.

"One day Guru went to Chennai," Sudha Auntie said,

"and sold the veena to a store. Not just any store but one of the most famous ones: The Chennai Music Palace."

Neela gave a start. This was the same store that had mailed her grandmother's veena to her in the first place!

"Parvati was very upset," Sudha Auntie continued. "That veena had been her life. But as it turns out, Guru's luck changed soon after. His veenas started selling like hotcakes, and he made money, and the bad time passed. Still, Parvati was so upset, that on the day Guru was at the store selling her veena, she put a curse on it, declaring that no one would ever be able to own her veena. Afterward, she gave up playing for good. As for her veena, it's said to disappear from anyone who tries to own it, and returns to that same store, to the same display case. Sometimes it returns immediately, sometimes it takes years, but it never stays with anyone for long before it disappears again. It's known as the *maya veena*, or 'vanishing veena.' People say the veena is still looking for Guru's wife."

"How tragic," Neela sighed, imagining Parvati without her veena.

"What happened to the veena?" Pavi asked.

Sudha Auntie shrugged. "Who knows? Maybe it's still vanishing. Maybe it joined an act on Broadway." She looked at Neela, who was deep in thought. "Hey, that was a joke. I don't really know. It's just a story, of course."

Pavi poked Neela. "You okay?"

She nodded absently. A tiny scrap of conversation from her parents came floating back to her, about Lalitha Patti being "spooked." Was this the curse her parents were talking about? Did her grandmother own Parvati's *maya veena*?

"And that's all I've got for today," Sudha Auntie said. "By the way, I talked with your parents. You may borrow my student veena again for as long as you need. Oh, and you might have noticed, but in the last few months, it got a small crack from where one of my dogs chewed on it. So unusual! They're normally very well behaved." She glanced at the clock. "Look at the time! From the top, Neela. This time, no skipping."

That evening after dinner, Neela made a beeline to the study. She had been waiting all day. On the computer, she opened a browser and entered *Veronica Wyvern veena player* into the search field just as Lynne had done in school. A list of links appeared.

Neela tried the first link, but it went to a site that didn't exist anymore. She kept trying until she clicked a link to a newspaper in India and retrieved an article from its archives. The headline read "Legendary American Veena Player Meets Untimely End," and it was dated December 18, 1995. Intrigued, Neela scrolled down to read the full article.

> CHENNAI, INDIA--Officials confirmed that one of the passengers reported dead in last night's train wreck was the noted musician

Veronica Wyvern. Wyvern, a rising star in South Indian music, was renowned for her mastery of the veena. The daughter of an American schoolteacher and minister, Wyvern began her veena instruction at the age of five after attending a South Indian concert in Boston.

"Ronnie was a master," said Alfred Tannenbaum, professor of music at Tufts University. Like Wyvern, Tannenbaum also rose to acclaim as an American-born veena player. Wyvern and Tannenbaum often performed together in the Boston metro area. "This is a dark day for all of us. She will be missed, both as a musician and as a friend."

Wyvern and her husband, R.S. Ramdas, had been on their way to Chennai for this year's South Indian Music Festival when they fatefully boarded the Chennai Express train from Bangalore. The train derailed and ran into a ditch after the train engineer reportedly applied the emergency brakes, possibly to avoid an obstruction on the tracks.

Both Wyvern and Ramdas perished in the accident, along with seventy other

```
passengers, who were primarily in the first
two compartments. Wyvern was thirty-four
years old.
```

So Veronica Wyvern was a veena player who had lived right here in Boston, until she died in a train crash in India many years ago. And Professor Tannenbaum knew her, too. But why would Lynne be interested in her?

Neela printed out a hard copy, then picked up the phone and dialed. "Go online," she said.

Pavi sighed. "I'm in the middle of math homework." But a few seconds later Neela saw Pavi's name turn bold on their messaging screen. She sent Pavi the link.

"Cool," Pavi said after she was done. "Er, sad, I mean."

Neela was remembering the list in Lynne's notebook. "Lynne wrote down a bunch of things about my veena, almost as if she were . . . comparing it to someone else's."

"Maybe she wanted to know if you have Veronica's veena."

"But that's impossible," Neela said. "There's no way her veena could survive a train crash . . . could it?"

"Unless she didn't have it with her that day," Pavi countered.

Neela heard typing on the other end. "What are you doing?"

"Wyvern looks so familiar," Pavi mused out loud. Then she said, "Try this link."

Neela clicked to the page Pavi sent. "It's a kind of dragon," she said.

"My cousin has this video game with wyverns in it. I've seen the cover, and it has the word on the back. I didn't remember it until now."

Neela looked more closely. "Pavi! Look how many feet the dragon has."

The dragon, done in black and white, was lean and serpentlike, its body arched so the scaly underside showed, and its wings spread out like curtains. It stood on two clawed feet, and its face was sharp, triangular, and birdlike, with a pointed tongue curling from its mouth. Next to the drawing, the caption read, "Wyverns are common in medieval art, and are depicted both as a symbol of vengeance and as a sign of valor, strength, and protection."

"The dragons in the church and Lynne's notebook are all wyverns," Neela said excitedly. "And this veena player has the same last name."

"Your grandmother's veena. It must be a wyvern, too," Pavi said.

"So what's the connection?"

"Isn't it obvious?" Pavi said. "This woman's name is Wyvern. She buys a veena with a wyvern on it. Bingo. You have your connection."

"What about my grandmother? What about Lynne, Hal, and Mary's embroidery?" And the curse, she thought to herself.

"Maybe they're not involved."

"Of course they're involved!" Neela exclaimed.

"Okay, maybe they are. We just need to figure out a few more things."

Neela sighed. "What's the point? Even if we do, I still won't get the veena back."

"Neela, you can't give up now. You have a lot more clues than you did before."

"Sure. It's just . . ." Neela hesitated. "What did you think of Sudha Auntie's story?"

"The vanishing veena? Eh. One of her usual kooky stories."

"But do you think it could be . . . true?"

Pavi blew her air out in a puff. "Sudha Auntie is a mental case. You can't believe for one instant any of that stuff she spins."

"Yeah," Neela said, unsure.

After they hung up, Neela felt out of sorts. She was frustrated with how difficult the mystery was, despite what she had figured out so far. Did Lalitha Patti's veena once belong to Parvati? Did it belong to Veronica Wyvern as well? How had the veena passed from so many hands, from Parvati, to Veronica, to her grandmother? And survived a train wreck in the middle? And what about the blond photographer who seemed to know about a Guru original in Boston? Neela couldn't even begin to figure out where the photographer fit in all of this.

On top of that, Neela was struck with a sudden yearning for . . . what? Whenever she felt confused and unsettled, she knew the best remedy was to practice. It didn't matter what, so long as she was playing something, *anything*, to block out the noise inside her brain.

She brought out the student veena and set it down on the floor of the living room, where she normally practiced. After months of playing on her grandmother's veena, the student veena felt strange and awkward, like a chunk of wood with strings attached to it, and a piece of duct tape wrapped around the bottom.

She paused to look at the peg box, which had a simple dragon head, just like the ones on all the other veenas Neela had ever seen. But to her, the dragon head felt incomplete compared to the one on her grandmother's veena with its spectacular, fully carved body and wings. This dragon was made from papier-mâché and painted crudely in bright colors, reminding Neela of her frog puppet from school.

She smoothed out the pages of the exercise book and began with the recital piece she had screwed up at the last lesson. She went over all the lines, repeating the ones where she had made mistakes. Her concentration grew stronger until she forgot the time, focusing on the notes and their exact pitches. If Sudha Auntie could only hear her now. If *anyone* could hear the way she played when she was by herself.

There was a rustling in the room, and Neela immediately stiffened. But when she turned around, she saw that it was only Sree, lying on his stomach under the coffee table.

"Go away," she said. "I'm practicing."

"No."

"Go away."

Sree stayed where he was, his chin propped up on his hands.

She turned back to her music sheets, deciding to ignore him. As she continued, the blood pumped through her body, flushing her cheeks, warming up her muscles. Slowly the area behind her shoulder blades relaxed. She ran through the piece a half dozen times and felt completely awake, as if a great eye inside her had opened. In the background, she could hear Sree stirring, but it didn't bother her after all. He didn't say a word, and it was actually nice to have someone listening who couldn't tell if she screwed up or not.

Her thoughts drifted to Parvati. It seemed impossible to go through life with just a single instrument. Yet Parvati had expected to do just that, and when she lost her veena, she gave up playing forever, and even put a curse on her lost instrument. Some people might call it crazy, but Neela could understand that feeling of dedication. And even if it was only a story, the part about Parvati had felt very real to her. After all, there *was* something special about her grandmother's veena, something Neela couldn't quite explain. She had felt it herself; she had seen it in the way her grandmother practiced on it, as if no one else existed in the world.

By now Sree had crept out from under the table and sat next to Neela. Out of the corner of her eye, she saw him beating his knee with the flat of his hand.

She stopped practicing, surprised. "Sree, are you tapping the beat?"

He shook his mop of hair from his face and looked at her.

"Where did you learn that?" she asked.

"I watched you." He showed her by tapping some more.

Seeing him reminded her of the first time Lalitha Patti had shown her how to count the beats. Neela was only three. She barely understood anything. But it thrilled her that her grandmother thought her important enough to learn. Neela rested the student veena on the floor. "Not bad, Sree. That's almost right." And then she tapped the beat out slowly for him, until he joined in.

CHAPTER 11

Pavi came over on Friday. They were at Neela's window, which was frosted and covered in the corners by snow. "Maybe we should go to Lynne's house and spy on her."

Neela drew a smiley face on the windowpane with her finger. "I'm done spying," she said. "I suck at it."

Pavi drew a cat. She always drew cats. She had always wanted one, but couldn't because of her allergies. But that didn't stop her from drawing them everywhere.

Neela started to add a dog to the windowpane. "And I'm not going to Somerville."

"Somerville? How do you know she lives there?"

"I saw her address in her notebook."

"Why is Lynne living in Somerville and going to school in Arlington?"

Neela frowned at her dog. It was starting to look like a frog. "I don't know. Why does it matter?"

"Hello? Have you heard about school districts?"

Before Neela could answer, they heard a loud thud outside the house. She and Pavi bolted down the stairs. The mothers and the boys were already at the front door.

"Did you hear that?" Neela's mother asked.

"It sounded like something hit the house," Mrs. Sunder said.

They opened the door. A few tree branches swayed in the wind. But no one was there.

Mrs. Krishnan stepped out, frowning. "Was it snow from the roof?" She peered up to see if the snow had shifted.

They decided to look around the house. Mrs. Krishnan, Mrs. Sunder, and the boys went along the side nearest to the garage, while Neela and Pavi skirted the front, behind the azalea bushes. Pavi was the first one to shout out. "I found it!"

Everyone quickly gathered around. "It's a note," she said excitedly. The note was attached to a rock with several rubber bands. "Somebody threw this and ran off."

"Why didn't they put it in our mailbox?" Neela said. "What if we weren't home? We'd never find it behind the azaleas."

Pavi undid the note from the rock. The words on it had been formed from letters cut out of a newspaper.

NEELA, IF YOU KNOW WHAT'S
GOOD FOR YOU, STOP
LOOKING FOR YOUR VEENA!
YOU WILL NEVER GET IT BACK
AND IF YOU KEEP
ASKING QUESTIONS AT THE
CHURCH, YOU AND YOUR
GRANDMOTHER WILL SUFFER
THE CONSEQUANCE

"Grandmother?" Neela's mother repeated.

Pavi was excited. "This is just like the movies!"

"Why is there newspaper on it?" Sree asked.

"So we can't recognize the person's handwriting," Pavi explained. "They don't want us to be able to trace it back to them."

"Why didn't they just type the letter?" Neela asked. "Talk about dumb." Something caught her eye. "Look," she said, pointing toward the edge of the lawn.

Everyone walked to the end of the property, where they found a line of tracks crisscrossing the snow along the edge of the driveway.

"They're boot tracks," Neela said. "They stop here, where whoever it was threw the rock. And the tracks look pretty big. Like a grown man made them."

"Like Hal?" Pavi asked.

"Is that the man from the church?" Mrs. Sunder asked.

Mrs. Krishnan looked worried. "I thought he was a thief. Now he's psycho, too. And why is he bringing Lalitha Patti into this?"

"It might be some kids pulling a prank?" Mrs. Sunder suggested.

"Over her veena?" Mrs. Krishnan asked. "I thought kids just threw rotten eggs."

Pavi looked mildly insulted. "Kids are more sophisticated than that."

"Maybe there's a clue in the note," Neela said. She stared at the footprints in the snow. Was Hal warning her to stop trying to find her veena?

But Mrs. Krishnan wasn't interested in clues. "I'm calling the police." She asked everyone to come inside. "I don't want some nut out there to hurt you."

Mrs. Krishnan contacted the police department and gave a description of what happened. Within ten minutes, an officer came to their door. They showed him the rock and the footprints. He looked at one, then the other, and scratched his head.

"Tell him about the veena," Mrs. Sunder said.

"The what?" he asked.

Here we go again, Neela thought. She remembered her father spelling "veena" at the station a few weeks ago.

Mrs. Krishnan ran through the whole past month, including the report they had already filed.

The police officer listened patiently and said, "Ma'am, I wish I could say these all added up to something. You know what I mean?"

Mrs. Krishnan murmured something to the effect of, yes, she knew what he meant. Which was basically that he wasn't going to do much more about it.

The officer turned to Neela. "Even so, you be careful. Watch where you go, and don't talk to strangers." Then to Mrs. Krishnan, "If anything more happens, let us know." As he left, they heard him muttering under his breath, "Weirder stuff every day."

"Well, that was unhelpful," Pavi said after the policeman was gone.

The rest of the afternoon the mothers drank coffee in the kitchen, discussing many things but always returning to the same topic—who was this strange man after Neela's veena, and was he after her as well?

Neela and Pavi sat at the foot of the stairs, eating chips and having the same discussion.

"I was so caught up with Veronica Wyvern, I forgot Hal is still lurking out there," Neela said. She was actually relieved he was back in the picture. It was easier to deal with an actual person than a haunted veena.

"What if Hal has been following you all this time?" Pavi went to the window. "He could be watching from one of the bushes."

Neela chewed on a chip. "Why would the note mention my grandmother? Isn't it kind of strange?"

"Maybe he knew the veena belonged to your grandmother before."

Neela thought for a moment. "Come to think of it, I did mention her to him. But still, why threaten her? Unless he had a reason?" She ate another chip and looked at the note again. "Also, he misspelled 'consequence.'"

Pavi came back to look at the note. "I'd misspell it, too. Actually, I'd say something else like, Watch out or I'll brain you."

"But a grown man?" Neela was thoughtful. "He looked so well dressed and educated."

"Grown-ups can be idiots, too," Pavi observed. "Unless it was a kid. Like Lynne."

"She wouldn't misspell 'consequence,'" Neela said. "She's a good speller."

"Then it's back to Hal. Remember the boot track."

"Or," Neela said, "it could be someone else. Someone other than those two."

Just then, the phone rang. Neela answered it at the foot of the stairs.

"Can I talk to Neela or Lakshmi?" It was an older woman's voice.

"This is Neela."

"Don't know if you remember me; I'm Julia from the church. You came by with your mom the other day looking for, what was it now? A viola?"

"A veena." Neela gripped the phone. "Did you, uh, find it?"

"No, dear. Sorry to say I didn't."

"Oh." Neela was disappointed.

By now, Mrs. Krishnan had come to the stairs. "Who is it?" she asked.

"The church," Neela whispered.

"But I thought I'd call," Julia said, "because, well, something unexpected happened."

"Really?" Neela asked hopefully. Maybe Julia had some other information to share.

"It appears that since this morning, the teakettle has been missing."

"Missing?"

"Vanished. Mary's having a fit. She's crazy about it, with it being antique."

Neela mulled over what Julia said. "Are you sure it's really gone?"

"We searched everywhere. I told her to call the police."

"The police," Neela repeated. She wondered if the same officer who came to their house would go to the church, too. He would think things were getting even weirder.

"But Mary said no," Julia said. "As if . . ." Her voice trailed off.

"As if what?" said Neela.

"Maybe I shouldn't speculate like this, but as if she was *afraid* of something. She wants to wait, even though she keeps saying the teakettle is *priceless*. If you ask me, it's not worth the fuss. But I don't like the idea of Mary being afraid to go to the police. Anyway, I just thought it was a strange coincidence."

"What about Hal, the man I saw that day in the kitchen? What if it was him?"

"That's what I said. I remembered your story. But Mary said no. She seemed so sure, I didn't press her."

Why did Mary think it *wasn't* Hal? With all the stuff that had been happening with Lynne, and Veronica Wyvern, Neela had forgotten all about Mary. But now she remembered again the woman's strange behavior with the embroidery, and the squeaky shoes outside the kitchen door the other day. Was Mary protecting Hal, or just hiding something else herself?

After Neela hung up, she relayed the information to everyone. "Notice how," she mused, "the teakettle and the rock happened on the same day?"

Mrs. Krishnan got an anxious look on her face before disappearing into the kitchen. A few minutes later she returned with Mrs. Sunder behind her.

Neela groaned when she saw what her mother held in her hands. "But Mom, the aarti didn't even work the first time. Now we're getting rocks thrown at us."

Mrs. Krishnan lit the camphor on the brass plate. "Sometimes you have to do it a few times."

"Drishti?" Pavi asked. She and her mother watched as Mrs. Krishnan circled the burning flame clockwise and counterclockwise in front of Neela.

"Everything helps," Mrs. Sunder said.

Neela thought of the rock and the note. "We'll need all the help we can get."

CHAPTER 12

Neela looked at the clock. In India, where it was morning, her grandmother would be awake by now. Quietly, Neela slipped out of bed and got the phone from the hall. She had dialed her grandparents' number so many times, she knew it by heart, even the international and city codes for Chennai. As she heard the phone ringing on the other end, she glanced behind her. It was late, but her father wasn't home from work yet, and her mother was downstairs in the office, studying for an exam. Sree was already asleep. Neela climbed back into bed with the phone, just as her grandmother answered.

"Hi, Patti, it's me," she said in a low voice, speaking in Tamil.

"Neela! Shouldn't you be sleeping?"

"No, not yet." She fingered the edge of her pillowcase. She wasn't sure how to begin. "Something happened today, Patti. Something that has to with the missing veena."

Lalitha Patti's voice was immediately concerned. "Are you okay?"

"I'm fine. We're all fine." She described the rock and note they found earlier in the day. "But the strange part is that the note mentions *you*." She picked up the note from her night table and read it to her grandmother.

"I don't believe it," Lalitha Patti said. "This is getting worse and worse. Are you sure you're all okay? Did you call the police?"

"Yes, there's nothing to worry about," Neela said quickly. The last thing she wanted to do was scare her grandmother. That wasn't why she was calling. "But the note gave me another idea—about your other veena, the expensive one with the jewels?"

"It was stolen," Lalitha Patti said. "But you know that. Why are you thinking of that veena?"

"Because maybe whoever took *that* veena took the one you sent me, too."

"Neela, I think you should stop thinking about all of this."

"No, but what if the thief is trying to steal all of your veenas, and that's why he mentions you in the note, because—"

"He didn't want the expensive veena," Lalitha Patti cut in.

"But you just said it was stolen."

"Yes, but . . ." Lalitha Patti hesitated. "I don't think it's the one he wanted."

"How do you know?"

"I was about to go on a trip and wanted to take the sturdier case, so I switched the instruments the night before. But the thief didn't know that. He took the expensive one that was in the lightweight case by mistake."

"But wouldn't he open the case just to make sure?"

"I don't know why he didn't check," Lalitha Patti said, "but I'm positive." Here she paused again. "Neela, I have to be honest. I haven't told you everything. If you knew the rest, you would know why he wasn't after all my veenas. He was after only one."

"If it's the curse, I know about it," Neela said.

There was a silence. For a moment Neela thought her grandmother had hung up. But then she finally spoke. "I told them not to tell you. I didn't want to upset you."

It took Neela a second to figure out that Lalitha Patti meant her parents. "They don't know I know," she said. She thought about Sudha Auntie's story, but that would take too long to explain to her grandmother. "I overheard them," she said instead. "But don't worry about me, Patti. I'm old enough to know."

"Oh, Neela, it isn't just the curse. There's more."

"Well, tell me, then," Neela said. "Tell me what you didn't tell me before. Who is the thief?"

"I don't know," Lalitha Patti said. "But I can tell you

what happened before the veena was taken, and why he was after the other veena." She cleared her throat. "Many years ago, I was traveling and came across a music store in one of the villages near here. You know me. I can't resist instruments, especially something old and in good condition. That's when I found this veena. When I saw it, I knew right then it was . . ." Lalitha Patti searched for a word.

"Special," Neela said. She had heard this story before. It was one she had always loved, the one she had asked her grandmother to repeat countless times before going to bed when she was in India. But tonight, the story had begun to take on a new meaning.

"Little did I know how 'special' the veena was," Lalitha Patti said.

"That it was cursed," Neela said. "But what about the Chennai Music Palace? Isn't the store part of the curse, too? Doesn't the veena always return there?"

"You're jumping ahead. As it turns out, my good friend Govindar owns the Chennai Music Palace. Two of my veenas are from his store. But I only met him after he had sold the *maya veena* many years ago, so I never saw it in his store. And it never came up between us because, well, I didn't know *I* owned the *maya veena*. I certainly didn't know it when I bought it from that village store."

"And then what happened? The veena stayed with you? It never disappeared?"

"No, but here's the thing. After I bought the veena, my brother-in-law handled all the maintenance—fixing strings, adjusting and reapplying the frets. All the little things you need to do to keep your veena in shape. But over the years, he developed arthritis in his hands and had to stop. Last year, I had someone else come. Someone new."

"Govindar," Neela guessed.

"Oh no, not him," Lalitha Patti said. "He *sells* veenas, he doesn't service them. At least not anymore. This was someone from a different store. When he came over to the house, he recognized the veena right away. This is Guru's *maya veena*, he told me. He used to work at Chennai Music Palace long ago. He remembered the veena because of its story."

"So *he's* the one who took the instrument?"

"I don't know. But two days later the *Chennai Telegraph* did a big front-page article on how Guru's legendary cursed veena had been recovered. Someone leaked the information to the newspaper. Maybe it was him or someone else he told." Lalitha Patti's voice took on an angry tone. "From then on, I had phone calls, reporters bugging me at my door. All because of this veena, which, after so many years, had been finally unearthed. It became a huge scandal and a major headache."

"Then what happened?" Neela asked. "Someone tried to steal the veena?"

"No, no. Not yet. Govindar called. Why hadn't I told him I had the *maya veena*? I said I didn't know until the fellow who came to service my veena told *me*. At that point, Govindar and I discussed what to do next. He said the press would stop after some time. But that if the stress of owning such an instrument got to me, he offered to buy the instrument from me."

"Of course," Neela exclaimed. "He wanted the instrument back!"

"Govindar?" Lalitha Patti said. "Why on earth would he want that veena? More than likely, he had been trying to get rid of it all those years. But the last thing I wanted to do was sell my veena because of some stupid story. So I said no, thank you. Then over the next months, we started getting phone calls *every* day. Not just phone calls, but e-mails, letters in the mail, even people stopping me in the street, claiming the *maya veena* belonged to them. Most of them were real cuckoos. Even this I put up with. Then about a month before I mailed you the veena, that's when we had the break-in."

Neela reflected over what she'd heard so far. "It had to be the man who repaired your veena. Or Govindar."

"Why do you keep suspecting Govindar? Definitely no. He's a good man. But really, it could be *anyone*, Neela. Remember, the news was broadcast over all of Chennai." Lalitha Patti sighed. "The break-in is what finally did it to me. Your grandfather became so jittery after the incident, he began having palpitations, and with his heart condition, it was serious. And the thought of a complete stranger in our home frightened us. He had taken the wrong veena—maybe he would be back for the real one. I realized then that this veena would always be a source of trouble. It was cursed, all right, but not in the way I had expected. Unless I did something. So I called Govindar again."

"To sell the veena?"

Lalitha Patti was quiet for a moment. "I guess it was my own selfishness, wanting to hang on to that instrument. But it was unique and too beautiful to sell; I couldn't bring myself to do it. So instead, I decided to mail it away, someplace far. To my granddaughter, who was in need of an instrument."

"Then why was the package from Chennai Music Palace?"

"Govindar helped with the packing and shipping. His store ships to places internationally all the time, so he did me the favor and I reimbursed him."

"So then what happened?" Neela asked.

"Well, I announced to the *Telegraph* I'd sold the veena, which they published, and that was the end of that. The phone calls, the e-mails, the weird people in the street, all stopped. Still, maybe it would have been better to sell the veena to the store when I had a chance. The veena is missing again, and now I've got you involved in the whole mess, too."

Neela leaned back in her bed, taking in the whole story. "That's not so bad, Patti. Why didn't you tell me all of this before? Why did it have to be a secret?"

"Well, I didn't think it was worth sharing. I thought the curse was some silly story passed around Thanjavur and Chennai."

Neela frowned, trying to make sense of her grandmother's

words. "And you don't think that anymore? You think it's the curse that keeps making the veena disappear?"

Lalitha Patti seemed to hesitate. "I honestly can't say I know. There is something about that veena that's not . . . normal. It has some kind of pull, some kind of force."

There was one other thing she and her grandmother had not talked about yet. "Patti, do you know about Veronica Wyvern?"

"Veronica Wyvern?"

"Yes, the veena player who died about ten years ago, and—"

"Of course I know about her. What a ridiculous question."

Was it Neela's imagination or had her grandmother's voice turned sharp?

"I hear you are getting a new veena," Lalitha Patti suddenly said. The whole tone of her voice changed in just a split second, as if someone had wiped over it with a cloth. "I think that's the *best* news I've heard."

"But . . ." Neela paused. Why was her grandmother trying to change the subject?

"And now I must leave you," Lalitha Patti went on, "because the milkman is here, and I have to pay him." She ended the call with an abrupt good-bye.

Neela set down the phone. What just happened? At that moment, she looked up to see her mother standing at the door. She jumped. How long had her mom been there? Had she heard the whole conversation?

"Who were you talking to?" Mrs. Krishnan asked.

"Lalitha Patti," Neela casually said, hoping that would be the end of it.

"And what's this?" her mother said next, holding up a printout.

The article about Veronica Wyvern! She must have left it in the office the other evening. "That's mine," Neela said. She resisted the urge to snatch it from her mother's hands.

Mrs. Krishnan looked at the margin, where some notes had been scrawled. "'Veronica Wyvern killed?'" she read. "'Veena destroyed in crash?'" Her eyes narrowed. "Does this have something to do with Lalitha Patti's veena?"

Neela looked at the floor. "Sudha Auntie mentioned the veena player. I was curious about her," she mumbled.

"Curious about a train wreck?"

Neela said nothing.

Mrs. Krishnan sat down on the bed next to her and accidentally crunched a bag of chips. "You eat way too many chips," she said, picking the bag out from under her.

"It helps me think," Neela said.

"About what?"

"Stuff." Neela waited for a lecture to begin on the downside of eating too many potato chips.

Surprisingly, her mother said nothing. She opened the bag. "There are a few more left." She held out the bag like a peace offering.

Neela took it from her reluctantly. She was still trying to make sense of her conversation with Lalitha Patti and her grandmother's reluctance to talk about Veronica Wyvern when she had shared everything else. On top of that, ever since Neela had overheard her parents talking that night, she knew they weren't being completely honest with her either. How was she expected to tell her mom stuff if she didn't do the same in return?

Mrs. Krishnan reached over to stroke the ends of Neela's hair. Neela had always loved this since she was small. But lately, it had begun to annoy her, too, because it felt as though her mother was secretly trying to arrange her hair at the same time.

Still, it was a trick that never failed, and in spite of herself, Neela found herself relaxing under her mother's hand. She reached into the bag and ate the last remaining chips.

"Do you think the veena is a dying tradition?" she asked.

"Wh-at? Did Patti tell you that?"

"No, someone else. One of . . . Sudha Auntie's students," Neela lied.

"The veena is definitely not dying. It's beautiful and expressive."

"But what if no one wants to play it?"

"There will always be people who want to play it. Like you. Unless you're thinking of giving up. But you shouldn't let the rock stop you from playing."

"I'm not," Neela said. "Actually, I want to find Patti's veena even more. There has to be something special about it if someone wants it so badly."

"Don't you think you're confusing two different things?"

Mrs. Krishnan asked. "You can still go on playing, with or without Patti's veena."

"But it's only after I got her veena that I started to sound okay," Neela said, "and not twangy. It's bad enough I get scared to play in front of people. The last thing I need is a twangy veena."

"You're not that twangy. And you won't play on Sudha Auntie's veena forever. We'll get you a new one."

But it wouldn't be her grandmother's veena. It wouldn't be a Guru original. It wouldn't be the one with a strange curse that marked it special forever. Neela thought all these things, but she didn't say them out loud.

Mrs. Krishnan stared at the printout still in her hand. "Is there something else you're not telling me? Like this Hal, is he someone you know?"

"Of course not! I never saw him before in my life."

Mrs. Krishnan sighed. "The important thing to remember is that Patti's veena is gone. And some strange man out there wanted it and knows where you live. And God only knows if he has anything more planned. That veena isn't worth your safety. Forget about it and this Veronica Wyvern stuff. . . . It isn't healthy to be so fixated."

"How can you give up so soon?"

"There's nothing else we can do."

Neela remembered her mother saying how it was better that the veena was gone. "I think you're happy we lost the veena," she said. "Because it's bad luck."

"Of course not!" Mrs. Krishnan flushed. "I'm just being

practical. You should too. I don't know what Lalitha Patti said to you. But I'm telling you: stop thinking about that veena." She crumpled up the printout and threw it in the waste can on her way out.

When her mother was gone, Neela leaped from the bed and pulled the printout from the trash. She smoothed the paper out and stored it inside her backpack. She most certainly would *not* forget about the veena. So much had happened in just the last few days. And she was sure she was on the right track. The rock was proof. Her grandmother's story was proof. There was something her mother didn't want her to know, and Neela was going to figure out what it was.

CHAPTER 13

As the weeks went by, Neela found it hard to concentrate. She felt charged with excitement over all the things she had learned so far. At night she tossed and turned in bed and woke up the next morning tired. In class her mind wandered until Ms. Reese would call on her to pay attention. From her seat, Lynne would look over at Neela as if she wondered what was wrong with her. Sometimes Amanda would look at Neela, too, but to make a face at her.

The only thing that relaxed Neela was playing. Some days she practiced twice, once in the afternoon, and again before going to bed. The pads of her fingers, which in the past always became sore when she practiced for too long, had formed thick calluses, just like Sudha Auntie's, making it easier to press down on the strings.

"You seem to be practicing more these days," her mother

observed. "I thought you didn't like Sudha's veena."

"Well, the duct tape sucks," Neela said. "But I'm getting used to it."

It was true the duct tape was ugly and rubbed against her leg when she practiced. But she didn't notice it so much these days. She had finally memorized her recital piece, which meant she didn't have to look at her book anymore. Sometimes she closed her eyes and focused her entire mind on how she sounded, note by note. She was surprised by the results, that even with her own ears she could hear she was improving. If she had her grandmother's veena, she couldn't help thinking, she would sound even better.

"Why are you closing your eyes?" Sree asked. He was always there these days when she practiced.

"I can see the music better," she said.

Sometimes she asked, "Don't you get bored, Sree? Don't you want to watch TV instead?"

He shook his head. His hair, which had now grown past his ears, hung in big, curly locks around his face, making him look girly.

"Fine," she said. "Just don't get used to it, okay? I need my space."

She said that every time, but so far, she had never sent him away.

December arrived, and, one by one, Christmas decorations began to appear in the neighborhood. First it was white metal reindeer pulling a sleigh at the corner of Lambert

Street. Then several manger scenes along Winthrop. And finally, near the stone church came the giant inflatable snowman that her dad called the Pillsbury Doughboy. Some of the newer, flashier decorations came and disappeared in a season or two, but these regulars had been there every year as long as Neela could remember. The sight of them strangely comforted her as she walked to school and back, as if seeing a snowman that was almost as tall as her house meant there was still some normalcy in her life.

It had been weeks since the rock incident, after which not a single clue concerning the missing veena had cropped up. It made Neela wonder if her mother wasn't right all along, and that it was best to forget about the veena and the curse and everything that went with it. But just when she was about to give up hope, something unexpected happened.

One day after art class, Neela went to the church office to get an application for the next semester.

Julia, who was at her desk, saw her immediately. "Neela!" she exclaimed. "Come in!"

Neela hadn't talked to Julia since that day on the phone when the teakettle was stolen. She glanced at Mary's desk, which was empty. "Where's Mary?" she asked.

"She had a dental appointment," Julia said. "I'm glad you came. I have something to show you on my computer."

Neela walked gingerly around the stacks of papers and bags on Julia's desk, trying not to knock anything over.

"Don't mind my mess," Julia said cheerfully. "You

wouldn't guess looking at it, but it's an organized mess. I know where everything is."

"So, did you ever find the teakettle?" Neela asked. She looked at Julia's things. If it was here, they would never find it.

"No, but I found something else. I was scratching my head, trying to figure out how to track down Hal or your missing—uh, what was it again?"

"Veena."

"Right. So then I had this idea—what if I looked through the pictures from our fall picnic? Maybe Hal is someone who belongs to our church."

"That's a good idea," Neela said. "But you don't know what he looks like."

"Oh, I know just about everyone who comes and goes in the church. So I figured I would look for an elderly, well-dressed man—that's how you described him—that I *didn't* know. And bingo." She opened a computer file. "Is this your Hal?"

Neela watched the screen as the picture loaded. Then there before her was the very man she had met, a person she had almost come to believe didn't exist, until she saw his photo staring back at her. He was dressed differently, this time in navy slacks and a pale purple polo shirt, but he had the same hawkish eyes and the shortly cropped gray hair, and he was standing with a plate of food next to Mary Goodwin.

"That's him," Neela said excitedly. "And look, Mary

does know him. They're standing together."

"That's right," Julia agreed.

"So she lied," Neela said, then wondered if that was the right thing to say in front of Julia.

But Julia was more puzzled than anything. "Maybe she met him that day and forgot. It was a newcomer picnic, and there were so many people there. I have great respect for Mary. It isn't like her to lie."

Neela didn't say anything. Personally, she didn't trust Mary, but Julia did have a point about the newcomer picnic. She studied the photo. Mary wore a dark-colored, button-up blouse, and looked as if she were at a funeral instead of a picnic. Hal looked as he did the last time Neela saw him: well-dressed and nice. How could someone who looked like him steal her veena? Or throw a rock at her house?

"So, now what?" she asked.

"You tell me," Julia said. "We've got this picture of Hal."

And Mary, Neela wanted to add. "Is there a way to find out where Hal lives?" she asked instead. "If he belongs to the church, you could have his address somewhere, like an address book. . . ." Her voice trailed off. She looked at Julia's desk. How would anyone find anything in all those stacks of papers?

"Yes!" Julia said. "We have it in two formats—one in hard copy, which would be in . . . Now which stack would it be? Hmm."

Neela looked again at the heaping stacks. "What's the other format?"

"On the computer," Julia said. "How brilliant! Let's look him up on my computer."

Neela wasn't sure why Julia was so excited, but then again, it *was* exciting, like being detectives. But the only name they knew was Hal. When Julia typed it in, no records came up. And just like that, the search was over.

"Don't worry," Julia said, seeing Neela's face. "I'm not sure if it's allowed, but I'm going to e-mail you this picture of Hal. You hang on to it. Maybe seeing his face will jog your memory, and you'll remember something important about him that will help you find your vee—um—instrument."

Neela smiled and said thanks, but she was disappointed. Also, she wasn't sure if she wanted to look at Hal's face much longer.

They talked a bit more while Neela told her about the rock and how it had happened on the same day as the teakettle getting stolen. She didn't want to sound crazy, so she didn't mention Veronica Wyvern, Guru, or the curse. Then they moved on to other things, like Neela's art class, school, and finally music.

"I used to play the clarinet when I was a child." Julia laughed. "Boy, did I stink. The neighborhood must have been very happy when I gave it up."

"It's hard to play anything in tune," Neela said. "I sounded terrible when I began. I'm so much better now than before. But I still have to get over my stage fright."

"Oh, you have that? My daughter, who's grown up now, had the same problem. Her hands would shake like crazy during her piano recitals. I'd tell her to think of pink elephants."

"Thinking doesn't help," Neela said. "Not thinking does. But it's hard not to think when I play."

"Well, I still say you're very admirable, being so serious about music at your age."

Neela knew Julia was probably just being nice, but it was still satisfying to get a compliment. No one had ever called her admirable or serious before.

Just then the phone rang. As Julia answered, Neela noticed that the wyvern embroidery was back on Mary's desk. Here was her chance to look at it!

She went over and picked it up. The price tag on the back said Dray's Discount Store. Hardly a family heirloom, she thought. The only thing interesting was the banner across the top, in which the word *wyvern* was stitched in curlicue writing. Neela's heart leaped for a moment when she recognized the word, but then again, she already knew the dragon was a wyvern, so it didn't tell her all that much. So what was it that Mary didn't want her to see?

Her eyes met Julia's.

"Sorry, Neela," Julia whispered, covering the mouthpiece. "I have to take this one." She smiled at her before resuming her phone conversation.

Neela looked again at the embroidery. She had never stolen anything in her whole life. And yet she had the strongest urge to tuck the frame inside her cardigan and slip out before Julia noticed. The feeling was so intense, her arm tingled and her throat went dry. She told herself stealing was wrong and that Julia could get in trouble.

Still, Neela was sure there was something important about the embroidery. Could she take a picture of it somehow? Looking around the room, she spotted the photocopying machine behind Mary's desk.

She lifted the lid of the machine and turned to Julia. "Can I photocopy this?" she asked softly.

Julia, who was still busy talking, nodded distractedly.

Neela watched as the light from the machine crossed under the embroidery she had laid flat over the glass tray. When the copy came out, she surveyed the results. Wow! The copy of the wyvern was clear and crisp.

She put the frame back on Mary's desk, glad she had found a solution, but a bit unsettled by how close she had come to stealing. I'm getting as bad as Hal, she thought.

She waved to Julia before leaving. After weeks of nothing, she now had Hal's picture, a photocopy of Mary's embroidery, and she had made a friend in Julia. A pretty good day in all. Now if she could only figure out what Mary was up to.

CHAPTER 14

Sunday morning, Neela woke up to Sree howling in the bathroom.

"Sree, I'll be fast," Mrs. Krishnan said over his whining voice.

"No, no, noooo . . ."

Neela put her pillow over her head. Not again, she thought. She tried to ignore them, willing herself back to sleep. But the harder she tried, the louder Sree's voice became. Would the two of them ever stop? Finally Neela rose from bed. She wasn't quite sure what she was going to do, but by the time she reached the bathroom and saw the lollipops all over the floor, she had made up her mind. She held out her hand. "Give me the scissors."

Mrs. Krishnan stared at her. Behind them, Sree lay

in a quivering heap on the ground.

"But you don't know anything about . . ." her mom started. She looked down at Sree. "Honey, if you just had a lollipop and . . ."

Sree cried even harder.

By now, Mr. Krishnan had stopped by the bathroom, too. "Neela wants to help? Grab the chance!"

"But she's only eleven," Mrs. Krishnan said, alarmed. "Can we really trust her with the scissors? He moves around so much and—"

"She'll be fine," he said.

Neela closed the bathroom door behind her. After a moment, she heard her parents clattering their mugs in the kitchen. Her mom said, "How can we have coffee while she might be in there puncturing his face?"

Great, Neela thought. She was glad her mother had so much confidence in her. She looked down at her brother. "Get up," she said.

"No," he cried. He curled up into a smaller ball.

"I'm not cutting your hair," she said.

He looked up at her. "You're not?"

"No. At least not the way Mom wants."

She could see the gears turning in his head: *Where was the trick?* "No tricks," she said.

He sat up. "Are you cutting out my brain?"

"Of course not." She looked around the bathroom. Then she saw something that gave her an idea. "Sit on the toilet, Sree. With the lid down." From the shelf behind him, she picked up a bowl of seashells, dumped them into the bathtub, and dusted off the empty bowl. Then she put it upside down on his head.

Sree started squirming, then giggling. "What are you doing?"

"I'm protecting your brain. I'll only cut whatever is sticking out of the bowl."

He thought about it for a moment. "Promise?"

"Yeah."

Then he sat still as she carefully snipped the ends of his hair around the edge of the bowl—along his forehead, around his ears, and then behind his neck.

Halfway through, Sree looked up at her. "I hate lollipops," he said.

Neela nodded. "I know."

That evening, Sudha Auntie came for dinner. Mrs. Krishnan made it a point to invite her over a few times in the year so she and Mr. Krishnan could suck up to her. At least, that was how Neela saw it. Sudha Auntie arrived promptly at six o'clock in a mustard-colored sari and matching blouse, carrying a bag of oranges, which she gave to Mrs. Krishnan.

Everyone settled down in the living room, including Sree, who was still happily fingering his new haircut. He had liked it so much, he said he wanted it done with a bowl every time. When Mr. Krishnan saw Sree, he said something like, "Look, it's the fifth Beatle!" But mostly he and Mrs. Krishnan were relieved that nothing had been punctured or shorn and that Sree ended up looking half decent.

Sudha Auntie began by talking about growing up in Thanjavur, a city in India famous for art and music. "It's a place where music lives and *breathes*. All the leading instrument-makers reside there; even Guru did."

When she heard Guru's name, Neela sat up. Would Sudha Auntie say more about the *maya veena*? Neela had studied the picture of Hal and the photocopy of the embroidery what seemed like a hundred times, but so far, she had come up with nothing.

But today her teacher was more focused on her own roots. "My family, for three generations, have all been musicians. When I was only six years old, my mother began teaching me the veena. So you can just imagine how my family of musicians living in Thanjavur reacted when I said I wanted to be a veterinarian."

"What did they do?" Neela asked.

"They married me off, of course. At sixteen. My mother said girls from good families didn't become animal doctors."

Sixteen! Neela couldn't imagine getting married that soon.

"But I wanted to be a vet," Sudha Auntie continued. "I grew up with a Pomeranian. She was so sweet. She did not bark at anybody. So after I married, I made a deal with my husband's family: I would play the veena, but I would also go to vet school."

"Why did they care if you played the veena or not?" Neela asked.

Sudha Auntie turned to her. "My family were very noted musicians. My husband's family wanted me to continue that tradition. But they were open-minded and sent me to vet school. On our first day, we had to do dissection." Sudha Auntie made a scissoring action with her hand. "On dead animals. That day it was a fetal pig. Well, I took one look at the guts of a pig, and my vet career was over. I decided that playing the veena wasn't so bad. What do you say?" She tweaked Sree's cheek. He gave her a horrified look before darting behind his mother.

"The world is lucky because of that decision," Mrs. Krishnan said, covering up for Sree.

"Well, times are different," Sudha Auntie said. "You don't have to be so traditional to be a veena player. Heck, you don't even have to be Indian anymore."

"Like Tannenbaum," Mr. Krishnan said. "We were amazed by how authentic he sounded that day. Right, Lakshmi?"

"Very authentic," Mrs. Krishnan murmured.

Neela had an idea. "What about Veronica Wyvern?"

"Veronica Wyvern?" Neela's mother repeated. Her eyes flashed.

"She's an American player," Neela said innocently.

"Lovely musician." Sudha Auntie smiled widely. "Trained entirely here in Boston."

"Did you ever hear her?" Neela asked. "In person, that is?"

"A few times," Sudha Auntie said. "We were friendly."

"You were friends?" Neela asked, trying not to look too excited.

"I said we were *friendly*, not friends," Sudha Auntie corrected. "Why do you seem so interested, Neela? Is there something about her you wanted to know?"

Neela paused. There *was* something she wanted to know ever since she first talked about Veronica with Pavi over the phone. It was the one mystery element that stood between the veena belonging to Veronica, and then to her. "I wanted to write a report about Veronica Wyvern," Neela said slowly, thinking as she spoke. "And it's always more interesting to include quirky information. Like, did she own a million veenas, or just one?"

"That's what people want to know?" Sudha Auntie said. "Humph. How about how she had mastered hundreds of *ragams* by the age of twelve? That would be more relevant." Then she saw Neela's impatient expression.

"Oh, all right," Sudha Auntie continued. "I think she owned only one. Most players own at least two or three. Not her. And"—she scratched her head thoughtfully—"I'll tell you how I know. It might be the kind of 'quirky' information you're looking for. One day I went to the grocery store in Cambridge, when I ran into her in the parking lot. We stopped and chatted for a few minutes. Her hands were full of grocery bags. She opened her car door to pile them into the back. I spotted her veena. 'Off to a concert?' I asked. She said no. 'Master class?' No. Then, if I wasn't so nosy, I'd have kept quiet. But people rarely carry around their veenas, so I had to know where she was going with it. I pestered her some more, and she told me she was going nowhere but the grocery store. 'I always take my instrument with me,' she said. 'No matter where I go.' 'Every day, everywhere?' I asked. 'Rain, sun, and snow?' She said yes, and I thought this was the looniest thing I'd ever heard. Especially when she told me it was the only veena she owned. But I guess that's dedication for you. And *quirky*."

Neela listened intently to Sudha Auntie's story. It did sound strange to take your veena to the grocery store. But maybe Veronica had a reason? "Did you ever see her veena?" she persisted. "Would you recognize it if you saw it?"

"Neela, why this morbid curiosity in a dead musician's instrument?" Mrs. Krishnan said.

Sudha Auntie nodded. "I don't recall what it looked like. I guess I was too busy listening to her play. Poor lady. She met an untimely demise."

Mrs. Krishnan said, "Maybe we can change the subject to something more cheerful?"

"What happened to the pig?" Sree suddenly asked.

"Pig?" Sudha Auntie asked.

"He means the fetal pig you had to cut up," Neela said. "Who cares, Sree? That wasn't the point of her story." She couldn't help sounding cross. It seemed with every chance she got, Neela's mother was steering her away from her grandmother's veena.

Still, Sudha Auntie had managed to answer Neela's question. A woman who carried her only veena with her everywhere she went would certainly have had it with her when she was on the train that crashed in India. Case closed. So where did that leave Neela?

Sudha Auntie gave a wink at Sree. "Would you believe that fetal pig was reincarnated as a little boy? Ha!"

Sree shrank back behind his mother again, and Neela caught her parents exchanging looks as if they thought Sudha Auntie was a very strange woman.

After dinner, everyone returned to the living room.

"You have to do the honor of playing something for us, Sudha," Mrs. Krishnan said.

Sudha waved her hand. "You don't want to be subjected to my playing on an evening like this."

"Are you joking?" Mr. Krishnan asked. "All our friends will say, *You had Sudha Rajugopal at your house and you didn't hear her play?* It would be a hard thing to live down."

Sudha Auntie grinned. "That is a nice thing to say, even to an old donkey like me."

Neela listened as her teacher and parents went back and forth. She knew this pretense of Sudha Auntie not wanting to play, and her parents insisting, was all just an act. It was only a matter of time before Sudha Auntie "gave in" and did what she had been hoping to do all evening long. At last her parents "won," and Mr. Krishnan got out the student veena.

"Glad to see it's still here," Sudha Auntie quipped.

Neela bit her lip. Would she ever hear the end of it from her teacher?

Sudha Auntie gestured to her. "Neela plays first."

Neela started. "No, you can go ahead." She hoped that would be enough to avoid playing.

Sudha Auntie was adamant. "All musicians play. Besides, we want to hear you."

"Go on," Mrs. Krishnan said gently.

Mr. Krishnan smiled encouragingly. "How about the recital piece?"

Neela sighed, seeing she had no choice. She sat down next to the student veena. It seemed she had been practicing the recital piece for so long. But she had been getting better. Even Sudha Auntie, who used every opportunity to harp on all the things Neela was doing wrong at their lessons, had been criticizing her less these days. Still, practicing was not the same thing as performing. When you performed, you didn't stop in the middle. Unless you messed up.

Neela began softly, building volume as she continued with her song, entirely conscious of everyone watching her. Why couldn't she concentrate the way she did when she was alone? Then halfway through the piece, Sree crept next to her to tap the beat on his lap. And usually it was annoying to have him so close to her elbow. Yet that little thing made her feel as if it were just the two of them in the living room, as it had been all these past days. She started to relax, the great eye inside her opened at last, and she was able to focus. When she finished, she had counted three wrong notes, but she was sure she hadn't left out any lines this time, and she had even improvised the last notes the way she did when she was alone. Everyone clapped.

"Sree, you counted the beats!" Mrs. Krishnan said. "When did you learn that?"

"Neela taught me," he said.

Her parents looked at her, surprised.

"He's been sitting with me when I practice." Neela shrugged as if it was no big thing, but secretly she was glad he had done a good job.

"Not bad," Sudha Auntie said. "Neela, you're improving."

Neela smiled. "Thanks."

"Of course, you'll have to learn to sound more musical," Sudha Auntie added, "and less like a trained monkey."

Her parents and teacher laughed. How typical of Sudha Auntie. Yet wrapped inside that monkey comment was an actual compliment—maybe the first Neela had ever heard from Sudha Auntie directed her way. She felt a glimmer of satisfaction flash through her. When Sree sat on the couch next to her, she didn't shove him away like she normally did.

Next came Sudha Auntie's turn. She started first with a scale known as a *ragam*, which contained all the notes she would play in the song. Then she continued with the main song, which Neela recognized immediately. It was "Sri Chakra Raja." Her mother sang it when she was scrubbing the kitchen or folding clothes. Neela always associated the song with housework. It never occurred to her that it could be performed in front of an audience.

Sudha Auntie took her time with the melody, her fingers gliding up and down the frets effortlessly. Neela remembered Lalitha Patti saying that Sudha Auntie made many appearances in her early days, with thousands of people coming at a time to hear her play.

As Neela watched, she was struck by something strange and lovely in her teacher's face, a kind of glow, as if she were lit from within. How was it that her teacher, who normally looked like a dried-up fruit, could look suddenly almost . . . beautiful? *Play for yourself and it will come beautifully.* Her grandmother's words returned to Neela. Was that it? Would it ever *come beautifully* for her? Tonight had been better. Her mind was on her music, with a little help from Sree. If only she could find a way to do that every time.

Neela continued listening to her teacher, and she imagined herself in the future, as she always did. But instead of seeing just herself, she saw a circle of veena players like Sudha Auntie, Veronica Wyvern, and Parvati, widening that circle to let her in. She pictured their music billowing out like an enormous knitted blanket, stretching and covering the entire world. The thought comforted her.

She looked through the window, watching as fresh snow fell over dead leaves and bare tree branches, covering the tops of houses and cars, turning the quiet, empty street white and new.

CHAPTER 15

By morning, Arlington was covered by more than a foot of snow. When Neela got to class, Ms. Reese was talking to Matt, and she didn't look pleased.

"Matthew, I've been very generous, but no matter how I add them up, they're much more than thirty." She looked at Neela sitting down at her desk. "Neela, I'm afraid I have to say the same for you. Please see me after class so we can make up your late minutes."

Neela stared down at the floor. No one in class had been punished yet for tardiness. She and Matt were the first ones for the whole year, and possibly for the first time in the history of Bay State Elementary. This was worse than getting punished in Art. Neela could feel the class watching them. Even Amanda, who would normally be snickering, was strangely quiet, as if she couldn't believe Neela was getting in trouble either.

Ms. Reese shook her head. "You're two of my best students. Why can't you come to school on time?" She gave them each disappointed looks. Neela felt her insides churn.

"The snow," she said helplessly. It was unfair to count minutes during bad weather.

"But what about the other days? It can't be the weather alone."

"Sometimes, Ms. Reese," Matt said seriously, "I run into Neela on the way to class, and we'll end up talking about a great book we read, and we just forget about the time because we're so *absorbed* by our conversation."

"Oh, please." Ms. Reese's voice was high and sharp.

Neela sighed. Matt could be such a twerp.

Ms. Reese made a note on her desk calendar. "I expect you both after school on Thursday. Who knows, maybe this will cure you of your tardiness."

"Yeah, right," Matt said.

Her parents weren't exactly pleased when they found out she had to stay after school for being late. They spent dinner discussing the virtues of punctuality, which, as far as Neela was concerned, no one in her family had mastered, least of all her parents.

"When I was young in India, the schoolmaster would smack our hands with a ruler if we were late," Mr. Krishnan said.

"Did it hurt?" Sree asked.

"Let's get a ruler and try it on you," Neela said.

Sree started screeching, and her parents frowned at her.

"I was kidding," she muttered. "Besides, you're making that up."

"I'm not!" her dad said. "Things were different then."

"And that's why you missed your dental appointment this week," Neela said. She was the one who had answered the call from the receptionist asking where her dad was. "I guess that ruler really helped."

"No one's perfect," Mr. Krishnan conceded. "Even a ruler isn't perfect."

"Start writing." It was Thursday after school. Ms. Reese had set them up with their "assignments" and was stepping out to the main office. "I'll be back in a few minutes," she said before closing the classroom door behind her.

As soon as she was gone, Matt turned to Neela. "Show me what you have so far."

She did.

"That's just your name." He leaned back in his chair. "This bites."

Neela had to agree. Lateness, she decided, was relative. You were late because someone else wanted you somewhere before you were ready to be there. But that was probably not what Ms. Reese wanted to read about in the essay that she and Matt were being forced now to write: "What I Missed by Being Late to Class," which, if she thought about it, was impossible to write. How could you know what you missed if you missed it?

"So did you find your veena?" Matt asked.

Neela was surprised he remembered. She put down her pencil. "No."

"Do you think a nun took it? She could slip it under her robe and walk out the church, and no one would notice. They'd just say, 'There's goes a really fat nun.'"

"My veena case has wheels," Neela said, "so she could just *roll* down the sidewalk."

"Yeah, a nun on wheels."

And then they smiled at each other. Neela's eyes widened. It might be the first time they had actually shared a joke and she didn't find him completely annoying. She thought for a moment. Maybe with all the mystery and sci-fi books he read, Matt might be able to help.

Before she knew it, Neela began telling him all that had happened with Hal, Lynne, Mary, the missing teakettle, and the rock. She even told him about the curse but said that it was according to her veena teacher, who was most likely insane.

Matt listened, and for once he stopped trying to say something goofy. "I'm not sure how Lynne fits in. Maybe it's just Mary and Hal that are in on it together. I bet you could get some information on Hal at the church."

"Julia and I already tried to look up his name on her computer."

They both sat, thinking.

"What if Mary's married to Hal," Matt guessed, "and they're one of those international criminal couples. Maybe there are ancient documents stuffed inside the veena, and they know about it because they make a living stealing valuable papers around the world."

"Hmm," Neela said. Matt was beginning to head in the ridiculous direction.

"You should break into the office and look up Mary's file."

"I'm not breaking into a *church*."

"I could do it for you," Matt offered. "I know how to open a lock with a credit card."

"That's just in the movies."

"Seriously. I have lots of practice. That's how I bug my brother in the bathroom."

"It doesn't make sense," Neela said. "If Mary and Hal were married, Julia would know. And besides, they're too old to be international criminals." She didn't know if age was a factor, but the idea was preposterous anyway.

She pulled out the photocopy of the embroidery that she had been carrying with her for the past couple of days. "But you're right, there is some connection between Mary and Hal, and it starts with this." She gave him the photocopy. "Only, I've been looking at it for so long I feel like my brain is about to explode."

"That's pretty serious, because there's this one case of a Russian chess player who was thinking so hard his brain actually *did* explode and—"

"I'm just saying," Neela said crossly. "Do you want to see the embroidery or not?"

Matt looked at the sheet for a moment. "It's a crest," he said.

"A what?"

"A crest. You know, like a family crest or a coat-of-arms. In the middle ages, the knights wore them on their shields and helmets to represent their family."

"Like the knights of the Round Table?" Neela asked.

"Yeah, kind of like that. And now some people are into their family crests, and they have stuff they frame and pass down in the family. This one aunt of mine ordered a coffee mug off the Internet with her family crest on it."

"So if this is Mary's family crest, what does it mean?" Neela mused.

Matt shrugged. "It explains why she's into wyverns."

"What if wyvern was a family crest *and* a name," Neela said. "Like Veronica Wyvern. That's her name. But it could be her crest, too. Which could mean that Mary and Veronica are . . ."

"Related," Matt finished.

Just then they heard Ms. Reese opening the classroom door.

Neela's thoughts were whirling. Mary and Veronica, related?

"What, done already?" Ms. Reese said. "I could hear you chatting."

"We were brainstorming," Matt said gravely.

Ms. Reese laughed. "You have an answer for everything, don't you, Matt? What about you, Neela? Are you done?"

With effort, Neela focused on her teacher's words. "It's kind of a hard assignment."

Ms. Reese smiled. "You've got another ten minutes. Keep writing, both of you."

Neela sighed. She didn't want to write. She wanted to talk more with Matt about Mary and Veronica. From his expression, she could tell he felt the same way.

The last ten minutes seemed to drag on forever as Neela forced herself to write. What had she missed by being late? She was missing a great many things, not to mention a four-foot veena, but she didn't write that.

When it was time to go, Matt and Neela handed their assignments to Ms. Reese, but she waved her hand. "They're for you to keep. But I hope this is the last time we have to stay after. Tomorrow I'll see you both in class and on time."

As they walked to their lockers, Matt asked to see what Neela had written. She shook her head. But before she could say more, he grabbed the sheet from her hand.

"Hey!" Neela was indignant. She tried to take it back from him, but he was too quick.

"*I learned about the virtues of punctuality . . .*" Matt read aloud. "Oh my God, you're such a goody-goody." He handed her paper back. "Anyway, Mary must be the one who took the veena, because she's Veronica's grandmother."

Neela was still mad he'd snatched her paper. "What did you write?"

He stopped while she read his sheet. When she finished she looked at him. "You wrote about *Star Wars*? You wrote about a movie?"

Matt shrugged. "I knew she wouldn't read it."

Neela shook her head. How could he be so sure of himself all the time?

"So you think Mary's the grandmother?" she asked. "But she isn't old enough."

"Then she's the mom."

Neela thought about it. "But she didn't know what a veena was the day I went to the church. At least, she didn't know about it the way a mother would know about an instrument her daughter played, especially a famous dead one. Can you imagine having something so awful happen to your kid? You couldn't pretend you knew nothing about it afterward."

By now they were outside and had reached the sidewalk.

"Well, I'm heading this way," Matt said. His breath came out as a puff in the cold air.

Neela nodded in the other direction. "I'm going that way."

There was a brief pause before they each mumbled good-bye.

As she kept walking, Neela thought about the afternoon. Most of the time he acted like a dork, but maybe Matt wasn't so bad after all. He was certainly the smartest boy in class. And when he wasn't goofing around, he actually did come up with some pretty good ideas.

As she neared a corner, she spotted a familiar face on

the other side of the street, standing at the city bus stop. Lynne was facing the opposite direction, watching for the bus. Neela hid behind a tree.

School had gotten out a long time ago. Where was Lynne going when everyone in class either walked home or got a ride on the school bus? No one she knew ever rode the city bus, which went all the way downtown.

"Why are you spying on Lynne?" a voice whispered behind her. "I thought you said it was Mary or Hal."

Startled, Neela turned to find Matt standing behind her. "You scared me. And I never said it was just Mary and Hal. I still think Lynne is involved, too."

Matt peered around the tree. "What's she doing?"

"She's waiting for the T," Neela said. The T was the name for the bus and subway that went to Cambridge and Boston. "Why would she be doing that?"

"Maybe she's going downtown. It's not a big deal." Matt paused. "Unless you want to follow her."

"Follow Lynne?" Neela leaned against the tree. Pavi was always telling her to do that. Here was a chance. "I've never been downtown by myself. How would I get back? And if I'm home late, my mom will kill me. She's already upset I got punished in school."

He looked at his watch. "Ms. Reese let us out early. You could follow Lynne for a little while and head back, then call your mom and pretend you got delayed at school. She'll never know the difference. And I've been downtown before, so, uh, I could go with you."

"Really?" Neela considered his offer.

He nodded toward the road. "It's coming. Hurry up and decide."

She saw that the bus was only a block away. "All right," she said. "Let's do it."

She tucked her long hair inside her coat and slipped the hood on. It was the best disguise she could come up with at the last minute. Matt put on a Boston Red Sox cap that he got out of his backpack.

As soon as Lynne stepped inside the bus, Neela and Matt darted across the street. Neela had just enough time to read 77 HARVARD SQUARE on the front of the bus before they climbed aboard, keeping their faces down in case Lynne looked back. A moment later, the doors closed and the bus pulled out into the street, taking Neela and Matt along with it.

CHAPTER 16

The bus driver was crazy. At least he acted as if he were, speeding faster and faster down the street, weaving around cars and other buses, so that Neela, who clung to the sides of her seat, was sure they would die in a horrible crash any minute. Matt sat next to her by the window. "We're on Mass Ave," he said, which was what everyone called Massachusetts Avenue. He pointed to a street sign when the bus screeched to a halt at a red light.

Neela nodded, keeping an eye on Lynne, who sat halfway down the bus behind them, looking at a photography book. "Maybe we're going to Harvard Square," she said, remembering the bus label. She had been to Harvard Square many times with her family. Sometimes they stopped at the Au Bon Pain for chocolate croissants. But she had never been there by herself. Or alone with a boy.

Which brought up something else in her mind: she had never been alone with a boy anywhere in her whole life. Pavi's little brother didn't count. Nor did the boys that came to her prayer class on Sundays and played kick-the-can with her outside when the weather was warm. This was different. This was a situation that her parents would, with every inch of their lives, disapprove of. She glanced at Matt to see if he was registering the fact that they were alone together. *Alone together*. Could you even say that?

"Oh my God, did you see that?" he exclaimed, his eyes glued to the window. "The bus driver just ran a stop sign. He almost swiped a BMW."

At that point Neela decided that if Matt wasn't freaking out about their alone-togetherness, then neither should she. She looked at the road, watching as they sped by different stores—clothing boutiques, haircutting salons, rug stores, a Japanese steakhouse, and several furniture shops. She felt a thrill pass through her. I'm on an adventure, she thought. She was doing something real and exciting that she would remember afterward. The thought made her tingle all over.

Finally she recognized the bricked walkways of Harvard Square, with fresh snow on the rooftops of buildings and along the sidewalks. She smiled without realizing it. She loved Harvard Square. They circled around and entered the bus terminal. Inside, the bus came to a stop and everyone rose from their seats, including Lynne. She headed to the back while Neela and Matt moved to the front.

They hurried off the bus, following Lynne through a set of glass doors. It was important not to lose her in the crowd. The T station was full of people, most of them hurrying through the turnstiles. Inside the terminal, Lynne climbed up an escalator that wasn't working, taking the steps two at a time. When Neela and Matt got to the top of the same escalator, the cold air and the smell of cigarettes hit their faces. They scanned the area for Lynne. Across the street were the iron gates enclosing Harvard campus.

"You think she went that way?" Matt asked, pointing toward the gates.

Neela shook her head. "Let's keep looking." At last she spotted Lynne's aquamarine coat heading down a street to the left.

She and Matt followed as closely as they could without being noticed.

"Where do you think she's going?" Matt asked.

"I don't know," Neela said, out of breath. "But, man, does she walk fast."

At last, Lynne came to the end of the street and stepped inside a camera shop called Tristar Media.

"Should we go in?" Neela asked.

"The store's too small. She'll see us right away."

Neela saw a mailbox a few feet from the store, surrounded by a heap of snow. She stepped gingerly into the snow and crouched behind the mailbox. Matt crouched next to her.

"What will people think we're doing?" she asked. They

looked kind of funny, peering around a mailbox.

"Maybe they'll think we're really short FBI agents," Matt said.

"Or really short postal workers."

"Can you see anything?" He craned his neck. "Move over."

"Ouch. You're stepping on my foot."

After they settled down, they were able to look into the store window. A man stood behind a glass counter, showing cameras to a tall lady with a pink woolen scarf tied around her neck. She took her time, laughing over something the man said. Neela wondered what Lynne was doing. Neela's hands were getting cold. She had forgotten her mittens and had to bunch up her fingers inside her coat sleeves. Matt's nose was already red.

"C'mon, lady," said Neela.

Matt changed his voice to a falsetto. "Excuse me, mister, but I'm looking for something to go with my scarf. Do you have anything in pink?"

Neela pretended to be the man. "Lady, weya all out of pink. Don't ya know, this is Hahvahd Squayah?"

"That was actually pretty good," Matt said, surprised.

"That's what Hal sounded like."

"Look," he said.

Neela had almost forgotten what they were supposed to be doing. By now the woman with the scarf was done, and Lynne was at the counter.

"What's she going to buy?" Matt wondered.

Just then Neela remembered the ad in Lynne's notebook that had fallen to the floor in the art room. "I think I know," she said softly.

They watched as Lynne pointed to something inside the glass case. The man pulled out a camera for her. It looked like the one Lynne had circled in the ad. Presently, the man pulled out a lens for the camera as well, the kind that Neela had seen professional photographers use. The man behind the counter didn't have a lot to say. In fact, he looked as if he thought Lynne was wasting his time while she examined a camera that was clearly very expensive. He took out another camera, but Lynne shook her head. Then she took out a wad of bills and laid it on the counter.

"Are you seeing what I'm seeing?" Matt said.

Neela's eyes widened, seeing so much money. The man also looked surprised. It took him some time to count out all the bills.

"How much does she have there?" Matt asked. "She's loaded."

Neela wondered the same. She knew that some of the kids in class got monthly allowances, but usually they spent them on things like a movie or a pair of jeans, never on something as costly as a camera. "I think he counted out at least a couple of hundred dollars," she said. "Those look like twenties."

Matt whistled. "I wonder what else she's getting. Laptop? Flat-screen TV?"

"I think she's done," Neela said. They watched as the

man packed the camera and lens boxes inside a bag and handed her a receipt. "Quick," she said. They ducked behind the mailbox as Lynne came out the door. Neela felt an odd twinge of guilt when Lynne walked by, as if she had witnessed something she wasn't supposed to see. Still, Neela couldn't help wondering about the money. It had come from somewhere. A job? A gift?

She and Matt watched Lynne's retreating figure. "Now what?" she asked. She brushed some snow from her coat.

"We follow her."

They got up, maintaining their distance behind Lynne.

"I see her looking at photography books all the time," Neela said. "And she's taking a photography class. Maybe she saved up."

Matt shook his head. "There's something weird about it. You know there is."

Neela had to agree. Such an expensive purchase—shouldn't she have done it with her mom or dad?

When they reached Harvard Square, they had to wait at the curb for the light to change before crossing the street. Lynne was already on the other side, on her way to the escalator that descended into the T station.

"What time is it?" Neela asked.

"Three thirty."

"I should have been home by now, even if Ms. Reese let us out at three fifteen, and it takes me about ten minutes to walk home, and . . ."

"Neela!"

A gray-haired Indian lady in a parka was waving from the other side of the street. Neela's insides withered. "Oh God," she groaned. "It can't be."

"What? Is that your mom?"

"Are you kidding? Would my mom be that old? It's worse. That's my veena teacher."

The light changed, and Neela and Matt made their way across the street. Behind the figure of Sudha Auntie, Neela saw Lynne disappearing into the T station. Gone. With no chance of following her. Instead of crossing the street, Sudha Auntie stood where she was, waiting until Neela reached the other side.

"Well, lucky surprise to find you here," Sudha Auntie said. Her eyes narrowed as she glanced at Matt. "I guess you're here with a friend?" The way she said *friend* made Neela wince. It was clear that Sudha Auntie thought Matt was something else.

"This is Matt, a friend from school," Neela mumbled. All the thrill and happiness she had felt at being on an adventure with Matt dribbled away at the sight of her teacher's hawky face. Why—why of all people did they have to bump into Sudha Auntie? She didn't even live near Harvard.

"Is your mother somewhere here?" Sudha Auntie made the pretense of looking around, as if Mrs. Krishnan might suddenly matcrialize before them.

Neela gritted her teeth, loathing her teacher at that moment. "Actually, she's expecting us home any minute.

I'm sorry; we have to run or we'll miss our bus. Good-bye!"

With that, she hurried off to the escalator, not even looking to see if Matt was following. When they reached the bottom, Matt practically ran to keep up with her. "What's the matter? She was kind of creepy, wasn't she?"

Neela whirled around so suddenly that Matt almost collided into her. "Don't you see? That's Sudha Auntie. First of all, she's not even human. Second of all, she saw me with you, and—" Neela couldn't finish what she was about to say. The implications were too awful.

Matt looked at her closely. "Are you, like, arranged to marry someone?"

Neela flushed. "What are you talking about?! My parents won't even let me go to the mall by myself. The last thing they want is me getting married."

"Just wondering," Matt said. "I read this really cool quest book set in India, but then there was all this stuff about child brides."

"I'm not a child bride," Neela snapped.

"All right. Don't freak out about it."

Neela still glowered. "Let's figure out how to get home," she said. So I can get into more trouble, she added to herself.

Matt walked over to a bus schedule posted in the main area of the terminal. "We have to find the seventy-seven. That's what we came on." Together they looked until they pinpointed the bus arrivals. "We have exactly two minutes," Matt said, looking at his watch.

No sooner had they walked out the double glass doors than the 77 swung around the corner and pulled up to the curb just a few feet ahead of them. They ran up and climbed aboard.

She and Matt rode silently back along Mass Ave. They didn't talk about Lynne or the expensive camera. Now that they were seated, Neela had a chance to reflect over what had happened. She hadn't meant to yell at Matt. But she hadn't meant for Sudha Auntie to see her alone with a boy. She could only guess what her teacher would say to her mother the next time they met.

In some way, though, she felt like she owed Matt an explanation. Because if it weren't for him offering to go on the bus with her, she wouldn't have followed Lynne. And though Neela hadn't figured out why, she knew seeing Lynne with all that money was somehow important. She turned to him and tried to think of a way to explain.

"My parents want me to be both Indian and American," she began. "That's why they started me on the veena. Well, that's not exactly true. I was the one who wanted to learn the veena. But I think because I picked something completely Indian, my parents went along with it."

"So if you wanted to play the bongos they'd be like, oh my God, you're not Indian."

Neela smiled. "No. My parents actually are cool about most things. But I don't think they've figured out about boys yet." As soon as she said that, she expected him to say something stupid and embarrassing.

"You're doing this to find your instrument," he said instead. "They should be glad."

Neela looked at him in surprise. She realized then that for most of today, he had actually been okay.

"Parents are always flipping about something," Matt went on. "Like my hair. It wasn't supposed to be orange."

"It's not *that* orange," Neela said, trying to be nice.

"My mom had a hissy fit when she saw me. She wanted to shave my head."

Neela giggled. "That would be dramatic."

"Eh. She got used to it. And then when I wanted to play the electric guitar, it was no big deal."

"I didn't know you played the guitar," Neela said.

Matt looked embarrassed. "I just mess around. But someday I want to be in a band." For the first time, his voice was uncertain, as if he didn't know if it would really happen.

Neela thought about his rock band sketches at school, and all the musty band T-shirts he wore. He wasn't so sure of himself as she had thought.

"My lesson's on Wednesday. Maybe Sudha Auntie will forget about seeing me in Harvard Square and telling my mom. She is kind of old." But Neela knew this was wishful thinking. Her teacher never forgot anything.

"Yeah, she's definitely in the senility category." Matt shook his hair back. In the evening light, it looked less orange and less like a mop. "And who knows," he added, "maybe Lynne won the lottery."

Neela grinned. “Maybe.”

The world seemed full of surprises, of strange secrets, hidden talents, and unexpected discoveries. Neela pictured Lynne on her way home with her shiny new package, all paid for and belonging to her, a present that no one knew anything about.

Or so she thought.

Next to her, Matt looked out the bus window into the darkening streets as they rode along the last stretch of Mass Ave into Arlington.

CHAPTER 17

"**Why are you whispering?**" Pavi asked.

"Because I'm in trouble and not supposed to be on the phone," Neela whispered. "I was so late from school today, my mother totally flipped." She told Pavi about Harvard Square and Lynne buying the expensive camera with her big wad of money.

"Sounds like crime money." Pavi was excited. "Maybe she robbed a convenience store."

"She didn't rob a convenience store," Neela said. Pavi came up with ridiculous ideas sometimes. "I don't think it was stolen money." She thought about the photographs in Lynne's locker and the big photography book Lynne looked at during recess. Maybe she wanted to be a photographer. "I don't even think it matters where she got the money. Maybe if we had followed her later, that would have helped."

"*We*?" Pavi asked. "Who's *we*?"

"Oh, this guy in my class, Matt." Neela tried to be casual. "He came along, too."

There was a silence on the other end. Then: "Is he friends with Penny?"

"No. The worst part is that Sudha Auntie saw us together in Harvard Square."

"Uh-oh. If my mom caught me alone with a guy in Harvard Square, she'd freak."

"So would mine," Neela said. "I guess."

"Of course she would. Remember what happened to Shoba?"

Shoba was a friend of theirs that lived in the next town. Her parents had caught her going to the movies alone with a boy from her school, and Shoba had been banned from seeing movies with anyone for the rest of the year.

"That's different." Neela remembered her parents talking about it when they thought she wasn't listening, wondering if Shoba's parents hadn't overreacted.

Her mother's voice floated up the stairs. "I hope you're not on the phone, Neela."

"So, did you tell your parents about him?" Pavi asked.

"No. I mean, yes," Neela said, flustered. "I mean, nothing happened."

"So he came all the way to Harvard Square on a bus for no reason?"

"He came to help me."

Pavi snorted. "Yeah, right."

"I'm warning you," Neela's mother called again from downstairs.

"I don't know why you're making a big deal out of it," Neela said to Pavi. "I just hope Sudha Auntie doesn't say something stupid to my mom, that's all. You know how she is."

"Maybe she'll forget about it."

"You know she won't."

"Well, maybe she has more important things to think about than you." Pavi's voice was sharp.

Neela was taken aback. She waited for Pavi to say "kidding," but she said nothing.

Until now they had never discussed boys. She knew Pavi's parents were a lot more strict than hers. That was one of the reasons why Pavi wore a bindi these days. But it went beyond that. Pavi's family saw themselves differently, as though it were *us*, the ones who were Indian, and *them*, the ones who weren't.

Neela's parents had never been this way. They had always made great pains to tell her she was Indian *and* American. "Take the best of both cultures," they said to her. "Be *both*."

By now, Neela's mother had appeared at the door. "Neela!" she said.

"I have to go," Neela mumbled, glad to get off the phone. "Talk to you later."

"First you're late to school," Neela's mother said, "then you get punished for being late, and then you're late coming home from being punished for being late. Does anyone see the irony here?"

"We already went through this," Neela said.

"I don't think so," Mrs. Krishnan returned. "When you were late, what was I supposed to think? We *just* had a rock thrown against our house, and a note threatening you."

"That was a month ago," Neela said.

"Maybe that man was just waiting for a chance to get you alone," Mrs. Krishnan said.

Neela rolled her eyes. "If Hal wanted to hurt me, he wouldn't have thrown a rock. He would have whacked me on the head when I walked to school."

"Neela!" Mrs. Krishnan said. But she seemed to buy Neela's logic, because she changed tactics. "Anyway, I still don't understand why you got on a bus when we're two blocks from home."

"My foot was hurting," Neela mumbled. "I thought it would be faster. How did I know the bus would go downtown first?" Even to her ears, this sounded far-fetched, but she decided a half-truth was better than a complete lie. After all, she did ride the bus downtown. And her feet were kind of tired by the time she got home.

"Something's going on," Mrs. Krishnan said. "The rock, these phone calls back and forth with Pavi, getting into trouble at school, and that boy who got in trouble, too. And don't tell me he's not involved. I have a note from Ms. Reese saying the two of you sit next to each other and are consistently late."

"But that's crazy. I didn't *choose* to sit next to Matt. We were assigned. It's just a coincidence we're both late to school."

"There are no coincidences," Mrs. Krishnan said.

"Maybe you just have to trust me instead of thinking I'm up to no good."

"I never said that," Mrs. Krishnan said. "It's just . . ." Her voice trailed off.

They looked at each other, and in her mother's eyes, Neela saw something she hadn't seen before: a look of sadness. She tried to ignore the twinge of guilt she felt. She had done nothing wrong. Well, maybe she had done things without asking permission. But they had been for a good reason, an important reason. Her mother, on the other hand, had seemingly given up looking for the veena, and with no good explanation—unless it was because of bad luck, which was barely a reason at all, as far as Neela was concerned. So Neela looked away and sat at her desk to do her math homework. She kept her back turned, and focused on her work until she heard her mother finally leave the room.

"We're in for a real treat today," Ms. Reese said. "You want to share, Amanda?"

Amanda stood up, twinkling in a powder blue sweater with glitter sewn in. "My mom's a photographer, and she's talking to us about what she does."

Three seats down, Lynne suddenly started coughing, as if she'd swallowed something wrong. Neela turned, remembering the camera shop. Lynne was probably excited to see a real photographer now that she had a fancy new camera of her own. Except, as Neela watched her, excitement didn't seem to be the right word. If anything, Lynne looked as though she was going to be sick. She shifted around in her chair and then took her glasses off, rubbing them nervously on the front of her jeans. Without her glasses, her eyes were unexpectedly large, and reminded Neela of classical Indian dancers who wore *kajal*, a black eyeliner, around their eyes when they performed. A few moments later, Lynne put her glasses back on and looked like the old Lynne again. Except that she seemed on the verge of a heart attack. What was the matter with her?

Just then, Matt sat down next to Neela. It amazed her that even after their punishment, he still came to class late. Today he wore a T-shirt with the words DEF LEPPARD on it, and orange sweatpants that matched his hair. "Check out my dad's old T-shirt. Def Leppard rules."

"I've never heard of them," she said coolly.

Ever since their bus trip last week, something strange had happened. The next day at school, apparently everyone seemed to know that Neela and Matt had been punished for late minutes. Maybe it was because it had never happened to anyone else before. A few kids even asked about it. Amanda came up to them and asked, "So are you guys like, BFFs now?"

Neela tried to think of a good comeback, but she drew a blank.

Matt kept it short and simple. "Bug off," he said.

Still, Amanda had made them self-conscious. Neela suddenly remembered all the weird, space-alien stuff Matt was into, and maybe he remembered he didn't usually speak to her outside of class. Whatever it was, Neela and Matt didn't talk about Lynne, Harvard Square, or Sudha Auntie. It was as if the bus trip had never happened.

"Whoa, who's that?" Matt asked.

"Amanda's mom," Penny said.

In front of them, Elizabeth Bones strode into class, wearing suede pants with tassels, a cream-colored silk blouse, a silver-buckled belt, and black leather riding boots. In one hand she carried a leather attaché, and in the other, an assortment of leather cases for her camera equipment. Her gear looked so complex and important that it seemed like Mrs. Bones was going on a safari or some other dangerous expedition instead of speaking to a bunch of sixth grade students.

As soon as she saw her, Neela recognized her. It was the blond photographer at Alfred Tannenbaum's concert!

"What is she, a supermodel?" Matt asked, gawking at her.

"She's too old to be a model," Neela whispered, feeling catty. She hadn't noticed the other day at the concert hall just how gorgeous Amanda's mother was.

Elizabeth Bones pushed her straw-colored hair back.

"Beauty is in the eyes of the beholder," she said. "Anyone hear that before?"

The class murmured yes, staring at her.

"In photography, beauty is in the hands of the photographer. The photographer controls what you see and how you see it."

Neela had never thought of photography that way. But Amanda's mom did seem like the controlling type. Neela remembered her rudeness at the concert.

Her heart started racing. She also remembered that Elizabeth Bones was at the café with the Indian man, asking all those questions about Guru originals, as if she had seen one before. Did Elizabeth Bones know where her grandmother's veena might be? Maybe Neela could go up to her after class and ask, if she could only work up the nerve.

Elizabeth Bones snapped open one of the leather bags. "I'm passing around the latest *Boston Living*," she said to the class. "You can look at my work while I'm talking." She continued, describing photographs she had taken of sea life on a trip to Hawaii.

Meanwhile, Neela was trying to figure out why Lynne looked as if she were having a meltdown. Was it her imagination or was Lynne trying to slide under her desk? In just the last few minutes, Lynne had slumped down with her legs and lower body hidden away. Neela couldn't understand it, especially when Elizabeth Bones was talking about photography. Was Lynne jealous because she wanted to be a world-famous photographer but she was only in sixth grade? Or did she have food poisoning? It was hard to tell.

Penny poked Neela in the back and handed her the magazine from behind. "There's an India page," she whispered.

"Really?" Neela whispered back. She flipped through the pages until she came to an article titled, "Rooms with a World View." The photo shoot! Elizabeth Bones had gone ahead with the article. Just think, if her veena hadn't been stolen, it would be in the magazine right now. Neela went through the photographs of rooms from Italy and France and Spain, until she came to the one with Indian decor, and a full-length photo of a veena by itself. Only . . . Neela stared at the photo, dumbstruck. Only it was *her veena* staring right at her from the inside spread of *Boston Living*. Without thinking, she clutched Matt's arm.

"Huh?" he whispered. He was in the middle of sketching an electric guitar.

Neela wrote on his paper: *It's my veena*. She pointed to the magazine spread.

Behind her, Penny was trying to figure out what was going on.

Matt's eyes widened. He wrote: *R U sure?*

Neela nodded. *Yes!!*

OMG! What R U gonna do??

Talk to Mrs. B!

Penny poked Neela in the back again. Neela looked at her and shook her head mutely. It was too much to explain. For the next few minutes, she could hardly concentrate on anything. She kept staring at the photograph. There it was, the same dragon with folded wings and a tail, the same bronze frets, the same initials barely visible against the wood. At first, Neela felt a sense of outrage. Amanda's mother had known about the veena all along! Here was proof. Had she stolen the veena herself? Or did she have a secret connection with the person who did? Maybe they were in cahoots, as part of an elaborate scheme to . . . to what? Take a photo for a magazine?

Neela began to slowly calm down. Because it soon occurred to her that if Elizabeth Bones had any interest in stealing the veena, the last thing she would do was publish a photograph of it in *Boston Living*. Or bring the magazine to her daughter's class. There had to be another explanation. At that moment, Neela met Lynne's stricken eyes, and she knew she had to talk to Amanda's mother right away.

At last, Elizabeth Bones wrapped things up and began packing up her equipment. As soon as she had answered the last question, Neela leaped from her chair.

Amanda, who was standing next to her mother, saw Neela approaching. Even with everything on her mind, it struck Neela, as she saw them side by side, how unlike each other they were. Amanda's auburn hair was in direct contrast to her mother's platinum blond. "You remember Neela," Amanda said. "The girl with the veena."

Elizabeth Bones smiled, but with a distant, puzzled look in her eyes. "This girl?"

"She lost her veena. I told you that."

Elizabeth Bones kept smiling. "You tell me so many

things, Amanda." She said it as if most of what Amanda told her was in between important deadlines at the office and therefore subject to being forgotten. Then she said, "But there was that other girl."

"What other girl?" asked Amanda.

Neela finally spoke up. She had been dying to talk during the whole exchange between Amanda and her mother. "Mrs. Bones, I really like your work, but there's something strange here about the veena photo."

"Oh, yes?" Elizabeth Bones asked.

"Well, here's the thing," Neela continued. "Where did you photograph it? Because—"

"What other girl?" Amanda repeated.

"The other girl who contacted me," Elizabeth Bones said to her daughter.

Why weren't they listening to her? "It's *my* veena," said Neela. "In the photograph."

"*Your* veena?" Amanda said. "I thought it was stolen."

Elizabeth Bones shook her head. "It was definitely another girl's. I would know. I went to her apartment."

Amanda turned to her. "Mom, who was the other girl?"

"She's in this classroom." Elizabeth Bones pointed. "That girl right there."

Even before she looked, Neela knew who it was.

CHAPTER 18

As Neela made her way across the room, she tried to think of the first question to ask. Lynne watched her, and it seemed she slid farther into her desk, her frizzy hair spilling over in sad waves. Behind Neela trailed Amanda, while her mother talked with Ms. Reese.

Neela held up the magazine article to Lynne. "Do you know about this?"

Lynne looked nervously at the photograph. "I can explain," she said.

"Yeah, right," said Amanda.

Neela pursed her lips. "Let's go somewhere else," she said to Lynne.

"Library?" Lynne whispered.

Neela nodded.

Amanda made a move, but Neela held her back with one hand. "Maybe you can stay and tell Ms. Reese where we went."

"I'll come with you, Neela," Amanda said. "In case you need backup."

"We'll be done in five minutes," Neela said firmly. The last thing she needed was "backup" from Amanda.

Amanda looked insulted. But at that moment, Elizabeth Bones motioned her daughter over.

"All right," Amanda agreed reluctantly. "But I'm totally telling Ms. Reese what you did, Lynne. I hope you get fried."

"I hope you eat crow," Lynne said evenly.

Neela wasn't exactly sure what that meant, but it sounded worse than getting fried. Lynne was tougher than she thought.

But once they were outside the classroom, it was a different story. Lynne's face fell and she spoke in a rush. "I know how it looks, but I didn't take your veena, Neela. I needed the money, and it was too good a deal to pass up."

"Start at the beginning," Neela said. "You said you didn't take the veena. But Ms. Bones said she photographed it in your apartment."

Lynne looked miserable. "I didn't take it. Someone else did."

"Hal."

"Yes, Hal." Lynne nodded, unwilling to go on.

"And who is he? How do you know him?"

Lynne gulped. "He's my neighbor."

"Your neighbor!" Neela exclaimed. "But why did he take my veena?"

In a tearful voice, Lynne began. Hal was an old man in her building that Lynne had befriended. He used to know a veena player a long time ago that he was still hung up over. Whenever Lynne went over to see to Hal, all he talked about was Veronica Wyvern.

"He's a very confused, sad person. And when he found out that someone in my class was bringing a veena, he said he was sure it was Veronica's."

"What?" Neela's heart started pounding. She had heard the first time; she just wanted to hear it again.

"He thought the veena belonged to Veronica."

"And did it?" Neela could hardly get herself to say the words.

Lynne shook her head. "I tried telling him he was wrong, but he didn't believe me."

How would Lynne know if the veena had belonged to Veronica or not? But there was more to Lynne's story, so Neela kept listening.

"Anyway, I wish I hadn't told him about the instrument unit we did in the fall, because I never thought he would come to school and follow you home."

"He followed me from school?" Neela asked. "But I never saw him."

"You weren't looking for him. He just snuck into the church and pretended he had been there the whole time, and, well, you know the rest."

"I thought I heard someone behind me," Neela mused slowly. "And that's why he was wet, too. But he also seemed like he belonged to the church. He knew where everything was. And someone told me he volunteers there."

Lynne shrugged. "Maybe he does."

Neela didn't know whether to get angry or cry. "The whole time you knew where my veena was," she said in disbelief. "The whole time you let me believe I'd lost it, and you *lied* about it to me even when I asked you about Hal."

Lynne's face wavered. "I'm sorry. It was so wrong, I can't say how sorry I am, except that I never stole your veena, and I always meant for you to get it back safely." When Neela didn't say anything, she went on. "I found the business card from Amanda on the ground. So I called her mom and pretended it was my veena, and offered it for the photo shoot. She came to Hal's apartment to take photos, and I pretended I lived there, too. But I never meant to keep your veena. I was planning to get Hal to return it to you as soon as the photo shoot was done. It's just that I really needed the money. There was something . . . special I needed to buy."

"The camera," Neela said flatly.

Lynne's eyes widened. "How did you know?"

Neela looked away. "It doesn't matter."

"I would give you the money I got from *Boston Living*, but I already spent it. So"—Lynne swallowed—"you can have my camera."

Neela's palms started to sweat. "I don't want your camera."

Lynne stared at the ground. "But I don't have anything else to give."

"I don't want anything from you," Neela said slowly. "I just want my veena back. So maybe if you can tell Hal to return it to me, then we can forget about the whole thing."

Lynne shook her head. "I'm sorry, but I can't."

"But you just said you were going to get him to do that."

"Well, I can't anymore." Lynne's voice was tight.

"Then tell me where he lives. I'll talk to him myself."

"No."

Neela was getting exasperated. "You can't keep protecting Hal, and—"

Lynne looked up, tears spilling from her eyes. "He *can't* give the veena back to you because he doesn't have it anymore!"

"What?" Neela exclaimed.

"Someone else took it. I don't know, but it's gone."

Neela stared at Lynne. The veena had vanished . . . *again*?

Maybe the curse was true after all.

CHAPTER 19

Between sobs, Lynne finished the worst part of her story—the end. Last week, someone broke into Hal's apartment and stole the veena. Now Hal was more upset than ever, especially at Lynne, because she was the one who had arranged for the photo shoot. He was sure that someone from *Boston Living* had stolen the veena.

"Why does he think that?" Neela asked.

By now Lynne's sobs had quieted down. "They were the only ones who saw the veena in the apartment. And they arranged for the complimentary dinner."

"What complimentary dinner?"

"I got a call later in the day from their office, saying Hal and I were entitled to a free dinner that evening at Swilley's."

"I love Swilley's," Neela said.

"I know. Their pizza rocks. But now I can't stand the place because when I got back from there, *that's* when we discovered the veena was stolen from his apartment."

"But it could be anyone. Maybe a different neighbor?"

Lynne shook her head. "I didn't tell anyone about the veena or the photoshoot. It had to be someone from *Boston Living*."

"When you came back from Swilley's, do you remember anything else that was strange? Any clues? Try to remember."

"All I know is that when we came back, the living room window was unlocked, and so was the door."

"Because whoever it was walked out the door?"

"Yeah, but he or she must have come in through the window. The apartment is on the ground floor."

"And it was just Mrs. Bones that came that day."

Lynne shook her head. "Oh, no. There were lots of people. A lighting guy, an assistant, someone writing notes, and an Indian guy who looked at the veena. But I didn't get anyone's name except for Mrs. Bones."

At that moment, the door opened. It was Ms. Reese. "Girls. Amanda told me where you were. Please return to your seats, and save your discussions for after school."

Back in the classroom, Neela sat at her desk, feeling drained. She couldn't believe what she had just heard. Hal was Lynne's neighbor. Not only did Lynne not tell her, she found a way to make money out of the whole thing. And most important of all, the veena was missing . . . again. Was it the curse that made the veena disappear twice in a row—first from her, then from Hal?

Meanwhile, Matt and Penny were looking at her expectantly.

"What happened?" Matt whispered.

"Yeah, Amanda won't stop talking about it," Penny added.

"It was Lynne's neighbor," Neela whispered to them. "Except now the veena is missing again."

"Neighbor!" Matt repeated.

"How weird," Penny whispered. She glanced at Lynne, who was staring down at her desk.

Amanda leaned over from her desk. "But it was Lynne, right?"

Neela frowned. "Not exactly."

"Who else could it be?" Amanda continued. "You might as well tell, because you know I'm going to get the whole story from my mom later."

"Your mom doesn't know the whole story," Neela said.

"Is it true?" Amanda said to Lynne. "Did you take Neela's veena?"

"Sshh," Neela hissed. What had gotten into Amanda?

By now, everyone in the classroom was watching Lynne.

Lynne looked like a small animal cornered by a pack of wolves. "It was complicated. . . ." she started, then stopped, on the verge of tears again.

"Because you're a thief?" Amanda asked.

"Amanda," Neela said.

"I'm just trying to help you," Amanda said gravely. "Until this year, no one in our class has ever stolen anything from anybody. What's different this year? *She's* different."

A wave of anger overcame Neela. "Maybe it's okay to be different," she said fiercely. She looked over at Penny, who didn't say anything. But Penny never said anything. That was how she was.

"How can you defend her?" Amanda exclaimed. "She stole your instrument!"

"She didn't," Neela said.

"How do you know?"

"I know!" Neela's voice rose. "So you can stop hating her. And me."

Amanda stared at her. "I never said I hated you."

Neela flushed. "Well, you aren't exactly nice to me."

"Yeah, you're a pain in the butt," Matt added.

This was so unexpected, Neela laughed out loud, then stopped when she saw the hurt look in Amanda's eyes.

By now, Ms. Reese, who had finished saying good-bye to Elizabeth Bones, had noticed the conversation. "Girls, enough. Please, everyone, get ready for your next class."

Amanda turned back in her seat unsteadily. Neela watched, feeling a nagging sense of shame. She hadn't meant to lash out. But she did stand up for Lynne when Amanda was being hateful. Wasn't that the right thing to do?

Though, if Lynne was grateful, it was impossible to know. Not once did she look up from her desk during that whole conversation. And afterward, not once did she speak to anyone, either. Occasionally she drew back a curly strand and wiped her eyes. Except for that, she was perfectly still. Then, after class ended, everyone rose—noisy, relieved, banging the edges of their tables with their chairs. In the midst of that end-of-class ruckus, Lynne silently disappeared.

CHAPTER 20

Several years earlier, when the sound stopped working on the DVD player at home, it didn't stop Neela from putting on her favorite Scooby-Doo DVD every day. She watched as Scooby and his gang of detectives scrambled through deserted buildings, swampy rivers, and creepy caves, solving mysteries without a single word. Finally her parents got around to buying a new player. That day, the sound of Scooby-Doo came crashing through the speakers as Neela heard what the gang had been really saying the whole time.

That was how Neela felt now—as if the sound had suddenly been turned on, and all those mysterious, muted actions of the last few months at last made sense. Lynne taking pictures of her veena. Lynne in the kitchen of the church. Lynne buying a camera with all that cash. All because she had known where the veena had gone.

When she came home from school, Neela was in such a state of confusion, she didn't say a word about what had happened. In fact, when her mother said she was going to the grocery store with Sree, Neela was relieved. It would give her time to figure things out. Which is where Pavi came in. Her best friend always helped her think.

"Why didn't you say anything when Lynne left class?" Pavi asked over the phone.

"I didn't know she left. No one did until she was gone. The worst part is, I can't even contact her." After school, Neela had gone to the office to find out how to reach Lynne. One of the secretaries explained that Lynne had an unlisted telephone number that they weren't allowed to give out.

"But she disappeared in the middle of the day," Neela had sputtered. "Even Ms. Reese doesn't know where she went."

"Our attendance sheet says she's sick at home," the secretary had said. "Her family called to notify us." She smiled. "Don't worry. Lynne will be back when she feels better."

When Lynne felt better? When was that—when Hal stole another veena?

"So now what?" Pavi said.

"I wish I could talk to Lynne," Neela said. "I wish I could find out where Hal is. Most of all, I want to know who stole the veena from him. I never expected another thief. Unless . . ."

Pavi waited. "Unless?"

"What if," Neela said, "the curse was real?"

"You can't be serious," Pavi groaned.

"It would explain why the veena disappeared from me, and then from Hal."

"It disappeared from you because Hal took it," Pavi said.

"Yes, that's *how* the veena disappeared. But I want to know *why*. Let's think. What does the curse say? No one can hold on to the veena for too long because it eventually returns to the Chennai Music Palace, where it was first sold."

"Yeah—because the veena is still looking for Parvati," Pavi said.

Neela's thoughts leaped ahead. "So then, what if the veena was back in that store?"

"I never thought of that," Pavi said. "Too bad we can't call and ask, *Did you by any chance find a vanishing veena in your store?*"

"No," Neela said slowly, "but my *grandmother* could. She's in Chennai. Govindar, the owner of the store, is her friend. It would be no big deal for her to call him."

"Ooooh, what if it *was* there?" Pavi wondered.

Outside, Neela heard the sound of a car door slamming. "Gotta go," she said.

A few moments later, Neela's mother entered the kitchen with two grocery bags and Sree trailing behind. Her mother had a funny expression on her face. "Guess who I ran into at the store?" she asked.

Neela thought of all the usual possibilities. But a second

look at her mom's face told her it was someone that could only mean bad news, and that Neela was in trouble.

"Sudha Auntie?" she asked.

"Try a different teacher. One closer to home . . . who knows something about missing veenas."

Except for Sree, everyone was up late in the Krishnan household.

"I still don't understand, Neela. If I hadn't run into Ms. Reese today, were you ever going to tell me what happened at school?" Mrs. Krishnan asked. "That Lynne knew who took the veena?"

"I was," Neela mumbled. Though the truth was, she wasn't sure. What reason had her mother given that she wanted to know? "But I thought you wanted to forget about the veena."

"I never said that," Mrs. Krishnan said.

"That's what you said to Dad after he told Patti about the veena."

Mr. Krishnan turned to look at Neela. "What?"

"Yeah, I was standing outside your door." Neela flushed.

Mrs. Krishnan let out her breath. "Well, I never said I would keep looking for it. Especially when the risks outweigh the benefits. Just think, a strange man followed you home from school. He must be the same person who threw the rock."

"But it's not just Hal," Neela said. "Don't you get it? It

was stolen *again*. Twice. So there's someone or something else that made the veena disappear."

"Some*thing*?" Mr. Krishnan repeated.

Neela shrugged, trying to act like it was no big deal. "I know about the curse."

Her parents looked at each other.

"More standing outside the door?" Mr. Krishnan asked.

"It doesn't matter how I found out," Neela said. "But I know about it, and maybe . . ." She was about to share the idea she had come up with on the phone with Pavi, when her mom cut in.

"Is this what you were talking about that day with Lalitha Patti?" her mother said.

"Yeah, but . . ."

"And was she the one who told you to look up Veronica Wyvern?"

"No. That was from following Lynne into the library. I told you that already."

"What I don't understand," Mr. Krishnan mused, "is how anyone could think Neela owns Veronica Wyvern's veena. Didn't she die in a train wreck *with* her instrument?"

Neela sighed. Her parents kept interrupting. It was impossible to tell them about the great plan she had come up with.

"The whole thing sounds creepy," Mrs. Krishnan said.

"It sounds bizarre," Mr. Krishnan said. "How do we know there is even such a thing as that curse? Someone must have made it up."

"But it's the same story Sudha Auntie told me," Neela said. "Everyone in Thanjavur knows about it. And this is what I was trying to say before. If the curse *is* true, that means my veena might be back in the store." She jumped up. "Which is why we have to call the store. If it's there, we'll get the veena back."

"Call the store?" Mrs. Krishnan repeated. "Of course we're not calling."

"What if it's there?" Neela asked.

"Then I *definitely* don't want that veena back." Mrs. Krishnan shuddered.

"But what's the problem in calling? We're going to India in ten days, and Lal—"

"Neela." Mrs. Krishnan's voice was sharp. "We're all set to buy you a new veena—from a different store, I might add. Why can't you be happy with that? Why can't we forget about this cursed veena and start over fresh?"

"But, but . . ." Neela said helplessly.

"Anyway, Neela, you know who took your veena," Mr. Krishnan said. "Hal did. It didn't 'vanish.'"

"But it did afterward," Neela countered. "That's what Lynne said."

"Maybe Lynne lied," Mrs. Krishnan said.

"Lynne didn't lie. She didn't even want the veena. She needed the money for a camera."

"That's another thing. How do you know she didn't use the money for something else or—"

"I *saw* her buying the camera in Harvard Square. I

followed her on the bus that day when I—" Neela stopped. "When I stayed back at school to make up late minutes," she finished.

Her mother stared at her. "But you could have gotten lost, and—"

"I didn't get lost. I was fine." Neela thought of Matt, but if she mentioned him, her mom would flip out even more.

"All I can see is that you've lied about everything," Mrs. Krishnan said.

"Maybe if *you* were honest with me in the first place about the curse," Neela said angrily, "I wouldn't have taken my veena to school. I'd still have it with me today."

"That's silly," her mother said. "It's *your* fault for talking to Hal. It's *your* fault you lost Lalitha Patti's veena."

Mrs. Krishnan's words hung in the air like a hero from a kung-fu movie, mid-kick, before nailing the bad guy in the gut.

She and Neela stared at each other.

"I . . . I didn't mean that," Mrs. Krishnan finally said. "It's late. Maybe we all need some sleep." She scooped Sree from the couch, then looked at Neela with a slightly kinder expression. But Neela wasn't in the mood to be nice. She turned away as her mom walked past her.

Neela's father patted her back. "She's just trying to help."

"No, she's not," Neela sniffed. "She's trying to make me feel bad about everything."

"No, she loves you and worries about you."

"Yeah, by blaming me for everything."

Mr. Krishnan put his arm around Neela's shoulders. "Maybe we're all a little tired. And a little to blame, too."

"Do you think the curse is real?"

Mr. Krishnan paused, as if measuring his words. "I don't know about the curse, but I think there's something special about that veena. It seems like it draws certain kinds of people."

"Like Veronica Wyvern?"

"Well, actually I meant my mother." He smiled at her. "And you."

As they went upstairs together, Neela thought about how her mother had reacted just as she'd expected. Without an ounce of open-mindedness. But there was one thought that gave Neela hope. Through their whole discussion of what to do and not do, no one had said anything about *not* calling Lalitha Patti.

CHAPTER 21

"**So, what did your** grandmother say?" Pavi whispered. They were standing in the mudroom of Sudha Auntie's house while Mrs. Krishnan chatted with their teacher about the impending trip to India. Neela shook her head. She didn't want to talk in front of her mom.

Not that there was much to say. Neela had tried her grandparents' house a half a dozen times, and no one picked up. That was last night. This morning, she had no better luck. No one, it seemed, would answer her grandparents' phone.

"Thanks so much for lending your veena," Mrs. Krishnan said. She said this at every lesson, right before she left. That's when Neela remembered how she'd been spotted last week in Harvard Square with Matt. Great. That was all she needed—another fight with her mother.

"No problem," Sudha Auntie said, giving her usual reply. Then, just as Mrs. Krishnan walked out the door, Sudha Auntie continued. "Just the other day I was at Harvard Square, and you'll never guess what I saw."

Neela braced herself. Here it was.

"Oh?" Mrs. Krishnan looked as if her mind was already on her shopping.

"A lovely book on veenas at the Harvard Bookstore," Sudha Auntie said.

"How—nice," Mrs. Krishnan said politely.

Sudha Auntie looked meaningfully at Neela before adding, "See you later, Lakshmi."

Neela let out her breath. Sudha Auntie had let her off the hook!

"Get your instruments out," she said to Neela and Pavi. "I'll get a cup of water."

After they were alone, Neela and Pavi looked at each other.

"That was unbelievable," Pavi said.

Neela nodded, relieved. Maybe she had misjudged Sudha Auntie. Still, she couldn't help wonder why her teacher decided to be nice. Did she have something else up her sleeve?

"I'm still thinking about your veena," Pavi said. "Man, you're lucky."

"Why is Neela so lucky?" Sudha Auntie asked. She had returned with her water.

"Someone thinks Neela's lost veena belonged to Veronica Wyvern," Pavi announced.

"Pavi!" Sometimes her friend was such a blabbermouth.

"Veronica Wyvern," Sudha Auntie repeated. "Why on earth do you think that?"

Neela pursed her lips, debating how much to tell. Maybe Sudha Auntie would use the information to find a way to scold Neela to practice, which was about the only thing she ever did. On the other hand, her teacher had just done a nice thing by not squealing to her mom about Matt. Sudha Auntie was also the one who had told her about the *maya veena* in the first place.

Slowly, Neela filled her teacher in on the whole story. Before they knew it, they were seated in the parlor, their lessons forgotten, eating samosas, a snack made of curried potato stuffed inside a pastry.

"Interesting," Sudha Auntie said through a mouthful of samosa. "So you think your veena is the *maya veena*, *and* that it belonged to Ronnie Wyvern?"

"Ronnie?" Pavi asked.

"That's how she was known here in Boston," Sudha Auntie explained. She paused. "So what does this whole adventure have to do with you and that boy in Harvard Square?"

Neela swallowed. How did her teacher know the two were related? "Nothing," she mumbled. It was one thing to talk about Veronica Wyvern or the *maya veena*, but she wasn't sure she wanted to talk about Matt.

Sudha Auntie was watching her. "If you think I'm going to tell your mother, you can rest assured I won't. It may be hard to believe, but I was once a young girl." She smiled faintly. "I grew up in a different time and place, but we all have the yearning to make our own decisions, unencumbered by our parents. So if it's your interest to befriend boys with strange-colored hair, that's no business of mine."

"What's wrong with his hair?" Pavi asked in delight.

"Oh, you haven't met him?" Sudha Auntie asked. "Think of a flaming sunset."

Pavi snickered, then stopped when she saw Neela.

"But if he has something to do with the mystery, spill it, I say," Sudha Auntie said.

Neela felt herself turning red. She hated being the butt of their jokes. But more surprisingly, she hated it that Matt was becoming the butt of their jokes, too.

"He helped me spy on Lynne," she said. "That's when we saw her buy the camera."

"Yes, Matt was a big help," Pavi said, licking some potato from one of her fingers.

Neela glared at her. She waited for her teacher and Pavi to continue with the jokes.

Instead, Sudha Auntie had a thoughtful look on her face. From one of the coffee table drawers, she pulled out a box of photographs. A few minutes later, she found two photos. "I thought you might get a kick out of these." She handed the first one to Neela. "That's me, fourteen years ago. And that's Ronnie Wyvern after a concert in Boston."

Surprised, Neela leaned in to have a closer look. On the right was a younger version of Sudha Auntie, without her glasses, dressed in a sari, and wearing her hair up in a bun. On the left was a tall, thin-framed woman in a flowery kurta pajama set. Her light brown hair hung straight across her shoulders, pinned on both sides by barrettes. "She's so pretty," said Neela, then remembered herself. "And so are you," she finished lamely.

Sudha Auntie waved a hand. "Don't be ridiculous. Even fourteen years ago, I was old." She handed over the other picture. "This one is about two years later in Providence. That's her husband, Ramdas, standing on the other side."

In the second photo, Veronica wore a pink salwar kameez with her hair braided loosely, and dangly earrings showing through on the sides. Her husband was a few inches shorter than her, with a swirl of curly hair.

Pavi scooted next to Neela to get a look. "Her husband was Indian?" she asked.

"Yeah, remember the article?" Neela said. "They both died in the train wreck."

Pavi looked at the pictures some more. "Veronica is pretty," she agreed, "though she looks a bit chunky in the second photo."

"Pavi!" Neela said.

"Chunky?" Sudha Auntie repeated. "What are these strange expressions you use?"

Pavi looked embarrassed. "Forget it. I was being mean."

Sudha Auntie looked at the second photo. "Oh, I see

what you're saying. She was expecting, that's all."

Neela looked carefully at the photos, both of which showed Veronica posing in front of a stage with people milling around her. "Do you have other pictures of her? Or CDs of her music?"

Sudha Auntie shook her head. "Those are the only two photos I have. I'm surprised I even remembered about them." She nibbled on another samosa. "And believe it or not, Ronnie didn't record much. I think she only had one CD out before her death."

"Did it have a picture of her veena on it?" Neela asked hopefully.

Sudha Auntie finished chewing. "Hmm . . . You want to see if her veena is the same one as yours? First of all, there was nothing on that CD cover—just some traditional Indian design. Second, forget about whether her veena was the same one. Who cares? That veena is gone. And it's just the kind of thing that will distract you from what's important."

"But it was my grandmother's veena," Neela said.

"And Lynne's neighbor shouldn't have stolen it," Pavi said. "It isn't fair."

"And . . ." Neela stopped. She looked at them both. "You'll think I'm silly."

"What?" Pavi asked.

Neela thought about her grandmother playing wordlessly in the evenings on the old veena. "When I practiced on Lalitha Patti's veena, I sounded so much better. I thought it was because her veena brought me luck."

"Some luck," Sudha Auntie said, unimpressed. "Ever since that instrument entered your life, you've had nothing but misfortune. Maybe your grandmother's veena is the *maya veena*. So you have Parvati's bad luck stamped all over it. Maybe it's the one Ronnie died with on a train. More bad luck. I say good riddance. It's practice that makes you a great musician, not the instrument."

Neela scowled. Sudha Auntie was lecturing her to practice—again?

By the time Mrs. Krishnan came to pick up Neela and Pavi, the samosas were all eaten. As the girls were leaving, Sudha Auntie pulled Neela aside. "I saw that look on your face a while back. The one where you were mad enough to wring my neck."

"I was just thinking about Hal," Neela lied.

"Don't think you're fooling me. Anyway, before you do wring my neck, just remember what I said: it's practice, not the instrument."

In the car, Mrs. Krishnan asked, "So, how did lessons go today?"

"Fine," Neela muttered. She stared out the window, still feeling angry at her teacher.

"I'm so happy I got all my shopping done," Mrs. Krishnan said. "I even got a wedding gift for Arun. Too bad we'll miss the wedding. At least Lalitha Patti will be able to go. Which reminds me, I have to get those gardening books for her. She hasn't told me what she wants us to bring her, and since she isn't home, I can't ask her."

Neela looked up. "Lalitha Patti's not home?"

"She's in Bangalore. Remember, your cousin is getting married. Do you listen to anything, I wonder."

So that's why no one had answered the phone. "When will she be back?"

Mrs. Krishnan sighed. "The same evening we arrive. Isn't that crazy? How will she ever swing it?" She went on, still wondering about Lalitha Patti "swinging things."

Neela stopped listening, disappointed by this unexpected news. With Lynne gone, the veena gone, and now her grandmother out of town, Neela felt as if she was running out of options. Not to mention her patience.

Maybe it was time to take the matter into her own hands.

CHAPTER 22

That night, after what seemed like an eternity, the Krishnan household became still, as everyone but Neela fell asleep in their rooms. Quietly, she tiptoed down the stairs to the office. She stopped in the kitchen to look at the clock, which read eleven thirty, and get a bag of potato chips. The crunching would help her work up the nerve.

Now that she was actually downstairs, she was getting cold feet. Also, she wasn't sure who would pick up, Govindar or someone else. If only she could talk to Pavi or Matt. But not at this hour. And if she waited until the morning, her parents would be awake.

She chewed on a few more potato chips, recalling the first time she had tasted them in preschool at a birthday party. She could still remember the sensation of something hard and crunchy turning soft inside her mouth, until all that was left was the salt. It was that feeling that comforted her now, the soft, buttery salt flavor, and the memory of preschool, back when life was simple.

Finally she wiped the crumbs from her palms on her pajamas. It was just one simple phone call. She could do it. From her pocket she pulled out the small slip of paper on which she had copied down the number for the Chennai Music Palace from the Web. Then she picked up the phone. The call went through on the first try. On the other end, she heard the crisp, double-staccato ring of the telephone: *dring-dring . . . dring-dring.*

A man's voice answered. "Chennai Music Palace," he said with a heavy accent.

Neela cleared her throat. "Can I speak to Mr. Govindar?"

The man's answer was immediate. "This is Govindar speaking."

Neela's stomach lurched. She didn't know where to begin.

"Is someone there?" he asked.

"Yes, hello. I am Lalitha Krishnan's granddaughter."

"What?"

Neela began to think that calling was a bad idea. She repeated herself.

"Lalitha Krishnan, what? Please speak up," he replied.

She decided to switch to Tamil. Maybe he would understand better. "I'm her granddaughter, and—" She took a deep breath. "I'm calling about the *maya veena.*"

There was a silence on the other end.

"Are you there, sir?"

"Yes, I am listening. So you are Neela Krishnan."

How did he know her name? "Uh, that's right. According to the curse, the *maya veena* always returns to your store. So then, um, has my veena come back?" Said out loud, it seemed ridiculous. She felt as if Govindar would start laughing any minute and tell her the whole thing was an elaborate joke.

Instead there was a pause. "As a matter of fact, it arrived just yesterday to the store."

Neela's heart started beating. "Really? The veena? Someone brought it?" She could hardly believe what she was hearing.

"Yes, the package was delivered to our store."

Delivered? "What do you mean?" she asked.

"Isn't that why you are calling? To see if the package arrived?"

"What package?" Neela said. "You mean . . . the veena? Someone mailed it to you?"

It was Govindar's turn to sound surprised. "Of course. The veena was shipped from Boston . . . by *you*."

"Me?" Neela's voice came out as a squeak. "But I didn't mail it."

"That's the name on the package. I admit I was surprised, because I mailed the veena to you only eight months ago. Only, I didn't send it to a Boston address. I sent it somewhere else."

"Arlington."

"That's right. Did your family not mail back the veena?"

"Of course not," Neela said. "It was stolen from us."

"Stolen!" Govindar said.

"I've spent the last two months trying to find out what happened to it," Neela went on. She was still digesting what Govindar said. Obviously, whoever had stolen the veena from Hal was the one who sent it and then used Neela's name to disguise his identity. But why? And why would the thief send it back to the Chennai Music Palace?

Govindar sounded equally surprised. "I assumed you did not want the instrument anymore. I called your grandmother right away. But no one answered."

"She's at a wedding," Neela said quickly. "But my family and I will be there in a week. Can you hold the veena until then?"

"This is strange, so very strange," Govindar murmured, as if he was talking to himself.

"It *is* strange. But can you hold it for me? Just for ten days?"

"Yes, okay."

"Thank you! I felt so bad to lose the veena. I didn't want another one, even though my parents are buying me a new one." She was blabbering, but she was so relieved, she hardly cared.

"But there is one problem. I want to tell you, but you talk so much."

"You're scared because you think the veena is cursed. That it might be bad luck?"

"No, no. Not that. But you see, you are not the only one."

Neela didn't understand. "I'm not the only what?"

"You were not the only one to call."

Neela became very still. "Another person called?"

"Yesterday. A man."

"Hal," she whispered.

"He wants the veena, too. And he is coming in a few days to get it."

"But it's my grandmother's instrument," Neela cried. "It belongs to us."

"He seems to think that it's his," Govindar said.

Neela had been so happy for about thirty seconds, and now things were worse than before. Hal still wanted the veena, and he was going to India to get it.

She could hear the sound of someone talking behind Govindar. "Neela, we have a customer here who needs my attention. But I suggest that when you come, you and Lalitha resolve the issue with this man, yes?"

"Please don't give away the veena," Neela begged. "We'll be there, December twentieth."

"December twentieth," Govindar repeated. "Okay. Let's meet on that day. But so you know, there are no guarantees." The next sound Neela heard was a click, as Govindar hung up the phone.

CHAPTER 23

It had been three days since Lynne was first absent from school. Every morning, Neela would ask Ms. Reese about Lynne, and every time her teacher would shake her head. "Still sick. That's what the office tells me." She sounded like she didn't quite believe it, either, but there wasn't much she could do.

"How long can she be sick?" Neela wondered.

Mrs. Reese wasn't sure. She mentioned something about "going through the proper channels," which, as far as Neela could see, didn't amount to much.

At recess, Neela told Matt about the phone call to Govindar.

"Why does Hal want the veena so bad?" Matt asked. "Even if it belonged to Veronica."

"I'm not sure," Neela said. "But he's going to be in India in a few days. Unless I can figure out how to stop him."

"There has to be a way to get his phone number from the church. Do you have any clues—*anything*?"

Neela thought for a moment. "Well, there's that photo Julia e-mailed me of Hal. But I've looked at it a gazillion times, and I still haven't found anything."

Matt took out his cell phone. "Do you still have it on e-mail?"

Neela nodded. "Sure. You want to see it?"

She logged on to her e-mail account with Matt's cell phone and clicked open the photo.

Matt looked at it for a moment. "He looks so normal."

"I know," Neela agreed. "He doesn't look at all like a veena thief."

Matt grinned. "Is there a way that veena thieves are supposed to look?"

Neela studied the photo again over Matt's shoulder. She had seen it so many times, she had it practically memorized: Hal balancing a paper plate in one hand while half turned to Mary, the two of them looking as if they were discussing the weather, the Boston Red Sox, or something else just as ordinary. Why couldn't there be some clue she had overlooked?

"Can you zoom in on his plate?" she asked, without much hope. "Maybe we can tell something by what he ate."

"Sure." Matt zoomed in. "Hmm . . . Watermelon, corn

on the cob, pasta salad. Yep, seems like a pretty devious meal."

But then something caught Neela's eye. "Zoom some more to where the picnic tables are behind them." She waited as Matt zoomed. "Look!" she said. "See that person?"

Matt leaned in. The screen on his phone was small, but they could both make out a girl standing in the food line with glasses and curly hair, wearing . . . a feathered shirt.

"Lynne," Neela said.

After school, Neela's toes felt like marbles inside her boots as she and Matt trudged through the snow on their way to the church. Once they realized that Lynne was a member of the church, Neela knew that the only way to find Hal was to go back there.

"Aren't you cold?" she said to Matt. "It's freezing." It had started snowing early in the afternoon and continued steadily as drifts began to build along the sides of streets and in people's yards. Her hat was pulled down as far as it would go, and she had wrapped her scarf around her face so only her eyes showed.

"Nah." Matt had on a light jacket with his bare hands stuffed into the coat pockets. "You're sure Julia will help?"

"Positive. She let me look at the address database last time. If Lynne is part of the church, her address will be in that database."

"So then we can find Lynne?"

"Forget Lynne. I want to find Hal. But if they're neighbors, maybe I can still get to him by finding her." She noticed his teeth were chattering. "Are you sure you're not cold? Do you want my hat or something?"

Matt looked at her pink woolen cap with a silvery tassel on the end. "Uh, no thanks," he said, his teeth still chattering. "But maybe we should hurry up before my fingers fall off."

After that, they didn't talk anymore until they rounded the corner and the stone church came into view at the end of the street.

When they got inside, they were greeted by the sweet, sharp scent of pine from the Christmas tree in the foyer. Neela and Matt shook the snow off themselves as drops of water clung to their hair and eyelashes.

"How about some cocoa?" Matt said.

"Ha-ha."

Neela peered around the Christmas tree. She didn't want to run into Mary. She gestured to him. "Come on."

They walked down the hall to the church office. She was so happy Matt was coming along with her to talk to Julia. She didn't even have to ask; he decided to come as soon as he heard her plan.

When they reached the office, Neela said, "Mary might be there. Let me check first."

She gingerly opened the door. Mary's chair was empty, which made Neela open the door wider. But what she saw next was completely unexpected. Before she could react, a person who was not Julia, but sitting at her desk, saw her and said, "Can I help you?" She looked like a teenager, with lots of hair and big teeth. But she wore bright red lipstick and tons of mascara, which made Neela think she was older.

"Is Julia around?" she asked.

"No!" The girl seemed very excited by this. Or maybe that was just the way she talked. With exclamation marks. "Julia is away on a health emergency!!" More exclamation marks.

Neela paled. "Health emergency?" Was she dying? In a car accident?

The girl's face altered only slightly. "Impacted wisdom teeth! She had to get those suckers out!" She said it as if she were reporting sun in the forecast for the week.

Neela and Matt glanced at each other.

"If it's important, Mary Goodwin is here. I'm on my way out, but she's just downstairs—"

"No, that's all right!" Neela said quickly. Darn. It was so disappointing. "When will Julia be back? Maybe I can leave her a message."

"Sure thing!" The girl looked at Julia's desk, puzzling over where the Post-its could be. She pushed around the papers and miraculously found a stack. Then she pulled out her handbag. "Just leave the note on her desk. She'll get it when she's back after the holidays!"

"After the holidays!" Neela exclaimed. She was starting to sound like the girl, but this piece of news was a disaster—it meant Julia wouldn't be back in time to help. Neela was about to say more when she saw Matt shake his head slightly. "All right. Thanks," she said instead.

After the girl was gone, Neela said, "That was kind of irresponsible of her, leaving the office with strangers still here."

Matt nodded. "Exactly."

She looked at him and then at Julia's computer. "Are you thinking what I think you're thinking? But that's . . . Mary will be back any minute."

"I'll stand watch."

"You don't know what she looks like!"

"What does she look like?"

"Uh, gray hair in a bun, plump, looks pissed, and her shoes squeak."

"All right. Go for it." He walked to the door.

"Matt," she called.

He stopped. "What?"

She wanted to say it was wrong to look at Julia's computer without asking, and that she didn't do things like that. But the thought of being so close, the thought of the veena being so close, gave Neela a bolt of energy she had never felt before. So she said, "If you see Mary, say you're looking for the clay class. She'll show you, and it will buy us more time."

"Yeah." He turned to go, then said, "Just in case, let's have a warning system: two raps if the coast is clear, three if she's coming back, and four if it's someone else, like the police."

"Huh?"

"Two raps after she leaves, three if . . ."

"Okay, okay," Neela interrupted. Honestly, how many raps did they need?

After Matt went out, Neela slipped behind Julia's desk. She looked down and found the main unit of the computer underneath, next to the chair. Surprisingly, the computer had not been turned on. Maybe the lipstick girl was only there to help with the phones? The computer hummed to life as soon as Neela pressed the button. At first she worried about needing a password to get in, but a few moments later, a window opened on the monitor, displaying everything. Neela was amazed by how easy it was. It was like being in a detective movie, she thought, where everything was going right. Until something went wrong, of course.

She found the link to the address database and clicked on it. Just then, she heard a tapping sound on the wall and froze. Then she remembered, Matt had said something about rapping twice. After starting the program, she searched for *Lynne Rao*.

There were zero results.

Surprised, Neela stared at the screen. She had been so sure Lynne would be in the database. Had she gotten the name wrong? But she was certain of the spelling because Lynne's last name was the same as Neela's favorite brand of spaghetti sauce.

She cleared the search and tried *Hal*. Still nothing. But she had already known that. It was hard to believe she had reached another dead end so quickly. Behind her came more raps, this time three muffled ones. Neela looked up, alarmed. Three knocks already?

She had to hurry. What if she searched by location? Didn't Lynne live in Somerville? That was what she'd written in her notebook. She typed *Somerville* by itself, and this time she got three records:

```
Maurice Linden
Ester Linden
Harold Wyvern
```

Neela stared at the last record: *Harold Wyvern.* Just like Veronica! She clicked the name, which brought up a street address and phone number, as well as his job title: *retired minister.*

Outside, she heard the quiet but distinct sound of voices approaching.

Quickly, she found a blank sticky note and jotted down the details from the screen. The voices were getting closer. She could hear, not too far away, the *phsst phsst* sound of Mary's shoes. Neela wrote faster. . . . She was almost done.

But now there was really no time left. The voices were outside the door, and they sounded like Mary and Matt. She shut off the screen, slid down from her chair, and hid under the desk, just as the door opened.

"I'm not sure how much more I can help you, son," Mary was saying. "The class is downstairs with a big sign on the door. Now, if you'll excuse me, I'm about to close the office." She tried to block his way, but Matt was too fast for her and slipped inside.

"Sometimes I have trouble with directions," Matt said, as if he had no idea Mary was trying to kick him out. "My mother got a book for me, *Following Directions for Dummies*. But you know, I have trouble following directions, so how can I follow a book about directions?"

Mary gave the kind of sigh that Ms. Reese gave when Matt said something exasperating. "Even so, you have to leave. The office is closed."

Matt pretended not to hear her, and walked farther inside. From under Julia's desk, Neela held her breath, trying not to make a sound. Her mind was still on what she had written down. Harold Wyvern, if that was Hal, had the same last name as Veronica. What did that make him? Husband? Brother? He was too old for either.

Just then, she caught Matt's eye as he walked past Julia's desk. He had been looking for her. He looked surprised but said nothing.

"Do you have a handout?" he said to Mary. "Handouts are good. I just read them over and over, and then I know what to do. Unless I lose them. Which happens sometimes. Actually, all the time. Which is why I try to get *two* handouts of everything, and . . ."

"All right, all right," Mary said impatiently. "Maybe I can find a schedule."

Neela remembered the newspaper article on Veronica—her father was a retired minister. *Just like Harold Wyvern.*

Which meant . . . She was so excited she wanted to yell out to Matt, but she didn't dare make a sound from underneath the desk.

"Does the church offer other classes, too?" Matt asked. "Because I love art. My teacher says I should be an artist. She says I'm naturally talented, but I need plenty of *inspiration*. What could be more inspiring than an art class?"

"Do you always talk so much?" Mary asked wearily. "Maybe you ought to come back tomorrow, because I really have to go now and . . . Wait a minute." Mary stopped. And when she stopped, it seemed like a whole bunch of things stopped at the same time: Matt's feet, all movement in the room, Neela's heart. There was one thing unfortunately that had *not* stopped.

"I know I turned off Julia's computer today. And yet now I hear it running." Mary began walking toward the desk.

"Can I get one of those schedules?" Matt tried desperately.

"Just a minute, son."

Neela saw Mary's shoes—the ones that went *phsst phsst*—come around the corner of the desk. Then she saw Mary right in front of her, as she huddled under the desk, with no place left to go.

CHAPTER 24

"Sometimes," Matt called out across the room, "you can press the restart button by accident instead of the shut-down button." His voice rang out in the office as he waited to see if Mary would believe him or not.

She stopped. "Oh?"

Matt crossed the room and came quickly around the side of the desk. Now Neela could see his shoes next to Mary's, a pair of worn-out sneakers with faded stripes. He bent down, looked straight at Neela, who stared at him mutely, before standing up again. "Yep. That's what you did. We have a bunch of computers at home, so I know all about them."

"Well, I'm no wizard," Mary murmured, apparently buying his logic. "Computers are so complicated these days. Safety features, viruses, people breaking into your computer!"

Which is closer to the truth than you know, Neela thought, inches away from Mary. She swallowed hard.

"That's why I didn't want one of the girls working here today to turn the computer on and troll the Internet," Mary said. "But she turned on the machine anyway. I will have to speak to her tomorrow. Well, I better shut it down again."

"I'll do it for you," Matt said quickly. He reached down and pressed the power switch until the computer turned off.

Mary frowned. "Aren't you supposed to log off first?"

"Sometimes it's okay to press the power button. That's why it's there, right?"

Again Mary considered his words, then sighed. "You kids are so smart these days."

Neela watched (and heard) Mary's squeaky shoes disappear around the desk.

Thank goodness. Things weren't over yet, but at least Matt had prevented a complete disaster from striking. Now, if he could just manage to get Mary out of the office without Neela getting caught . . . She was dying to tell Matt what she had just figured out.

Mary flipped through some papers on her desk. "And here. An art class schedule."

Matt feigned excitement. "Oh, wow. My *first* art class."

Mary cleared her throat. "Glad to see such interest." She turned off the lights.

"It's always been my dream," Matt said. "You know, Picasso, Renoir, Van Gogh."

"Come along. The office is closed." Her voice was firm. She grabbed her coat from the rack and closed the door behind her and Matt. All was silent in the office again; the sound of *phsst phsst* disappearing in the distance.

Neela crawled out from the desk and stretched out her legs.

Hal was Veronica's father. He had to be. This was the biggest discovery Neela had made so far. And if Hal was Veronica's father, then it explained a lot of things, like why he wanted the veena so much and why he was willing to go all the way to India for it.

It didn't explain everything, though. Because even if the veena had once belonged to Veronica, how would Hal have known he was stealing the right one? When had he had a chance to see the veena and confirm it was the same one before he stole it?

Just then, Neela heard a light rapping on the door, followed by an odd whizzing sound. She shrank back under the desk, worried Mary was back.

"Neela?" a voice called softly.

She climbed out. "Matt," she whispered, relieved. She stared at the open door. "Did you just slide the lock?"

"So I don't get rusty," he said, sticking a card back in his pocket. "Let's get out of here."

They closed the door behind them and hurried down the hall. A few minutes later, they were outside, blinking against the brightness of the fallen snow. It had stopped snowing at last.

"Did you find the address?" Matt wanted to know.

"Yeah, and a lot more." Neela told him Hal's full name.

"Wow!" Matt said, amazed. "What about Mary? And the crest?"

"Mary has to be related to him. Maybe his wife? Or his sister? I don't know. . . ."

"Which is why she would be protecting him. This is totally a whodunit mystery." Matt was excited. "So, are you calling him?"

Neela slowed down as they reached the snowy sidewalk. "Call him, just like that?"

"Wasn't that your plan? To stop him?" Matt pulled out his cell phone and offered it to her.

Neela did want to stop Hal, but that was before she knew who he was. She thought about that day in the church, and the far-off look in his eyes when they were talking about her instrument. He must have been remembering his daughter. "I don't know," she faltered.

"Call," Matt said. "Call before you change your mind."

He was right. Neela took the phone from him and dialed the number on the Post-it note. As she heard the phone ring, something surprising started to happen: her knees began shaking as if she were about to give a performance. Stage fright? Or in this case, phone fright?

This had never happened before, not even that day she phoned Govindar, and she was nervous then, too. The phone continued to ring, and Neela gripped it hard as if that would somehow lock down her knees. When she didn't think she could wait anymore, she heard the click of an answering machine come on. And then it was Hal's voice, the same one with the heavy Boston accent, and it seemed as if he were inside her brain, talking to her.

The strangeness of it almost undid her as she strained to make sense of the message. When it was done, she snapped Matt's phone shut and handed it back to him.

"What? What happened?" Matt asked.

In a daze, she repeated the message on Hal's answering machine: "We're on vacation. Call back at the end of December."

"Who's 'we'?"

"Maybe his wife?"

Matt smacked his forehead with his palm. "Man, you were *so* close. That bites."

"Yeah," Neela said, trying to understand the mixture of emotions inside her. She was just as disappointed as Matt—at least, she *ought* to have been. Then why had her knees stopped shaking as soon as she hung up the phone?

She watched as Matt scooped up snow from the ground and hurled it in the air until bits of snow fell down around them. "You'll have to nab him in India, then," he said.

Neela wondered just how she would do that. She still didn't know if Govindar would wait for her before giving the veena back to Hal. Who would he think more worthy? A girl who barely knew how to play? Or the father of a famous dead musician? Suddenly the task of getting back her veena felt daunting. And just a few hours ago she had been so sure of herself.

They walked in silence until they passed the inflated snowman on Winthrop.

"That snowman is butt-ugly," Matt said.

"I kind of like it."

"I had nightmares when I was little. Seriously. Attack of the killer snowman."

"My dad thinks it looks like the Pillsbury Doughboy."

"Attack of the killer doughboy. Same difference."

They stopped to watch the snowman sway from one side to the other in the wind, its enormous head bobbing up and down as if it were nodding at them.

"Isn't it strange," Neela said, "how different people can see the same thing and have completely different ideas about it?"

"Yeah, like completely *wrong* ideas," Matt said.

"But it's good, isn't it? We wouldn't all want to be scared by the same thing."

"I'm not scared of it anymore."

"I'm just saying *hypothetically*."

They walked until they came to the end of Winthrop, where they had to continue in opposite directions. Neela couldn't help thinking that if Matt had been Pavi, she could have invited him over to her house now. But imagine what Neela's mom would do if she showed up with an orange-haired guy at their door. She'd probably say his hair was bad luck and do an aarti.

Matt kicked the curb with one of his scuffed-up shoes.

“I guess you’re headed out to India in a couple of days.”

She nodded. “My best friend will be there. You haven’t met her. She goes to Pilgrim. Her family’s visiting at the same time.”

Matt shivered and rubbed his hands together.

Behind him, Neela saw a figure approaching in the distance. She was coming from an adjoining street, turning onto Winthrop. Neela stared, trying to get a better look. Was it who she thought it was?

Amanda was wearing a powder-white quilted down jacket that would have made her blend in with the snow if it weren’t for the brown suede of her winter boots. She stopped when she saw them. “Hi, Neela,” she said. She glanced at Matt but didn’t say anything to him. “I was on my way to your house, but I might as well give this to you now.” She opened her book bag. “Here,” she said gruffly. “I thought you might need it, and my mom had extras anyway.” She handed over the copy of *Boston Living* that was brought to class. “I guess my mom didn’t bother to make sure she was borrowing the veena from the right girl for the photo shoot, huh?”

Neela stared, unsure of what to say. “Thanks,” she finally stammered, taking the magazine from Amanda’s gloved hand.

Even Matt, who normally had insults ready to hurl at Amanda, said nothing. It was as if he also knew he was witnessing a rare event. He gave Neela a small salute. “I’m taking off,” he said. “So long, and stay away from the snowman." Neela could hear him whistling to himself as he walked away.

She and Amanda looked at each other.

"I remember this snowman," Amanda said. "Once in kindergarten, I walked home with you and your mom, and we pretended he was secretly Santa Claus, filled with presents." Before Neela could answer, Amanda turned away and walked off, her boots clomping quickly through the snow. Neela looked on in amazement, wondering what had come over Amanda.

She turned toward home, thinking through the events of the day. In more ways than one, the afternoon had ended on a high note. Now Neela just had to worry about the bigger issue at hand—"nabbing" Hal, as Matt put it. What would she say if she found him in India? *Excuse me, can I have back that veena you think belonged to your dead daughter?* Just thinking that gave her stomach a funny sideways ache. It was as if everything in her head had turned upside down, and all the things she once thought were true about the veena and herself had changed. Who did the veena really belong to—Hal, her grandmother, or her?

CHAPTER 25

The next few days there was a flurry of activity as the Krishnans got ready for India. The day before their trip, Mrs. Krishnan dropped Sree off at his friend's house and took Neela with her to the bookstore.

"Lalitha Patti wants a book on gardening," her mother said. In the home-and-gardening aisle, they found rows and rows of books. "How am I supposed to pick one?"

"Get a bunch," Neela said. She hated shopping with her mother. It always took forever because her mother would get sucked into a black hole of indecision.

"Did you see the size of these books? How will we carry more than one in our suitcase?" Mrs. Krishnan stared at the titles as if the answer would come to her.

"I'm going to the kids' section," Neela announced. She

figured it would be a while before her mother escaped from the black hole.

She was actually not in the mood to read, so she wandered through the store instead. She was too preoccupied with all she had found out in the last few days. Until she learned who Hal was, she had not even thought much about Veronica—who she was, how she'd lived, how everything had ended so suddenly for her. But now her mind was filled with images of the brown-haired woman posing in Sudha Auntie's photos with her flowing kurtas and crooked smile.

As Neela walked past the magazine rack, she spotted a tall man with poofy hair standing in one of the aisles, looking at one of the magazines. It was Professor Tannenbaum from the veena concert last month. Tannenbaum continued reading, engrossed in an article. Every now and then he chuckled and turned the page. He seemed to be enjoying himself, his whole face lighting up when he laughed. Neela remembered the comment he'd made about her string. She was embarrassed by the whole thing now, especially since she had overreacted by running away afterward. He looked pretty friendly, actually.

In fact . . . Neela drew in her breath. *He was someone who knew Veronica Wyvern.* She remembered his quote from the article: "She will be missed as a musician and as a friend."

If he had known her as a musician and a friend, he would know Veronica's veena if he saw it. If only Neela had the magazine with her. Then her eyes went straight to the magazines covers along the aisle until she saw *Boston Living* peeking out from one of the shelves.

What were the chances she'd run into Tannenbaum in a bookstore *and* with a copy of *Boston Living* nearby? She snatched up the magazine and walked slowly to him, her heart beating.

"Professor Tannenbaum?" she asked, holding the magazine tightly in her hand. He was so tall she had to crane her neck to look up at him.

Tannenbaum turned to her in surprise. He took off his glasses. "Yes. Can I help you?"

Now she had his attention, she didn't know what to say. She fumbled over her words. "Um, I'm Neela, Sudha Rajugopal's student."

He waited, still puzzled by the sight of her.

Neela sighed inwardly. "I'm the one with the snapping string," she said.

Tannenbaum's face shone with instant recognition. "Oh, yes! Dear heavens, hello!"

Again, Neela felt the embarrassment of her performance weigh down on her, but she decided she had more important things to talk about.

"Sorry to bother you, but I have a question and I think you might have the answer."

"Really?" He smiled curiously. "You've got me hooked. What's your question?"

Neela held up the magazine. "There's a picture of a veena in here." She turned the pages until she got to it.

"Could you tell me if this was Veronica Wyvern's veena?"

"Veronica Wyvern's veena?" he repeated. He looked at her as if she had lost her mind. Then he cleared his throat. "I'm sorry, dear. You might not know, but Ronnie passed away many years ago in a terrible accident. Her veena was with her. So the answer is no." He smiled politely as if the matter was closed.

Neela knew he was her only hope at this point, so she pressed on. "I know about her death," she said, "and I know you were friends. Could you please check anyway? It's very important to me." She held the magazine up to him again.

"Child, I'm certain her veena wouldn't be in a magazine today." Still, he must have been curious, because he put on his glasses again and took the magazine from her.

Neela watched as Tannenbaum's face changed from polite indifference to slow recognition. He stared a long time at the photo, then took off his glasses and looked at her. "How did you find this photo?" he asked.

"A photographer took it last month. Her kid is in my class."

He shook his head. "But Ronnie died in a train crash with her veena. I don't know how the photographer took this photo."

"You're sure this is her veena?" Neela asked.

"No doubt. See that peg box? It's a special kind of dragon with two feet and a tail."

"I know, a wyvern," Neela said.

"Yes, exactly. Ronnie found the veena in India a long time ago, and I remember her telling me she felt like it had been made just for her. You know, because of her last name."

As Neela listened, a mixture of wonder and dread crept through her. She felt an unmistakable thrill that came from knowing that she and her grandmother had owned an instrument with a legendary curse, which had belonged to a famous musician as well. In some small way, Neela had become part of a strange and mysterious history. Yet, the very thought of it made her sick to her stomach. Because it meant Hal had guessed correctly about the veena. He had been right all along.

"So it was hers," Neela said, stunned. "It was really Veronica Wyvern's veena."

"And how did you say the photographer came to take this picture?" Tannenbaum asked.

"It's a long story," Neela said.

She did her best to explain, as Tannenbaum listened with interest. "I can't believe her veena survived the crash," he said. "It's of great importance to me, not just because Ronnie was my friend, but because I have a scholarly interest in the history of Indian instruments. You see, that year when she went to India to perform, there was another reason for her trip. She was on her way to find out something significant about the instrument."

"The curse," Neela said quickly.

"The curse? Oh, yes, the curse of Parvati." He chuckled. "That story has persisted for so long."

"It isn't true?" Neela asked.

He shrugged. "I'm a scholar. I have no interest in such things except in what they mean historically."

"Then there was something else? Other than the curse?" Neela wasn't quite sure what she meant.

Tannenbaum regarded Neela for a moment, as if he were noticing for the first time that he was talking to an eleven-year-old girl. "You sure you want to know all of this?" He looked around. "Did you come alone? Is your mother somewhere here?"

Neela pointed to the gardening aisle at the other end of the store. "She's there," she said. "And please, could you go on, if you don't mind?"

He scratched his head. "It's far too much information. I can't get into it all. Maybe one of these days we can meet, along with Sudha, and talk more at length."

Neela glanced at the gardening aisle and saw her mother with an armload of books. Neela's time was about to run out.

"Please!" Neela's voice was urgent. "Please tell me, what was it that Veronica so badly wanted to know? I'm leaving for India tomorrow. I might be able to get the veena back, but I need to know as much as I can."

"Well, I'd have to start with Guru," Tannenbaum said.

"I know who he was. The veena-maker," Neela said, one eye on her mother.

"And then I'd have to tell you what a Guru original was," he went on.

"I know all about that, too," Neela said. She saw her mother put several books back on the shelves. In her hand were two. Was she ready to buy them?

"Oh." Tannenbaum was surprised. "Well, if you know all that, then I can tell you that out of the dozen or so Guru originals still circulating out there, there is great interest in locating the first one he made, the *original* Guru original, if you will."

"The original Guru original?" Neela repeated.

"What, you know about that, too?"

She shook her head. She was still watching her mother, who had now put back the two books in her hand, as well. What was she going to do? Not buy anything at all? If only Professor Tannenbaum would hurry. "Please. Why is the original Guru original important?"

"Well, it's the first one," Tannenbaum said. "It could be worth crores of rupees—hundreds of thousands of dollars, we're talking. But really, it's the value of owning the first one made by Guru that makes that veena priceless."

"And Veronica thought she owned the original Guru original?" Neela asked.

He shrugged. "That's what she wanted to find out. She thought maybe the person who sold it to her might know. She was going to consult a veena historian, search records."

Neela marveled over this new information. It seemed at every turn she was learning something more extraordinary about her grandmother's veena.

"So do *you* think she had the first Guru original?" Neela asked.

He smiled. "I don't know if there was any way of fully knowing. Dating rare instruments is a profession itself. First of all, you'd have to confirm that all the *parts* of the instrument are the original ones. Instruments can break and be repaired and have things replaced on them. That takes away some of the rareness factor. Once you verified that you have all the original parts, then I suppose you could look at the varnish, at the initials, at the other signs of craftsmanship to determine if what you have is a Guru original. But the *original* one? That's beyond my expertise." He looked past her. "I see someone; I think it's your mom."

Neela turned around to find her mother standing some feet away with two huge books in her hands. She seemed to recognize Tannebaum, from the way she looked at them.

"I'll be there in a second," Neela called to her mom.

Maybe because Tannenbaum was watching, Mrs. Krishnan went along without any questions. But Neela could see the checkout line was short. She had only a few more minutes left. "Thank you so much for your help, Professor Tannenbaum," she said to him.

"No problem," Tannenbaum said. "So you said you're off to India tomorrow? And you think you might find this veena?" He looked at her curiously.

"That's my hope," she said.

"Well, let me know what happens. And be careful. That veena of Ronnie's . . ." His voice trailed off.

"What?" she asked.

He hesitated. "I don't know in the end how much happiness that knowledge brings. Sometimes when you have something precious, it interferes with the rest of your life. It's like owning the Hope Diamond. You're not going to wear it to the playground. In fact, you'll stop going to the playground." He shrugged. "So, good luck. And watch out for snapping strings."

Somehow his remark didn't bother her now, and she actually smiled. "I'll try," she said.

When they got outside the store, Mrs. Krishnan said, "What were you talking about for so long with Alfred Tannenbaum? That was him, wasn't it?"

Neela paused. If she told her mother what she had found out, her mother might not think her so strange for wanting her instrument back, now that she knew it once belonged to a famous musician and that it might be the original Guru original. And the more Neela kept from her mother, the harder it became to share the next big thing. But in some strange and selfish way, Neela wanted to hang on to this information for herself just a little longer.

So she said, "Nothing—just the concert last month and what I'm playing now."

Mrs. Krishnan nodded agreeably as they walked to the car. As they were getting in, she said, "I'm glad, because for a moment, I was worried you were talking about your cursed veena with him."

Neela gave a start, then tried to keep her voice steady. "Why would that be wrong?"

Her mother made a face. "It's just not something to talk about with normal, sane people."

"What are you saying? We're not normal, sane people?"

"No, I meant the story about the curse is not normal or sane. And frankly, I'm not too keen on hearing about it. I'd like to think about something else, like our trip and seeing our family, not some creepy curse about a veena looking for a dead wife."

"That's *not* the story."

"Even so."

Meanwhile, a rage was building in Neela. "What if the veena did have something special about it, wouldn't you want to know? What if we went to the Chennai Music Palace and it was there, like the story says? Isn't there a part of you that—"

"No," Mrs. Krishnan said. "Not one little tiny part. Actually, I don't want to ever see that veena again. Let who ever has it, keep it. We'll get a brand-new veena. Without any curses."

Neela clenched her fists. She had been so close to telling her about what she knew. But now she was glad she hadn't. Her mother would never understand or try to help Neela get the veena back. It was clear—whatever Neela would do when she got to India, it would be on her own.

CHAPTER 26

When the day of the trip arrived, it came on one of the most blustery stretches of bad weather Boston had experienced in a long time.

"Drive slowly," Mrs. Krishnan warned, as they made their way down the slippery roads toward the airport. "They haven't plowed the streets yet."

Outside, soft, billowy flakes fell from the sky, landing on the car windows. Neela watched the snow with a mixture of excitement and gloom. Here they were, at last going to India—possibly to see her veena again—which would be the most thrilling adventure of her life, if only they could make it to the airport.

"We should have left an hour ago," Mrs. Krishnan announced, as if saying that could be useful to anyone.

Mr. Krishnan's eyes were glued to the windshield. "If anyone talks to me now, I'll crash the car."

After an hour of more snow and Mr. Krishnan's threats, the car pulled into Logan International Airport. Then, just as final boarding was announced, Neela and her family arrived at the gate, out of breath but all in one piece.

"What took you so long?" Pavi wanted to know. In spite of the bad weather, she and her family had arrived at the gate more than an hour earlier and were waiting dutifully. How did they do it? Neela wondered if they had ever been late to anything in their lives.

Neela said to her father, "Can I buy some chips?"

Mr. Krishnan looked at her as if she were insane. "The plane is leaving in three minutes. We don't have time for chips."

"Rats," Neela said.

"I have two boxes of Cracker Jacks in my backpack," Pavi offered.

"Cracker Jacks?" Neela repeated. "Man, that sucks," she muttered under her breath.

They hurried onto the plane after showing their boarding passes to the flight attendant. Once Neela and Pavi were seated in a row away from their parents, Pavi asked, "So, are you getting cold feet?"

Neela looked at her in surprise. How did Pavi always know what she was thinking? "Did I tell you who Hal was?" she asked.

"Only a million times. I don't get it. Who cares who he is?"

"Don't you see?" Neela said miserably. "He's the *father*. Of someone dead."

"Look, I'm not trying to be an evil person," Pavi said. "But even if that veena belonged to Veronica, it still was your grandmother's, too, and then it was yours. And it's not just any veena—it's a Guru original, and it's got a cool story behind it."

Neela was about to interrupt, but Pavi held up a hand. "I get that you feel guilty about Hal being Veronica's father. But she's dead. And he's not going to play that veena. He's going to put it in some corner of his apartment, maybe light a bunch of candles, or I don't know. But he's not a musician. And instruments—you have to play them. You will. *He* won't."

Neela considered her friend's words.

"Besides," Pavi went on, "if that veena meant so much to him, why didn't he call you and ask for it? Why did he steal it? And throw a rock at your house later? That makes him a creep in my book, no matter who his daughter was."

"It's just that I don't want to do the same thing," Neela said slowly. "I don't want to be . . . dishonest. Does that make sense?"

"But you never stole the veena from anyone. All you're doing is going to Govindar's store and asking for the veena back." She clasped her hands. "I mean, don't you want to see if the veena is in the store? Aren't you, like, dying of curiosity?"

Neela grinned. "Actually, yeah. It's killing me, not knowing." She sat back in her seat. Suddenly she felt better, as if a dark cloud that had been hanging over her had passed. "I guess, then, all I have to figure out now is how to get to the music store without my parents knowing."

"I'm coming too," Pavi said. "Since you don't have your boyfriend to help you."

Neela stared at her. "What are you talking about? Do you mean Matt?"

Pavi sniffed. "Why else did he go with you to the church? You didn't even ask me."

Neela sighed. "Because you don't live in Arlington. There was no way you could come with me after school." Then she added, "And he's not my boyfriend."

"Hmm," Pavi said.

Neela opened her backpack and pulled out the magazine from Elizabeth Bones. She had brought all her "clues" with her: the magazine, the printout from the computer, the note that had been attached to the rock, and the photocopy of the wyvern embroidery. She figured the magazine would give her something to do until Pavi simmered down.

"What are you looking at?" Pavi asked gruffly, in spite of herself.

Neela held back a smile. She knew the magazine would do the trick.

"*Boston Living*," she said. She turned so Pavi could

look at it, too. As they read, Neela came to a quote by K.R. Mohan, who was described as a leading expert on South Indian instruments: *The veena is one of India's oldest and finest instruments. If one talks about the music of India, one must start with the veena.*

And if one talks about the vanishing veena, Neela thought to herself, one must start with the Chennai Music Palace. And just like that, an idea popped into her head on how to get there.

"You hungry?" Pavi opened her backpack and handed Neela a box of Cracker Jack.

Neela looked inside the box of caramel-covered popcorn and peanuts. "What's this?" She pulled out a shiny packet.

"It's a prize. Don't you know anything about Cracker Jacks? Every box has one. That's why they're so famous."

Neela opened it. "Baseball cards," she announced. "Just what I need." Then she saw Pavi's face. "Thanks, anyway," she finished meekly. She realized she was being a pain.

The girls chewed on their Cracker Jacks, each thinking about their trip as the plane cleared the runway.

One stopover, two in-flight movies, several meals, a nap, and thirty hours later, Neela, Pavi, and their families landed in Chennai, India, sometime after the stroke of midnight.

CHAPTER 27

The air was balmy as Neela and her family stepped outside the airport building and were greeted at the curb by Ravi, her grandparents' driver. He led them to the car, and they set off for home. The streets were bumpy and crowded with motorcycles and lorries, even in the middle of the night. Neela stared out the window as they drove past darkened stores and the silhouettes of coconut trees framing the night sky.

Neela's grandparents lived in a bungalow on a quiet, tree-lined road in the heart of Chennai. Their house had been built more than three decades ago, but it had been updated over the years with screened windows, a new fridge, microwave, and washing machine. In the bathroom, her grandparents had even installed a ceramic bathtub, something unheard of in their neighborhood, to make the house more comfortable for Neela and Sree.

It was strange to arrive at her grandparents' house without Lalitha Patti there to greet them. Instead it was just Thatha, Neela's grandfather, who waited at the door as the car pulled into the gated driveway. He helped them with their beds, and without much talk, everyone fell asleep until morning.

At breakfast the next day, the family sat at the table while Thatha served *idlis*, or rice dumplings, and coffee. Neela's father asked him why he didn't go to Arun's wedding with Lalitha Patti.

"I went for the first half of the celebrations and came back. Someone had to be here to let you in when you arrived. Besides, weddings are too much noise and confusion for me." Since his stroke last year, Neela's grandfather declared himself "good as new." Still, he rarely went out of town for more than a day or two.

"When is Patti coming back, Thatha?" Neela asked.

"This evening," he said. "Soon."

Just then, Neela heard the sound of the front gate opening. At last! She had been waiting for that sound all morning. While everyone was talking, she slipped outside, the address to the music store tucked in her hand.

As it turned out, Pavi's family was staying only about twenty minutes away in an area of Chennai known as Royapettah. The good news was that the Chennai Music Palace was in the same neighborhood, only a few streets away from Pavi's house. And now the way to Pavi's, as well as to the store, had just arrived. Sure enough, Ravi was out front near her grandparents' car, with a bucket and sponge. He beamed when he saw her.

"Already up and about?" he said in Tamil. Ravi dipped his sponge inside the bucket of soapy water, the suds running onto the cement. He had been the driver for her grandparents for as long as Neela could remember. She wanted to talk to him the night before, but it had been impossible with her parents there.

"I like being here," she replied in Tamil. Behind them, the morning traffic droned with the sound of car horns, rattling bullock carts, and people. It seemed as if there was always traffic in Chennai. Neela watched as a vegetable vendor, several women carrying water jugs on their heads, a few stray dogs, and a group of schoolgirls with their hair in neat braids walked by. She decided there was no other way but to ask directly.

"Ravi, I need you to do a big, big favor for me." Neela showed him the address to the music store. "Could you take my friend and me there? Please?"

He glanced at the address. "Of course. Find out from your parents when to go."

"You don't understand. . . ." She stopped. She realized that Ravi would never take her anywhere without her parents' permission. "I have to go without them," she said slowly, "because . . . it's their wedding anniversary . . . and I'm surprising them with a gift."

Ravi shook his head. "Neela, what would they say with me driving you around by yourself? I would get sacked from my job."

"But it's just to my friend's house and the store down the street."

Ravi was firm. "I cannot risk upsetting your family. They have been so good to me."

Neela frowned. There had to be a way to convince him. He was her only hope unless she took an auto-rickshaw, which sounded scary, especially when she didn't know her way around the city. Or wait. Maybe that was it. "If you can't take me, maybe I can take an auto-rickshaw. I've never done it before, but how hard can it be?"

Ravi looked alarmed. "Don't! You don't know those auto-rickshaw drivers. It isn't safe for a young lady, and they'll spot you as a foreigner immediately."

Neela tried to look crushed. "If you can't take me, I don't have any other choice."

Ravi scowled. "Don't think I don't know what you're doing. I should tell your parents right now."

"Please don't," Neela begged. "It's a short ride. I'll be done in an hour."

"But what will you tell them?"

"I'll say I'm going to the neighbor's to play computer games. I'll be back before they find me gone. And they'll be so surprised with the gift I'm bringing home."

Ravi scowled even more, but at last he relented. "It better be an extra-special gift."

Neela thought of the veena. "It is," she said.

On the way to Pavi's house, Neela trembled with excitement. She had felt awful lying to her parents and grandfather. Her parents had barely looked up to say yes to the neighbor's house. Little did they dream that their daughter was actually heading down a dusty road to Royapettah.

When Neela had phoned Govindar, he sounded as if he was expecting her call.

"When can I come?" she asked, her heart thudding in her throat.

"Four o'clock. The same time as the other gentleman. You must resolve this problem together."

"Of course," she said. But she decided to go an hour early.

If she could talk to Govindar, she might convince him to give the veena to her. After all, all the things Pavi had said were true: Neela was a musician who would play the veena, not Hal. And wasn't Lalitha Patti a good friend of Govindar's? Didn't he owe something to their friendship? The important thing was to get him on her side. Then maybe he would let her take the veena home before Hal even got to the store. Because Hal was the last person Neela wanted to see. She wasn't sure how much resolve she would have if she looked into his eyes and saw them filled with the memory of his dead daughter.

Ravi turned down a narrow street lined with coconut trees and houses on either side. Neela peered out the window until she spotted her friend standing outside a pale green house. "There she is," Neela said to Ravi.

Pavi climbed in after the car came to a stop. She was wearing a lemon-colored kurta-pajama set with a thin, gauzy veil wrapped around her neck.

"What did you tell your parents?" Neela asked.

Pavi hesitated, looking at Ravi.

"He doesn't speak English," Neela said.

"I said I was taking a nap. They never check up on me when I'm sleeping." She readjusted her veil.

Neela yawned, starting to feel the effects of jetlag. "What's with the outfit?"

"Well, you know the saying: When in Rome, do as the Romans do." She eyed Neela's Disney World T-shirt and jeans. "Your clothing screams 'foreigner' to me."

Neela let out her breath. "Pavi, we're not going undercover. Govindar *knows* we're coming." She clutched her backpack, in which she had brought her "clues." She wasn't sure she needed them, but it was comforting to have them just the same. She had also brought her passport, in case Govindar asked for proof of who she was.

Outside, Ravi pulled onto a busy commercial street with shops. At the end of the street, between Meera's House of Saris and an auto-rickshaw stand, they saw it. The sign for the Chennai Music Palace was done in big, decorative writing. They were really here.

"We'll be back soon," she said to Ravi in Tamil. "Thanks for taking us."

Ravi glowered. "You both hurry. If Thatha finds out, I'm a dead man."

Neela resisted the urge to hug him, because he would get embarrassed. So instead she smiled and thanked him again as she and Pavi shuffled out of the car. Outside, the air was heavy with the smell of exhaust fumes and the sound of engines puttering noisily from the auto-rickshaw stand.

"Ever heard of mufflers?" Pavi muttered as they walked by. The auto drivers peered back curiously at the sight of two young girls alone on a busy commercial street.

The ground was littered with candy wrappers, scraps of food, old cigarette butts, and a stray animal or two. "Watch out," Neela said as Pavi almost stepped on the tail of a dog sitting next to the store. They walked up the front steps, past a window display of violins, veenas, flutes, a set of drums called mridangams, and a few instruments that looked like inverted clay jugs.

"How does anyone wear this?" Pavi grumbled, readjusting her veil.

"Here, give it to me." Neela took it from Pavi and stuffed it into her backpack. As they were about to go inside, they heard another car door slam behind them. Neela turned around. Just a few feet away, a car pulled away from the curb as a girl made her way toward the shop. She stopped when she saw Neela.

"What are you doing here?" Neela blurted.

Pavi turned to Neela. "Who's that?"

"*That's* Lynne."

CHAPTER 28

For a moment, no one said anything. Neela stared at Lynne, who was also dressed in a kurta-pajama set, hers a navy blue with multicolored embroidery along the neckline. Her curly hair was tied back, and she wore a bindi. Where had Lynne learned to dress like an Indian? And what was she doing in front of the Chennai Music Palace, thousands of miles away from home?

At last Neela found her voice. "You're here because you want to steal the veena again." When she spoke, she was surprised by how angry she sounded.

Lynne stood very still. "I know you're mad at me. I'm sorry about what happened. But I don't think you know the whole story."

Neela crossed her arms. "I know Hal is Veronica

Wyvern's father, and he thinks my veena belonged to his daughter. So I kind of feel sorry for him. But you just took advantage of him because he was your neighbor, and he thought he could trust you."

"That's not true." Lynne's shoulders gave way, and she seemed suddenly small and frail.

Pavi, who had been listening, spoke up. "Neela, maybe you should hear her side. You know, like why she's here in *India*?"

Lynne pushed up her tortoiseshell glasses. "Um, who are you?"

Pavi tossed her head. "I'm Neela's friend. I know all about the veena mystery."

"I thought you told me everything you knew," Neela said to Lynne.

Lynne motioned to the door. "Let's talk inside."

Neela blocked her way. "Why can't we talk out here? There's plenty of room." Behind them, Ravi was staring from the car in puzzlement. He signaled to Neela, but she shook her head.

Lynne sighed. "Because it's noisy and dusty out here. I'm not sneaking in and running off with the veena, if that's what you're worried about!"

Neela followed her inside—though, of course, Lynne stealing the veena was exactly what she was worried about. The three girls found themselves inside a small lobby. Neela and Pavi waited while Lynne took a deep breath and began.

"You're right about Hal being Veronica's father," she

said. "Ever since she died, he's been heartbroken. Sometimes he blamed himself because he was the one who found a veena teacher for her, and the veena was what brought her to India, where she died. It doesn't make any sense for him to blame himself, but that's the sort of person he is. And it might be because his wife passed away just a few years after Veronica Wyvern died. So he felt alone in the world without his wife and daughter. Well, almost. But I'm getting to that.

"Anyway, it wasn't until a year ago that someone sent him a newspaper clipping from India about a veena that kept disappearing and reappearing at the Chennai Music Palace. Some people thought it was haunted, some said it once belonged to Veronica Wyvern. When he read that, he flipped. How could the veena be hers when she died in a train wreck *with* her veena?"

"I wondered that, too," Neela said. "Unless she had some other veena with her that day."

Lynne shook her head. "No, she only owned one. So Hal got to wondering about this veena. Because the article was also about the woman who owned the veena now, a woman in Chennai."

"My grandmother," Neela said. "She said she later reported to the newspaper that she had sold the instrument. But she actually mailed it to me." Her eyes narrowed. "So how did Hal find that out?"

"The person who sent the article—it was the father of the man married to Veronica, her father-in-law—he met somebody at a concert here who knew your grandmother, and that person told him the veena had been secretly mailed off to her granddaughter in Boston. So when Veronica's father-in-law sent the clipping, he added a note that the veena was really in Boston, owned by a young girl."

"Where Hal lived," Neela said.

"Right," Lynne said. "But Hal had no idea how to find the veena or the girl. Boston's a big place. So he started looking for music recitals—anywhere a student learning the veena might perform. Finally he saw a listing at the temple last summer."

"My recital," Neela said. "With the snapping string." So even Hal had been there. Was there no one who *hadn't*?

"He got your name from the program list. Your mom was one of the volunteers, so her name was on it, too. Then just a quick look through the phone books for a 'Lakshmi Krishnan,' and he found your family in Arlington. Which, if you think about it, is a strange coincidence, since this whole time he had a granddaughter the same age, and the two of them were living over in just the next town, Somerville."

Neela instantly thought of her mother's saying: *There are no coincidences*. But then something much bigger struck her. "Granddaughter?" she repeated.

Lynne flushed. "Yeah, granddaughter."

A look of understanding crossed Neela's face. "You're not Hal's neighbor, are you?"

Lynne shook her head.

"What? What?" Pavi wanted to know. "What are you guys talking about?"

Neela turned to Pavi. "Don't you get it?"

"I'm the granddaughter," Lynne finished flatly. "And Veronica Wyvern's daughter."

Neela let out her breath. "I've got to sit down." She looked around and found no place to sit. "Veronica Wyvern had a child. Of course. Why didn't I think of that?"

"I was a year old when the train wreck happened," Lynne said. "And I've lived with my grandfather ever since."

Neela kept shaking her head.

"I wanted to tell you," Lynne continued. "But my grandfather made me swear to keep quiet. It was all part of his plan to get back the veena from you. I thought it was whacked-out, especially getting me to switch schools so I'd be in the same class with you. He thought if you and I became friends, you'd somehow give the instrument back to us."

"Why didn't you just ask? Why did your grandfather have to steal my veena?"

"He tried, he really did, but your grandmother said no."

"My grandmother?" Neela asked, confused.

Lynne nodded. "Ask her; I'm not lying. And stealing was never in the plan. I mean, I never thought my grandfather would do it. I didn't want to switch schools . . . I liked Somerville. But then I guess I wanted to meet you, too. I wanted to see if you really had the veena. Because, well, you know, maybe it belonged to my mom." She swallowed.

"Don't you know?" Neela asked, surprised.

Lynne shook her head. "None of our pictures are all

that clear, because the dragon part is always facing back, or someone is in the way. I don't remember her veena, of course, and neither does Grandpa. But he's convinced it's the same one because as soon as he saw your veena at your recital, he knew the dragon on it was a wyvern. I guess I want more proof than that, like someone who knew my mom to say, yeah, this is the same veena."

"Actually, there is someone. His name is Professor Tannenbaum. He knew your mom. He saw the photo in the magazine and recognized it right away." Neela felt suddenly sad.

Lynne's eyes grew wide. "So . . . it's hers?"

Neela nodded. The sick feeling that had been with her for days had returned. So now it wasn't just Hal, the long-lost father, but Lynne, the long-lost daughter, too.

Just then, the door to the lobby opened and Ravi appeared, looking cross. "What's going on? I've been waiting, and you haven't even gone inside; you're just standing here, talking, talking. Do you have something to do in the store, or do you just want me fired?"

Neela gulped. "I'm so sorry. We're going in. Please, wait just a few minutes more."

Ravi glared. "I cannot wait here. I must attend to the car. But be back soon. Time is ticking." He said the last sentence in English and left the lobby in a huff.

"Hmm, and I thought he didn't know any English," Neela remarked. She turned to the girls. "According to my watch, we've got about a half hour before Govindar expects us and . . . Wait a minute. Why are you already here?" she asked Lynne.

"I answered the phone when Govindar called," Lynne replied. "My grandfather doesn't even know I'm here. And I wanted to get here early because . . ."

"You wanted to talk to Govindar alone?" Neela finished. She smiled. "I guess great minds think alike."

"Well, let's go, then," Pavi said. "Time is ticking."

With that, the three girls entered the store.

CHAPTER 29

Inside, instruments hung along the walls, arranged in a semicircle around the showroom. The room was lit overhead with fluorescent bulbs that flickered, making a thin buzzing sound. There was a man at the counter, punching numbers into a calculator and entering them into a logbook. He turned when he heard the door open, but upon seeing three girls, he returned to his work as if they weren't worth his time.

Neela cleared her throat. "Excuse me."

"One minute, miss." He continued with his calculator.

Several minutes went by, and Neela began to wonder if he had forgotten them.

"Are you Mr. Govindar?" Pavi asked.

At the sound of the name, the man stopped. "You are looking for him?"

"We're a bit early," Neela said, "but he asked us to come. Can we talk to him?"

"He is not here, but you may talk to his son." He disappeared through a door behind him.

"Son?" Neela wondered.

Pavi was looking at a framed news clipping on the wall. "And you'll never guess what his name is," she said.

Neela and Lynne went to see what she meant. The article was about the Chennai Music Palace and the owners, K.R. Govindar and K.R. Mohan.

"Father and son," Pavi said. "They own the store."

"K.R. Mohan!" Neela said. "The expert from the magazine article."

"But if they're father and son," Lynne said, "why don't they have the same last name?"

"They do, it's just the order that's reversed," Pavi explained. "That's how it's done in South India. K.R. are the initials of their surname, and Govindar and Mohan are their first names."

"I've always found that confusing," Neela said.

"Mohan," Lynne said slowly. "You know what, I remember that name. I think he was at the photo shoot."

"Elizabeth Bones must have brought him along," Neela said. "I guess that makes sense. Though I'm not sure why you need an expert to take a photo of a veena."

Before anyone could say more, the door to the back room opened and a young man stepped out. He wore a tan-colored shirt that looked freshly starched and pressed, setting off his thin, delicate face. Behind him, the man they first saw came out, headed for the front door.

"I met you at the concert," Neela exclaimed. She was about to add, *You're the guy with the ruby ring*, but decided it might be weird to say that to a stranger.

"You were at the photo shoot," Lynne said next.

Mohan was just as surprised as them. "What are you all doing here?" He peered from one face to another. Neela saw the ruby ring on his finger shine under the fluorescent lights.

"We came to see Mr. Govindar about a veena," Neela said. She was still trying to wrap her head around what she had just learned. Could this Mohan really be so many people at the same time—the owner, the son, the young man at the concert, and the guy at Lynne's photo shoot?

"Veena?" he asked. He twirled the ruby ring on his finger, as he did that day with Elizabeth Bones. Was it Neela's imagination or was he completely taken off guard?

She was puzzled. Didn't Govindar tell him? "The special veena," she said, not knowing how else to say it. "I'm Neela Krishnan."

"*You're* Neela Krishnan?" he said. "And you're with her?" He looked at Lynne, then Pavi. Neela could tell he was utterly confused. But her name had meant something to him. Maybe, like his father, he had seen the name on the package and was now putting two and two together.

"Yes. We're here because he was supposed to give the veena back to . . ." Neela was about to say "me," then remembered Lynne. She flushed. "To one of us."

"Really?" He said the word slowly. An unmistakable look of anger flashed on his face. It was so brief, one could have missed it. But Neela did not. Clearly he knew nothing of his father's plans. And now, with his father not here, he was suddenly faced with three girls, unsure what to do. She glanced at him again, still remembering how quickly he had spotted what was wrong with Professor Tannenbaum's veena, how he said the veena was dying, with complete certainty.

By now, Mohan had recovered. "I'm surprised my father said he could meet with you," he said, more politely. "Because he isn't here."

"But I spoke to him this morning," Neela said, surprised.

"I talked to him, too," Lynne said. "He was very clear about it being this afternoon."

There was a silence as they all tried to make sense out of this strange turn of events.

"I'm sure there's a good explanation," Mohan said. "Maybe you can come back tomorrow? My father will be back and can clear up the confusion."

"Don't you know anything about his meeting with us?" Neela asked. "He said the veena was back. That is true, isn't it?" A note of doubt crept into her voice.

"The veena," Mohan said, and smiled sadly. "There are so many veenas, after all."

"But this isn't just any veena," Neela said, taken aback.

"Are you saying the veena *isn't* here?" Pavi asked.

He sighed. "Of course it's here. Why would my father lie to you? But I suggest you discuss it with him, not me, since he is the one with whom you arranged the meeting."

Something began to bother Neela. At first she wasn't sure what it was, but now a question had come to her. "At the photo shoot," she asked, choosing her words carefully, "didn't you recognize the veena?"

Mohan looked at her. "I don't understand."

"You were at the photo shoot, weren't you?" she asked.

Mohan glanced at Lynne. "Of course, yes." He sighed again, as if he had tired of the subject already, even though it had barely been discussed. "And of course I recognized the veena. Elizabeth Bones, the photographer, e-mailed me to request my help on an article she was doing on Indian instruments. I came to verify the veena was made by Guru, who you may or may not know was a veena-maker and—"

"Yes, a Guru original." Neela tried not to sound impatient. "But why didn't you *say* anything about the veena?"

"What was I to say?" Mohan asked. "Here is the veena that keeps vanishing from everyone who has bought it from our store? Besides, my father told me the veena was in Boston with a young girl. I assumed you were that girl," he said to Lynne. "I didn't know if it was proper to bring up those details at the time. So I kept quiet, like any well-intending businessman."

There was another silence now as each of the girls considered what Mohan said.

"And if you will accept my apology, you must come at

another time to discuss the rest with my father. I am on my way out."

Neela felt a wave of panic. She couldn't explain it, but something made her feel that if they left today without the veena, they might not have another chance to get it back. She steeled herself. "Even so, I'd like to take the veena home today," she said. "With or without your father here."

"What?" Mohan asked.

"The veena. I would like it back." She was surprised by how strong her voice sounded.

"As I said, this is something for you to discuss with my father at a later time."

Neela noticed an almost imperceptible shift in his voice. It wasn't so polite as before. She had nothing else to go on, but hearing that tiny change strengthened her resolve even more. "You have no legal right to that veena. My driver is outside; I'll call him in if I don't get back the veena."

Lynne caught on. "I have my cell phone and I can call my grandfather."

"And my uncle is the assistant police commissioner," Pavi declared.

Neela groaned inwardly. Pavi always carried it too far.

"Before calling anybody," Mohan said, "let us see if we can get to the bottom of this. First of all, I don't even know if you really are who you say you are without an ID."

Neela rifled through her backpack. "I brought my passport, and—"

Mohan cut her off. "Second, I do not know what my

father's intentions are. So I cannot hand over the veena to you—it is locked in a special room."

Neela was about to speak, but Mohan cut her off again. "What I can do is show the veena to you, if you want to verify it is here. Would you then go home and wait for my father to call when he's back?"

Neela hesitated. She turned to her friends. "What do you think?"

"We can take a look," Pavi said. "And decide what to do after that."

Lynne pushed her glasses up on her face. "I want to see it with my own eyes."

"As you wish," Mohan said. He went behind the counter. "Right this way, girls."

They followed him to the door in the back. He opened it. "There," he said, pointing.

The girls peered inside. By the wall where Mohan had pointed, a veena stood propped against a stand. A cloth cover had been thrown over it, concealing the peg box and frets.

"How do I know it's the same veena?" Neela asked.

Mohan shrugged. "If you don't trust me, see for yourself. Take off the cover."

Neela walked carefully to the covered veena, Lynne and Pavi closely behind. She lifted the cover and found a completely different veena with the peg box of a dragon head painted gold. Behind them, the door suddenly closed.

Neela whirled around. "No!" she cried, but it was too

late. They heard the sound of a click on the other side. Mohan had locked the door.

"Sit tight," he called out. "My father will not be coming, since I am notifying him that you girls could not keep your appointment."

"Wait!" Neela cried out, tugging on the door handle. "You can't lock us up. Maybe we can discuss this."

"There is nothing to discuss," Mohan said. "Good-bye, and rest assured that the veena is with its rightful owner."

"Come back!" Pavi shouted. But they could already hear Mohan's footsteps retreating.

The girls looked at each other in alarm.

Outside they listened to the sound of the front door closing, followed by the jingle of keys. Mohan had left the store and locked them inside.

"What do we do?" Lynne said.

"What about your cell phone?" Pavi asked her.

She shook her head sadly. "It doesn't have any coverage in India. I was just bluffing."

"I wonder what Ravi will think," Neela said worriedly. "This is so terrible."

She glanced at her friends. For the first time since the whole veena mystery had started, she was fresh out of ideas.

CHAPTER 30

"This room is like a jail cell," Pavi announced. "Not even a crummy trick ceiling." They seemed to be locked in a storage room for instruments. There were several veenas, a few violins, and a guitar; some inside cases, others on a table to be repaired. There was also a desk with a small shelf over it. But there were no windows, no phone, and no other door that led to a way out.

"I can't believe Mohan got away with the veena," Lynne said.

"I don't understand; was it Mohan all along?" Pavi asked. "How did he get the veena from Lynne? I thought it was mailed to the store."

"It was," Neela said. "And Mohan has to be the one who mailed it. Remember, he was in Boston last month.

And he was at the photo shoot. When he saw the veena, he stole it and mailed it back to India, only he used my name so it wouldn't be traced back to him."

"Why mail it?" Lynne asked.

"Did you notice how big a veena is?" Pavi asked.

Neela nodded. "He couldn't have carried it on the plane without drawing attention. It's too huge. But the bigger question is, why Mohan? Why this veena? And what about the curse?"

Pavi sighed. "Neela, you still don't believe in that curse, do you?"

"The veena did come back to the store," Neela said.

"But if the curse is true," Pavi said, "the veena should come back again. In fact, maybe if we wait it out, the veena will be here tomorrow. And maybe it'll bring me a large Coke."

Lynne giggled. "The article my grandfather read didn't mention anything about beverages."

"Did your mom know about the curse?" Neela asked.

"She had to," Lynne said. "She was paranoid about losing her instrument. She never explained why, but it was always with her, even when she traveled. My grandfather decided later it was because of the curse. And even though it sounded crazy, that's why Grandpa called the store a few days ago. Just to see if the curse was true. And sure enough, the veena was back."

"That's how I found out the veena was here, too." Neela stared thoughtfully at Lynne. "And yet, Mohan doesn't seem to think it will happen. I mean, why lock up a bunch of girls and run off with the veena if he thought it would come back *here*. . . . It's like something is different this time."

"Yeah, we're locked up in his store," Pavi said. "That's what's different."

"Not just that," Neela said. "It's clear that Mohan doesn't believe in the curse."

"Well, he's not the only one," Pavi said. "Look, this conversation is fascinating, but it isn't helping us get out of here."

"You're right," Neela said. "And we *have* to find a way to get that veena back. Which means finding Mohan."

"But he could've gone anywhere," Pavi said.

"Maybe he's leaving the country," Lynne said forlornly.

"We'll worry about that later," Neela said. "Let's see if there's a way out."

"Did that," Pavi said.

"Well, let's do it again. Maybe there's something we've missed."

For the next several minutes, the girls focused on the room. Not a single spot was overlooked. Lynne pored over the desk. Pavi searched the table area where the instruments were being repaired, while Neela turned her attention to the door.

It was an ordinary wooden one with a brass knob. She jiggled the knob. Then she examined the frame to see if there were any cracks. Nothing. She frowned. There had to be a way. Unless . . . She remembered that day in the church office with Matt, and the sound of the credit card whizzing along the door. She had never done it herself, but it was worth a try. Only she had no credit card. What else could she use? She rifled through her backpack and found the half-finished box of Cracker Jack. As soon as she saw it, a lightbulb went on in her head. She pulled out the box and dug through what was left of the sticky caramel popcorn.

"How can you eat at a time like this?" Pavi asked. "I thought we were searching."

"Just a sec," Neela said. She found the shiny cover and pulled out the baseball cards: Derek Jeter, Alex Rodriguez, and Hideki Matsui. The cards fit easily in her hand. They weren't exactly credit cards, but they were almost the same size. She inserted Derek Jeter's card between the door and frame. "Too thin," she said. She added Hideki Matsui and stuck them both back. "Better."

"What are you doing?" Lynne asked.

"Oh my God, are you going to slide open the lock?" Pavi was excited.

Neela ran the cards up carefully against the door jamb and felt it resist. "It's not giving."

"Try it again," Pavi said. "Do it more quickly."

This time Neela ran it up fast and as hard as she could. In the room all three girls heard the distinct sound of a click inside the door as the catch gave.

"Yeah!" Pavi shouted.

Neela grinned and leaned against the door, which swung open. "Come on," she called to Lynne, who had her head inside the large bottom drawer of the desk.

Lynne poked her head out, an intent look on her face. Her hand was inside the drawer, feeling around for something. She concentrated, tugging with her hand. "There, I got it off. There's a false bottom in here."

Pavi and Neela hovered over her as Lynne pulled out two items from inside the drawer. "They were hidden underneath this insert."

They looked through them quickly. One was a tattered book titled *A Chronology of Veena Makers of Thanjavur*. The other was an old photograph wrapped in oilskin.

"Let's *go*," Pavi said. "We've been here long enough. That's just another place for storing things."

"No, it's definitely a hidden compartment," Lynne said.

"Pavi's right," Neela said. "We have to go. Ravi's been outside all this time." She stared once more at the book and oilskin cover, then made a decision. "But let's bring them. Maybe they're clues." Lynne put them both in Neela's backpack.

When they got outside, Ravi was more than just mad. "Where have you been?" he shouted. "I wait one hour, and no sign of you!"

"Ravi, I'm so sorry," Neela apologized. "It was all a terrible mistake."

"What do you think, I am some idiot who likes to sit in a car while you goof off in your fancy music store?" he seethed. "Or maybe you think my home is lined with five-hundred rupee notes, and I drive your grandparents around for fun. Better yet, I was *hoping* to get sacked today."

"Ravi, please, you've got to believe there was a good

reason," Neela pleaded. She quickly told him about how she and her friends had been locked up in the back room of the store.

"Locked up? What's going on?" Ravi looked shocked. "What kind of present are you buying for your parents?"

Neela shook her head. "There is no present. It's too hard to explain. But we've been trying to find my lost veena, and now the man who locked us up has taken it away, and we don't know where he's gone."

"A man?" Ravi repeated, still glowering. He became silent. "Well, there was a man about twenty minutes ago that came out of the store."

"Yes? What did he look like?" Neela breathed.

Ravi shrugged. "A fancy kind of man, he smelled like perfume. I wouldn't notice him except he had something tall and big that looked like a potato sack with wheels."

"That was Mohan—with my veena." Neela was excited. "Did you see where he went?"

Ravi shook his head. "I didn't. But *he* did." He pointed to a man in an auto that had pulled up to the stand behind their car. "Looks like he just came back from dropping him off somewhere."

Neela regarded the auto driver, a lean, unshaven man with thick bushy hair, dressed in a dirty yellow uniform and chewing on a thin cigarette. "Ravi, do you think you could ask him where he took Mohan?" Neela pleaded.

Ravi glared at her. "Give me one good reason why I should talk to some random auto guy when your parents must be worried sick at home."

"Because I really have to find out where Mohan went with the veena," Neela said. "Don't you see? He wouldn't have locked us up if that veena wasn't so important. But it doesn't belong to him, he *stole* it, and that auto guy might be our only chance."

Lynne came forward. "I don't know Tamil, but maybe you can understand this." She bent down on her knees and looked at Ravi with her hands clasped. "Please help us."

Ravi stared at her. "What is this girl doing? Up, up, the ground is dirty." He made a motion with his hands to stand up.

Pavi knelt next to Lynne and did the same. Neela joined them.

"Please?" Neela pleaded.

Ravi looked at three pairs of imploring eyes. "Get up, all of you. Dear God, I hope today I am not fired."

Neela and the girls watched as Ravi spoke at length to the auto driver. Both of them spoke in rapid-fire Tamil, so it was impossible for Neela to tell what anyone was saying. After a moment, the driver nodded vigorously, pointing his finger down the street. He spoke for another minute or two. When he was done, Ravi slipped something in his hand.

"You bribed him?" Neela asked when Ravi got back.

"*Ayo*, not bribing, just greasing the path to information."

Neela felt a stab of guilt. "I will pay you back for—"

He waved his hand. "Forget it. So, you want to know what this fellow said?"

Neela held her breath. "Oh, Ravi. Where did Mohan go?"

CHAPTER 31

"Can you drive faster?" Neela implored from the backseat. If what the auto driver said was true, it meant they only had twenty minutes to stop Mohan from catching the five o'clock train to Thanjavur.

"Missie, it's a good thing I'm not driving you straight home for giving me a heart attack," Ravi shouted. Now that they were on their way, Neela knew he was just saying that to get some more scolding in, not because he wasn't going to help her.

"Where is Thanjavur, anyway?" Lynne asked.

"South, very old city," Ravi answered in English. Neela marveled at the level of English he actually knew.

"But if Mohan leaves, we'll never find him," Pavi said.

"Unless we stop him," Neela said. "But first, there must

be some way to contact Govindar. I have his phone number with me but no phone."

"You can use mine," Ravi said. He handed her his cell phone.

"What are you going to say?" Lynne asked while Neela dialed. "Your son locked us inside your store, and now he's headed to the station?"

"Something like that," Neela said.

Govindar's phone rang several times until the answering machine kicked in. Neela heard the beep and decided it was better to leave him something. "Hi, this is Neela Krishnan. We came to meet you in the store today, but your son, Mohan, tried to stop us. He is now headed to the train station. We are trying to stop him. I thought you should know." She hung up the phone.

Pavi stared at her. "What kind of message is that? You didn't even say anything about him locking us up."

"Or the veena," Lynne added.

Neela shrugged. "I didn't want to accuse his son on the machine. Kind of awkward."

"But he really did lock us up!" Pavi exclaimed.

"Details," Neela said. She opened her backpack. "Now we just have to figure out what these things are." She pulled out the book and photograph. The photograph was obscured by the oilskin cover, so Neela carefully undid it.

"Oh," Lynne exclaimed when Neela was done. The photograph was black and white and seemed very old. It was of a woman veena-player seated on a rug on the floor. "Do you mind?" Lynne took the photo from Neela. "It looks just like some of my grandfather's old photographs on my father's side." She turned it over gingerly. *Parvati, Mysore Palace, 1903*, it read.

"Parvati," Neela said. Lynne turned the photograph back to the front. Parvati was dressed in a traditional sari, with her hair in a long braid, covered in flowers, and diamond earrings, a necklace, and a nose ring adorning her face. She held a veena across her arms and looked very serious. "Is it the same veena?" Neela asked, squinting. "Looks like it, but it's hard to tell."

Lynne nodded. "I know from what my grandfather told me, people didn't get many photographs taken back then. See, this was taken at the Mysore Palace. It must have been commissioned. She must have performed there."

Ravi suddenly slammed the brakes, causing the girls to jerk forward.

"Sorry," he cried, glancing back at them to see if they were okay. Neela looked at the road and saw a flock of goats crossing in front of them. "Stupid farmers," Ravi muttered. "They act like they're still in the village. What, they don't notice twenty lorries coming down the road? Not to mention, me?"

When the car began to move again, Neela turned her attention to the book. The binding was coming apart at the seams, so she opened it carefully. "Look, it's printed in Thanjavur in 1948." As she thumbed through the pages, Lynne kept looking at the old photograph, murmuring to herself.

"I love photos," she said. "There's so little I know about my mom. Even though my grandfather went ballistic with this whole veena thing, he hardly ever talks about her or my dad. So all I have are photos."

"Is that why you wanted a camera?" Neela asked.

Lynne nodded. "I was always interested in photography. But I've never really had a good camera . . . until now." She flushed. "My grandfather isn't, uh, well off. He gets some money from his retirement, but it's not a whole lot, so we're always trying to save up. Also, he doesn't believe in buying 'expensive gadgets.' That's why we don't even have a computer."

"You don't have a computer?" Pavi tried to keep the astonishment from her voice. Neela knew that, for Pavi, a computer was like an additional limb.

"Yeah. It's really annoying. I can't go on the Web except at the library. I have to do everything by hand or type it out in the computer lab."

Neela thought for a moment. "So that's why you were looking up your mom in the library that day."

"Yeah. I wanted to see if I could find out more about her veena, and if the one my grandfather took was really hers or not."

"Hey," Pavi said, "was that rock with the newspaper cutout note from you?"

Lynne looked sheepish. "I had to think of something to make you stop asking around at the church. By then the veena was stolen again, and I didn't have it to give back to you."

"And I guess you misspelled 'consequence' on purpose," Neela said.

Lynne nodded. "I also made the boot prints with my grandfather's snow boots."

"And the teakettle!" Pavi exclaimed.

"Oh, right," Neela said. "Wait, that was you, too?"

Lynne sighed and nodded again. "You know Mary, right?"

"The church office woman," Neela said.

"Yeah, well, she's not just that. She's my grandfather's cousin. Twice removed or something."

Pavi hit her head with her hand. "You're kidding. Who else are you related to? Mohan?"

"Very funny. That's how we know about the church, and why my grandfather started volunteering there, because he knew Mary. In fact, we used her address for the school so I could switch districts. She didn't like the whole idea at first, but finally agreed to it."

"So she knew Hal took the veena?" Neela asked.

"No. But as soon as you came by and described what happened, she suspected him."

"And the teakettle? Did your grandfather take it?"

"No," Lynne said, squeezing her eyes shut. "That was me. I hid it inside the kitchen to make it look like it disappeared. I thought it would throw everyone off Grandpa's track. Because Mary knew he wouldn't take the teakettle. I'll have to return it to her when I get back." She looked at Neela. "I'm sorry. I guess I've created a mess. I can see why you'd be so mad at me."

Neela thought for a moment. "Actually, I'm not mad anymore. Because we're chasing down the real thief in India now. Together. Though who would have guessed?"

They smiled at each other.

Neela returned her attention to the book. It was exactly as the title said, a chronology of veena makers. She didn't recognize a single name until she came to a section on Guru, bookmarked with a slip of paper.

> Guru was a renowned veena maker whose earlier work was done in collaboration with his father, also a veena maker for many years (See L.V. Ramana and Son).
>
> In 1902, he married the veena player Parvati, and is said to have made his first solo veena for her. In crafting this veena, Guru departed from his father's traditional style, adopting a European design for the peg box (medieval dragon). It is also speculated that Guru adorned this peg box with jewels from his wife's wedding set, but no records have confirmed this.
>
> While the exact date of this first veena cannot be ascertained, the date of Guru's marriage can be used as an approximation. Legend has it the veena was sold preemptively, and lost from the Guru household thereupon.

And just like that, an idea formed in Neela's head.

"Of course!" she said. "I know what Mohan had this book for."

"What are you talking about?" Pavi asked. "Tell us!"

"I—" Neela started, and then before she could say

more, she glanced out the window and saw the clock tower of the train station rise before them. "I don't believe it," she said. "We're *here*."

It was a Saturday evening, and the Central Train Station was jam-packed with people. Neela kept her eyes open, searching for signs of Mohan, as she and the rest of the group headed for the Thanjavur platform.

She'd had no chance to explain herself, because at that moment, Ravi pulled into a parking spot, and they all had to jump out of the car immediately. Now they were inside, she had a moment to think, and the conversation she'd had with Tannenbaum a few days ago came rushing back to her. Mohan the veena expert, Mohan who wanted to be a musician, and Mohan who said the veena was a dying art—he was after the same answer as Veronica Wyvern, all these years later!

How it fit with the curse and the veena returning to the store, she still didn't know. But she would worry about that part later. Right now, they had to find Mohan.

Just then, Neela spotted a figure up ahead dragging something along the floor that was nearly his size, a shape so familiar she caught her breath. "Hey!" she shouted. She started running toward Mohan, jumping over someone's suitcase and almost running head-on into a man carrying a hen inside a wire cage.

As soon as Mohan saw her, he took off in the opposite

direction. Faster and faster he ran, weaving in and out of people drifting along the platform, the veena case rocking wildly behind him. He moved on, heading toward a train that was about to depart. To her horror, Neela saw that it was a train bound for Thanjavur, *his* train, and he was only a few feet away. With his speed he would make it to the train before they did. Neela willed her legs to move faster, as on the days she raced to class, but this time she had to make it count. He was almost there. She could see Lynne and Pavi now in her periphery, dodging passengers, all of them scrambling to beat Mohan to the train.

With a burst of speed, Neela tore down the last few yards, just as Mohan climbed aboard. Without thinking, Neela leaped onto the steps of the train car.

Mohan stared at her in surprise. "Get off the train!" he said. "You have no ticket." He stood between her and the veena case.

"Give me back my veena," Neela said. "You're stealing it!"

"Suit yourself," he declared. "They'll kick you off soon enough." With that he turned to enter the car, but Neela lunged forward to grab on to the hard plastic shell of the case. Around them, she heard the sound of the train whistle.

"Let go!" Mohan hissed. With a monstrous heave, he pulled the veena out of her hands, sending her reeling. She took a step back to steady herself and suddenly felt the ground disappear under her. She had fallen into the gap between the train and the platform, with her upper half still inside the train and her legs dangling over the edge.

"Neela!" Pavi shouted from the platform. "Get out of there! The train's about to start."

Neela tried desperately to gain a foothold. Her hands clawed the floor while she scrambled to stand up. Beneath her, she saw the ground starting to slide away, and felt the edge of the platform grazing the back of her legs. The train had started to move.

On the platform, Pavi screamed, "Stop the train!" By now, a small audience had formed a circle around Pavi, watching in horror as the train began leaving the station with a young girl wedged in between the platform and train. "Stop the train!" everyone shouted.

Neela felt dizzy, her fingers unable to catch a hold of anything on the cold, metallic floor of the train compartment. Then suddenly she saw a pair of black buffed boots standing squarely in front of her, as two powerful arms pulled her up in one swift motion and planted her, feet-first, on the floor that had been inches from her face only seconds before. She stared up at a tall man with carefully combed hair, a groomed mustache, and a double-breasted uniform with shiny buckles and stripes on the arms. He was the train's ticket collector.

"Are you okay?" he asked in Tamil.

Neela nodded, still dazed. In the background, Mohan tried to slink away, but with such a large instrument it was impossible. The ticket collector's white-gloved finger shot out, pointing to Mohan. "You, stay put," he said. Then he snapped his fingers at someone down the aisle and shouted, "Stop the train!" Another conductor nodded and picked up a white receiver at the front of the car. A few moments later, the wheels of the train ground to a halt.

"So, what is happening here?" the ticket collector asked.

"She tried to jump the train," Mohan said.

"That's not true!" Neela was indignant. "He stole my veena."

The ticket collector looked at the canvas-covered case behind him. "This is a veena?" he asked.

"It's *my* veena," Mohan said. "She's obviously a vagabond off the street."

The ticket collector looked at Neela's Disney World T-shirt. "She does not look like a vagabond to me. Do you have tickets, both of you?"

"Yes," Mohan said quickly, brandishing his. "I'm a valid passenger. *She* is not."

"I don't have a ticket, but I was trying to stop him from stealing my instrument."

The ticket collector looked at them. "Let us settle this on the platform. Out, both of you."

Mohan protested loudly, but a security guard appeared and forced him off the train with Neela.

"Frankly, I do not care who the veena belongs to," the ticket collector said, "but we cannot have young girls jumping onto the trains. And while you have a ticket, sir, I dislike you already for not rushing to the aid of this girl.

When she was hanging on for her life, why did you not help her?" He glared at Mohan.

"It happened so fast," Mohan said. "I did not have the chance before you stepped in."

By now, Lynne, Pavi, and Ravi had joined them.

"Well, you will have to settle this on your own time," the ticket collector continued. "We cannot hold the train for you."

"That's ridiculous," Mohan sputtered. "You have to let me back on the train with my veena."

"But it's not his!" Neela cried.

The ticket collector shook his head. "Who do I believe?"

"I think I can help you with that."

Everyone turned in the direction of the voice. A man had appeared from around the corner, accompanied by two police officers. He was thin, with hair graying along the sides of his head. When Neela saw him, she immediately guessed who he was. What was more astonishing was that directly behind him and the two officers were Neela's parents, Lalitha Patti, and Hal.

"Mom, Dad, Patti!" Neela exclaimed.

"Pa," Mohan said at the same time. "What are you doing here?"

Govindar looked gravely at his son. "The more important question is what are *you* doing here with *that* veena?"

CHAPTER 32

Everyone began talking at once. Neela couldn't help staring at Hal, who went straight to Lynne. After all these months, it was bizarre to see him . . . in *India*.

"How did you know we were here?" Neela asked her family.

"Govindar called to say you'd left a message," Lalitha Patti said, her arm around Neela in a hug.

"We called the police and came here," Mr. Krishnan said. "Computer games, ha."

"You're in big trouble," Mrs. Krishnan warned, her eyes moist. Her glance fell on Ravi. "You too." Ravi gulped silently.

Behind the group, the ticket collector jumped back on the train. Neela waved at him, because, after all, he had saved her life. He nodded as the rush of the wheels whirred past and the train disappeared into the distance. Mohan was watching the train, too. Neela could tell from his face that he wished he were on it. But it was hard to feel any sympathy for him.

"Mohan, tell me why you're here with the veena," Govindar said.

"He tried to steal it," Neela said. "He locked us in the store so he could get away."

"She's lying." Mohan's eyes flashed angrily.

"Neela slipped the lock open," Pavi said. "That's how we escaped."

"Mohan would have got away on the train if Neela hadn't jumped aboard," Lynne added. "He even tried to push her off, but the ticket collector stopped him in time."

"What?" Mrs. Krishnan exclaimed.

Govindar stared at his son. "Tell me this isn't true. Tell me you have more sense."

Mohan clenched his fists and said nothing. Seeing him with his father strangely reminded Neela of her mother and her. It seemed there were some conversations every family had. This was the one where the parent was suggesting the kid was an idiot. Although Mohan was hardly one. Because if Neela and her friends had come just a few minutes later, he would have been on that train and gone forever.

"I thought you had forgotten about this veena," Govindar said. "It is just an ordinary instrument, and—"

"But it isn't," Neela interrupted.

He stopped. "I beg your pardon?"

"It is definitely *not* an ordinary veena," she said. "In fact, Mohan knows exactly how extraordinary it is."

Pavi sighed. "Not the curse again," she muttered.

"No, something else." Neela pointed to the canvas case. "That's a Guru original."

Lalitha Patti said, "But we already know that, Neela."

"Yes, but it's not any Guru original. It's the first one, the *original* one." Neela saw the shock register on Mohan's face, confirming that what she said was true. She pulled out the book from her backpack. "Professor Tannenbaum told me about the original Guru original. Veronica Wyvern came to India with the hope of finding out if she owned it. She had a hunch; she had heard about the curse, but she wasn't sure if her veena was the first one Guru made."

"But what's the big deal if it was the first?" Pavi asked.

"It means it's a rare instrument," Neela explained, "and could be worth hundreds of thousands of dollars. So long as it's intact and with all its original pieces."

There was a silence as this information registered in the minds of everyone.

"So *this* is Guru's first veena?" Lalitha Patti asked.

"Neela, are you sure?" Mr. Krishnan said.

She turned to the bookmarked page. "Guru was the son of a veena maker. He had made many veenas with his dad. But this was the first one he made all by himself. And maybe because of that, he wanted to shake things up, be a little different. So he made the peg box European-looking, and chose a medieval dragon."

“A wyvern,” Hal said.

When he spoke, a range of emotions played through Neela: outrage, bewilderment, guilt. Why should I feel guilty? she thought. But all she said was, “Yes, a wyvern.”

She remembered then what Professor Tannenbaum had told her. “We can’t tell just by looking, though,” she said. “You would need an *expert*, someone to look at the varnish, the markings, and make sure that all the parts of the veena are *original*. But the peg box is a good starting place. Because how many veenas have you seen with a wyvern?” She was proud of herself for remembering so much. She could see from everyone’s faces that they were taking her seriously. Even Mohan was looking at her with grudging respect.

Hal nodded. “Ronnie knew right away it was a wyvern.”

“Sorry to be rude,” Mrs. Krishnan said, “but who exactly are you?”

“That’s Hal,” Neela said. “Veronica Wyvern’s father and Lynne’s grandfather.”

While her parents digested this piece of news, Neela heard Lalitha Patti draw in her breath. Surprised, Neela glanced at her, when she suddenly remembered her conversation with Lynne at the store: *He tried, he really did, but your grandmother said no*. Her grandmother had known about Hal. Just how, Neela would find out later.

“We found the book inside a secret compartment of a desk at the store,” she went on. “I suspect the book is Mohan’s. That’s why he stole the veena and mailed it to the store, using *my* name on the package. He knew the moment he saw it in Lynne's apartment, the veena was the original Guru original."

"I didn't know right away," Mohan blurted, then stopped in horror, realizing he had just incriminated himself. Suddenly he looked completely deflated, as if the air had gone out of him.

"It took me years to find that veena," he said at last. "If you knew who to talk to in Thanjavur—veena makers, vendors, and musicians—they had discussed the possibility for years, that the cursed veena was also the first instrument Guru made. They speculated about the value of the instrument. But no one knew for sure. Then I found that book in a tiny bookstore in Thanjavur, and it contained the first recorded information of Guru's work."

"What about the photograph of Parvati?" Neela asked.

"That was the other proof I had, which showed her as a performer at the Mysore Palace. It confirmed she was a player and that she owned this same instrument. That photograph came from a friend of a friend who acquires old photos of the Mysore Palace."

"What were you planning to do with all this proof?" Mrs. Krishnan asked.

"Originally I wanted to get the veena appraised. There are people who specialize in dating instruments. But now it doesn't matter anymore. I just wanted the instrument."

"Why didn't you tell me all of this before?" Govindar asked softly.

Mohan's voice was ragged. "You would have sold the veena. You did before."

"But weren't you going to sell it yourself?" Lalitha Patti asked.

"Of course not!" Mohan cried. "Don't you see? It's rare, a one-of-a-kind. It's meant to be played on. I would do that. I would *never* sell the veena."

"You *play* the veena?" Neela asked in surprise.

"Of course," Mohan said.

They stared at each other, and for a moment it seemed like there was a strange connection between them. For the first time Neela noticed how young Mohan was.

Just then an announcement blared over the loudspeakers, reminding Neela where they were and what was going on—that Mohan had almost pushed her off a moving train, and that she had forced a confession out of him in front of two police officers. Which was about as bad as it could get, unless, of course, you fell off a moving train. And just like that, the moment passed.

"So if he stole the veena," one of the police officers said, "are you pressing charges?" He looked expectantly at Mr. Krishnan, who had called them in the first place.

"Charges?" Mohan cried. "For what?"

"Stealing, kidnapping," Pavi said. "Being a horse's behind."

"Pavi!" Neela mumbled.

"If I'm getting charged, what about him?" Mohan pointed to Hal. "He stole the veena from Neela in the first place. And let's not forget someone else." He turned to his father. "Tell them," he said bitterly. "Tell them about the 'curse' and the Chennai Music Palace."

"Mohan," Govindar murmured.

"If you won't," he said," I will."

"I think we should stop right here," Govindar said. "I made a mistake, one I regret. But think of all I've done after that, how I've led an honest life as a businessman."

"That's the trouble with you, Pa," Mohan said. "You've always been a businessman, and just that. When I was twelve and I asked for the veena, you could have said yes. When I asked for veena lessons, you could have said yes. That day I stole the veena from the customer who bought it, and you found out, you could have done the right thing."

"And what would that have been?" Govindar barked. "When you have an angry customer in front of you, demanding to know why the veena she paid good hard money for is back in your store, what should I say? My son snuck into your house and stole it? Because he *wanted* it? I used the story of the curse to cover up for what you did."

"Like she would believe that," Mohan said.

"She didn't ask for the veena back, did she?" he asked. "She took a different veena home that day."

"But it didn't end there," Mohan said to everyone else.

"Mohan, please," Govindar said, his voice pleading.

"No, the story of the curse attracted everyone's interest," Mohan said. "We had people drop in, newspapers write about us, and tons of *other* sales. The curse lived on but with a twist—the Chennai Music Palace was cursed, too, because now not only could no one own this instrument, the store couldn't sell it away, either!"

"So you went on stealing the veena from customers who bought it, just to make people think the store was part of the curse?" Neela said in shock.

"No, but my father *lied* to make it seem that way," Mohan said. "He made up stories about how the veena was sold and reappeared back in the store. He told them to customers, to the newspaper, to anyone who wanted to hear. It was the same curse everyone knew about, only with the Chennai Music Palace built into it."

"I don't get it," Neela said. "The Chennai Music Palace *was* always part of the curse. It's the place Guru sold the instrument and—"

"No, it isn't," Mohan said. "That's all part of my father's lie. Guru never sold the veena to our store. Guru sold that veena to someone else long before—look at the date on that photograph of Parvati: 1903. Guru sold it soon after that. But the veena came to our store only about twenty years ago, from a different vendor. If you ask anyone living in Thanjavur before then, they will tell you about a curse, all right. They'll tell you how gifted Parvati was, how the veena was decorated with her own wedding jewels. They'll tell you she was the darling of the Mysore court, how she turned thin and sickly when she lost the veena, and never forgave Guru. They'll tell you the curse wore on, and no one could play that instrument again. But what they will *not* tell you about is Chennai Music Palace. That part was my father, fabricated and passed on by word of mouth, starting twenty years ago. And the updated curse was such a success that this is the only version you will probably hear today."

Govindar looked embarrassed. "It was publicity. And it did generate more interest in our store. But I never did anything disreputable. And when Veronica Wyvern came one day to the store and bought the instrument—"

"For a hugely inflated price," Mohan added.

Govindar glared at him. "After she bought the instrument, we didn't need that kind of publicity anymore. The store was doing just fine on its own. And yes, looking back, I'm embarrassed by what I did." He turned to Mohan. "But I never resorted to stealing."

As the two of them spoke, Neela stared at the circle of people standing around her with fresh eyes. Each person here, including herself, and even her parents in their own implausible ways, had engaged in some kind of deception. She thought of how she had lied, spied on people, and broken into a church computer, just for a chance to get closer to the veena.

She looked at the veena case now. It was monstrous, but she couldn't help thinking, just one simple tug at the handle, a few steps back, and she could sneak off with the veena, she could hop on any one of the trains departing around them, just as Mohan had tried to do. She imagined herself as she always did, fast-forwarded in time until she was all grown up. She would be giving concerts in India and around the world. And she would be performing on the legendary veena, famous for being cursed and for being the original

Guru original, with its unmatched sound, its haunting tone, and not to mention, its hefty price tag. She and her instrument would be the envy of veena connoisseurs everywhere.

But then, afterward, what would she do when the concerts were over? She would live a life of paranoia, as Veronica had, wondering who might steal the veena next. Or else she'd store the veena away in a bank vault, where it would never be played again.

Govindar now turned to look at everyone. "Neela, Mr. Wyvern, the rest of you, I suggest you go home and decide what is to be done with the instrument. It seems like Mohan and I have many things to work out. First, we must make a trip to the police station."

Mohan was stunned. "The police station? Why?"

"To show our customers that we are making honest people of ourselves," Govindar declared.

"Don't hand the veena over to them," Mohan pleaded. "I panicked. I shouldn't have run. Let's get it appraised, find out its real worth. And there's more."

"What more can there be?" Govindar asked, sounding tired. "Come, let's go." He signaled to the police officers to help him.

"You have no idea what you're giving away." Mohan's voice could be heard as the police officers led him away with Govindar following. "We'll see who has the last laugh. . . ."

"Well, *that* was weird," Pavi said.

"Did you really jump the train?" Mrs. Krishnan asked Neela.

"She totally did," Pavi said. "You should've seen it. She was cool."

"I was so scared," Lynne said. "You must really care for the veena to risk your life."

"Yeah," Neela said uncertainly. She hadn't planned to risk anything—it just happened. Before she knew it, she was dangling for her life until the ticket collector rescued her. Hearing Lynne now made Neela feel strange.

Mrs. Krishnan shuddered. "Do you know how many people are killed doing that?"

"On that note," Mr. Krishnan said, "let's go home."

"But what about the veena?" Pavi asked. "We have to decide who gets to keep it."

Mr. Krishnan stopped. "Oh." He looked uncertainly at Neela, Hal, and Lynne.

"But Prasant, he *stole* the veena from Neela," Mrs. Krishnan said in a low voice.

"Lakshmi," Mr. Krishnan said.

"It's okay," Hal said wearily. "I *did* steal it. All I can say is that I'm sorry. If you could only see in my heart how deeply sorry I am."

Why was Hal being nice now? Neela felt a queasiness in her stomach. At that moment, though, Hal's eyes were fixed on the veena case. He grasped Lynne's hand and said, "Strange that the veena made it back to Chennai. Wonder what your mom would have to say about that."

"She'd say that the veena isn't ours anymore," Lynne said softly.

In the din of the bustling train station, a silence fell on the party of people gathered around the instrument case. No one knew what to say, but they were all stirred by the same feeling of regret. Some moments later, Neela stepped forward; the effort was almost unbearable. But the decision was so clear she didn't stop to confirm it with her grandmother or parents. She wheeled the instrument case to Lynne and put the handle in her hand.

"Here," Neela said. "It belonged to you first."

"What?" Lynne stared at her.

"Oh, Neela, are you sure?" Mrs. Krishnan whispered. She looked ready to cry.

"I can buy another veena," Neela said, carefully and meaningfully.

Her grandmother nodded in silent approval.

"Unbelievable," Hal said, stunned. "I don't know what to say. Thank you."

"Yes, thank you," Lynne said quietly. "But are you really sure?"

Neela thought if someone asked her one more time, she would bolt down the terminal, clutching the instrument case in her hands. How could anyone be sure of anything? But the stomachache had subsided, and her palms didn't tingle anymore. So she said, "Yes, I'm sure. But you better hurry off or I might change my mind."

A few minutes later, Lynne, Hal, and the veena were gone.

Mr. Krishnan gathered Neela in his arms. "That was tremendous. After so many people trying to steal that instrument, you're the first one to give it up."

"You did the right thing when I couldn't," Lalitha Patti said.

Mrs. Krishnan nodded. "So courageous, Neela."

Neela didn't want to talk about it. "Let's go home."

As they walked back to their car, Pavi pulled Neela back. "What you did was totally cool. And I know how hard it was to give that veena up, after everything that's happened."

Neela flushed under Pavi's praise. It was different to hear it from her.

Pavi went on. "Listen, I've been kind of a twerp about Matt. I know he helped you a lot, and you wouldn't have figured things out without him."

"You helped, too, Pavi."

"I just didn't want things to change because of him. Because, you know, we barely get to see each other during the school year." Pavi's voice was gruff, but Neela knew it was because her friend always had a hard time sharing her feelings.

"But things won't change," Neela said. "And Matt's nice. You'd like him."

"You think so?"

"Sure. And anyway, we'll always have time to do stuff on the weekends and on the way to veena lessons."

"Oh, yeah, I forgot to tell you," Pavi said. "I'm quitting when we get back."

"What?" Neela was stunned. "I thought you loved the veena."

Pavi shook her head. "Dude, love is kind of a strong

word. Next fall my coach thinks I might be able to make the swim team. So my afternoons are shot—I'll be at the pool every day."

"Wow." Neela took a moment to let it sink in. "What about Sudha Auntie? She'll probably warn you that swimming leads to indigestion!"

Pavi laughed. "Yeah, I guess I'll risk it."

They continued walking. Neela felt sad thinking about Pavi no longer being there at the lessons. There would be no more trips together to Sudha Auntie's house. And no one to snicker with behind their teacher's back. But Pavi really liked swimming. And she had to do what was right for her, even if it meant giving up something else.

They reached the end of the platform, when a police officer stopped in front of them. "Pavitra!" he exclaimed. "What are you doing here?"

"I was involved with that veena escapade," she said. "That's why you're here, right?"

The police officer nodded, still looking surprised.

"They went that way." Pavi pointed in the direction Govindar and Mohan had left with the other officers. "But they left a long time back."

"Then I should hurry. Take care." The police officer dashed off.

"Who was that?" Neela asked.

"That's my uncle, the assistant police commissioner." Pavi saw Neela staring at her. "What, you thought I made that up?"

CHAPTER 33

That evening, Neela and her family sat on the rooftop, where several containers of jasmine were in bloom, filling the air with a soft, fruity fragrance. Neela and Sree drank Ovaltine, while the adults drank weak tea, and everyone talked about the events of the day. By then, Neela had also filled them in on the other details that had unfolded in Arlington.

"So, do you still think you did the right thing?" her grandmother asked. "Are you angry at that girl for taking your veena?"

"Lynne didn't take my veena, I gave it to her," Neela said. "And . . . I sort of had to do it. It wasn't just because she needed the veena. It was because . . . I didn't want to be like Mohan. He did so many wrong things because he wasn't happy with what he had. But I did wrong things, too. All because of an instrument."

"You're being hard on yourself," Lalitha Patti said. "I would not put you in the same category as Mohan."

"But maybe I would turn into someone like him," Neela said. "There's something about that veena. Everyone who's had it or been near it starts to do dishonest things."

"That's true," Mr. Krishnan said. "From Hal to Lynne to Mohan."

"And Guru," Neela said. "Don't forget him. He's the one who sold it in the first place without telling his wife."

"Yes," her father said. "And you. And my mother. Let's not forget the two of you."

"And us," Neela said. She looked at her grandmother, who at that moment turned away, as if she sensed the question that had formed in Neela's mind.

Instead, Lalitha Patti set down her cup and said, "Why don't we throw in the customs people at the airport while we're at it. Shame on them for not flagging a haunted instrument!"

"And Sree!" Neela said.

"And me!" he said, not knowing what he was including himself in.

Neela glanced at her mother, who had been quiet throughout. She saw her get up and walk around the rooftop, stopping from container to container to look at the flowers in bloom. Neela went to join her.

In her hand, Mrs. Krishnan held a few stray jasmine flowers, which she gave to Neela. "The scent of jasmine always reminds me of being a little girl," she said. "I would wear flowers in my hair every day in the evenings."

Neela held the sweet flowers up to her face and breathed in deeply. Above her, stars were appearing one by one in the darkening sky. Mrs. Krishnan began weaving the jasmine into her daughter's hair.

"I was thinking over the past couple of months," she said, "how we seemed to be misunderstanding each other."

"You should have told me the story about the veena," Neela said. "Not because it would have made a difference, but because it was important for me to know."

"I see that now. It's just that I could tell you were keeping things from me, and you just felt so . . . distant."

"I didn't know how to tell you what was happening," Neela said, "without you freaking out about it."

Mrs. Krishnan smiled. "Okay, I'll try not to 'freak out' so much from now on."

As Mrs. Krishnan continued adding more flowers to her hair, Neela wondered what Lynne and her grandfather were doing, if they were at home, looking at the veena that was now theirs. No more sneaking around, no more guilt. Just memories and photographs and the touch of sleek jackwood.

Neela's heart ached. She would miss that veena. It would be like a best friend that moved away and never came back. But she would get over it.

"One thing I wanted to ask," Mrs. Krishnan said. "Where did you ever learn to slide open a lock?"

"My friend taught me," Neela said cautiously. "We were talking about it at school one day." She still didn't mention Matt by name.

"Who? Penny?"

Neela took a breath. She didn't want to be dishonest anymore. "No, Matt," she said.

Mrs. Krishnan was silent for a moment, then continued with the flowers. "Is this that boy who sits next to you? The one who's always late?"

"Yeah, but—" Neela was about to get annoyed that this was the only way her mother could characterize him, but Mrs. Krishnan went on.

"Yes, Ms. Reese was telling me about him at the store that day when I ran into her," she said. "She said he was a good friend for you. And a bright kid."

Neela turned around. "She said that?" She searched her mother's face to see what her mother thought about the whole thing. "And you're okay with it?"

Mrs. Krishnan shrugged. "As long as he's a nice friend, sure."

Neela turned back to keep the surprise from showing on her face. Sometimes she had no idea what her mother would say or do.

Her mother glanced back at the group seated on the bamboo chairs.

"Well, Sree has certainly learned a lot from you," she said. "Maybe in a few years, he can play the veena, too, if he wants." She finished with the flowers and gave Neela's hair a final pat.

"Yeah," Neela said. "Sudha Auntie can have someone new to terrorize."

"Ha," her mother said.

As the days continued, a pall hung over the rest of the vacation for Neela. At night, she found herself dreaming of being back at the Chennai Train Station. Except in her dreams, the station was always empty of people, and she was standing alone with the *maya veena*, as if guarding it from something unknown. She wasn't sure why she dreamed about the veena now when she knew it was gone. Maybe searching for it had filled her life with more excitement than she'd ever known, and now her dreams were filling in the adventure that was missing from her waking life. Or maybe she just missed having such a special instrument. Whatever it was, she woke up each morning and moped around her grandparents' house, feeling strangely sorry for herself.

Lalitha Patti, who had been watching her, said one day, "Come with me, I'm going to the music store."

"What do you mean?" Neela asked from the couch, where she was lying down and reading a book she had already read before.

"Govindar found my veena, the one that got stolen by mistake, stored away under some sheets at the store. He's repaired it and polished it and says it's ready to be picked up."

"How can you think of going there after what he did?" Mrs. Krishnan said. She was sitting across from Neela, playing checkers with Sree on the floor.

"I do have to get my veena back," Lalitha Patti said. "And I think Govindar feels very bad about everything. Besides, he isn't the one who stole the veena. It was his son." She turned to Neela. "What do you say? Also, Govindar has something for you."

"What could he possibly have for her?" Mrs. Krishnan wondered.

"Well, she won't know unless she comes, right?" Lalitha Patti said.

Neela wasn't sure she wanted to see Govindar or his store again, but her grandmother had made her curious. She got up from the couch. "I'll go, but if Mohan's there, I'm leaving," she said.

"I'm sure he's saying the same thing about you," Lalitha Patti said.

At the store, Govindar saw them immediately and waved. His face looked weary, as if he had been through a lot in the last week. Neela noticed that Mohan wasn't around, and the framed newspaper article had been removed from the wall.

"Lalitha, Neela, good to see you," Govindar said. "I wish we could have parted on better circumstances last time."

"Mistakes happen," Lalitha Patti said graciously.

They sure do, Neela thought. Like having a crook for a son. Not to mention being a liar yourself. But she smiled and said nothing.

"Please follow me," Govindar went on. "We can talk in the back." He signaled to his assistant to step up to the counter.

"Um, are we going to the back room?" Neela asked.

"Yes, is that a problem?" Govindar asked. Then he saw Neela's face.

"It's fine," she said. "Just don't close the door. It still gives me the heebie-jeebies."

If Govindar was familiar with the heebie-jeebies, he didn't say. But inside the back room, he did leave the door wide open. "First item of business," he said. He directed Lalitha Patti to a worktable with two veenas on it, each covered by a heavy cloth. He lifted the cloth over one of them to reveal a shiny, freshly varnished veena that Neela recognized as her grandmother's. "I think you will see everything is in place," he said, "including the jewel work on the peg box."

Neela's grandmother bent over the instrument and studied it carefully. "Good work, Govindar," she said.

As they continued looking over the veena, Neela's eyes wandered around the room. It was hard to believe that just a week ago, she, Pavi, and Lynne had been stuck here with no way of escaping until a box of Cracker Jack saved the day.

Govindar noticed Neela looking around her. "Undoubtedly your mind is filled with the heebie-jeebies of last week," he said.

"Um," she said, trying not to giggle at the way this sounded.

"I am deeply sorry and ashamed by my son's actions," he went on. "For as long as I can remember, Mohan was obsessed with that veena. After we sold it away so many years ago, I was sure he had forgotten about it. But clearly he hadn't. And he knew a lot more about the veena than I did."

"So the girl and her grandfather, are they now insanely rich?" Lalitha Patti asked. She spoke casually, but Neela knew her grandmother well enough to hear in her voice a twinge of envy. It was hard not to feel it herself. After all, it wasn't every day you gave up a rare and valuable instrument because it was the right thing to do. The wrong thing to do, it seemed, would have been so much easier. Neela sighed unconsciously, waiting for Govindar to confirm what Lalitha Patti had asked.

Instead he shrugged. "Veenas weren't meant to withstand the test of time. Think of the heat and humidity. In Guru's case, his veena *did* last for so long, and we don't really know why. Still, an instrument is only worth what someone is willing to pay for it."

"Wait a minute. The original Guru original is rare and priceless, but no one wants to buy it?" Neela crossed her arms.

"Well, I didn't say no one," Govindar said with a note of sadness in his voice. Neela realized then that he was thinking about his son. "There are people, just not a lot of them."

There was a silence, and then Lalitha Patti spoke. "Govindar, when you're ready, could we talk about the other matter?"

Someone cleared his throat. Govindar's assistant was at the door, motioning to him.

"I will be right back," Govindar said. "But yes. We will get to the other matter shortly."

Neela and Lalitha Patti stood next to each other at the table while they waited for Govindar to return.

"Did you want to be insanely rich?" Neela asked.

"It isn't important," her grandmother said. "But one can't help being curious."

Neela nodded. She ran her finger along the sides of the worktable where the other covered instrument rested. Then at last, because she couldn't help it, she lifted the cloth. It was another full-size veena, this one made in a honey-colored jackwood. The varnish looked like it had been recently applied. The frets and strings gleamed. And the peg box . . . Neela looked at it again. It wasn't a dragon, but a fish painted in blue. She had never seen a fish on a veena before. Instinctively, she looked for a set of initials on the neck and was disappointed to see none. That would have been impossible, she thought. Guru was no more.

"Beautiful," Lalitha Patti said.

Neela agreed. The veena wasn't as ornate as the old one. There was no ivory inlay in the pegs or along the sides. But it had been stained in two tones, the top a lighter honey, and the back and bottom, a darker, richer shade.

It reminded her unexpectedly of butter melting in a pan. Without thinking, she plucked the strings. They had not been tuned, and vibrated off-key, but the tone was warm and gentle. She continued to pluck the strings, listening to the notes fill the small room. It had a bigger sound than she expected. She noticed that the frets were closer together and that the whole veena seemed smaller than her original one. When she spanned the width of two frets with her fingers, she saw that they fit her hand perfectly.

Just then Govindar returned. She pulled her hand back, embarrassed.

He smiled. "Go on. That veena is new."

"It's beautiful," she said. "Really big sound."

"You think so?" he asked. He glanced at Lalitha Patti.

Neela shrugged. "I'm no expert. It just felt like it was . . . filling up the room."

"Well . . . it's yours," Govindar said.

Neela gave a start and checked his face, then her grandmother's, to see if they were joking. Lalitha Patti beamed. "I told you Govindar had something for you."

"Yeah, but a veena?" Neela said in surprise.

"Govindar threw in a huge discount, but the veena is from me, and—"

Govindar waved his hand. "No discount."

Lalitha Patti stopped. "Govindar, I thought we had a deal," she said, her voice rising.

"No discount," he said, "because the veena is free. Courtesy of Chennai Music Palace. And Mohan."

"Mohan?" Neela repeated.

"Believe it or not, he wanted you to have a veena. He was very angry that you found a way to separate him from the veena of his dreams. But you made an impression on him, too. Using money from his own bank account, he had this veena bequeathed to you. He said it wasn't every day he met a girl in America that wanted to play the veena. So there you go. Your own veena. Not a Guru original, but would you believe it, a veena made by a fellow named T.G. Mukund, also known as Guru's grandson. Yes, grandson! And it's his first one. So you have an original, after all!"

Neela was speechless. Mohan, the person who stole the *maya veena*, who locked her in the store and tried to push her off a train, was now giving her . . . another veena? Had she understood correctly? Or had the world started spinning in the opposite direction?

"Here," Govindar said, reaching into his pocket. "He asked me to give this to you. I have not read it. I guess he wanted to explain for himself."

Neela took the letter from him and began reading it.

Dear Neela,

I heard what you did, giving up the maya veena, and I must comment on how silly and foolish you were. When you are grown up, you will look back at the day with regret.

Still, something about your gesture moved me. Not to tears . . . but to caution. Remember what I told you in Boston? How the veena is a dying art? Never has this been more true. All of us, friends and enemies alike, must join forces to see that this beautiful music tradition remains with us. I accept the torch and pass it on to you. This veena, which I ask you in turn to accept, is a measure of my desire to see you continue playing.

Best of luck, though I must say with all sincerity that I hope to never run into you again.

—R.K. Mohan

Neela stared at the letter when she was done. What did it all mean? Was Mohan a decent person after all?

"What does it say?" Lalitha Patti wanted to know.

"He wants me to keep playing," she said, still surprised. She turned to Govindar. "What happened to Mohan? Is he here? Or in . . ." She didn't know how else to say it. "Is he in jail?"

"Dear God, no," Govindar said. "We went home immediately after we went to the station. The police aren't interested in such things, just a big fat bribe. It's funny, but it took this whole experience to make me realize how unhappy Mohan had been. The two of us had a long chat. He said he was sorry, and I was sorry, too. And now he is in Thanjavur. I sent him. He is taking care of his uncle, who hurt his back, and he is learning the veena with one of the master teachers there."

"Wow," Neela said.

"I miss him," Govindar said. "But it was the right thing to do."

"Yes," Neela said. She knew all about doing the right thing.

~

On the ride home, Neela brought up something that had been on her mind ever since the day at the train station. "You knew Hal was Veronica's father all along, didn't you?" she asked.

A look of guilt came over Lalitha Patti. "I was wondering if you would ever ask me that. The truth is, I didn't. That is, I didn't believe him when he called me. After the newspaper article ran, I got so many phone calls, so many weird people approaching me with all kinds of phony claims. How was I to know he was telling the truth?"

"Would it have mattered?" Neela asked. "Would you have given him the veena?"

"I—I don't know. But what I do feel bad about is . . ." Lalitha Patti swallowed. "I knew I had Veronica's veena, from the time I bought the instrument. I remember her performing on it at the concert before her crash. The instrument was so unusual, so striking, and when it comes to veenas, I have a photographic memory. I remember everything, every little detail about anything that strikes my fancy. So when I saw it a year or so later in a tiny store about forty minutes from here, I was baffled—how could her veena survive the crash? Yet, evidently, it had. The salesman had no clue about what he had. He didn't even know what a Guru original was. But I did. I bought the veena cheap and took it home. It became my secret. I told no one, not even my husband."

"So when I lost the instrument and I told you about Hal . . ." Neela started.

Lalitha Patti shook her head. "It was too late by then. Honestly, I didn't put the two things together. I never realized that your Hal was the same man who phoned me." She looked down at her hands. "But I did know about Veronica, and I didn't tell you. Maybe if I had, *you* would have connected the dots sooner."

"But what was so wrong with having Veronica's veena, anyway? Why *didn't* you tell me or Thatha?"

Lalitha Patti let out a sigh. "I can't explain it, but I was ashamed to buy a veena that belonged to someone who had died in a horrible crash. It seemed like bad luck."

"You could have performed an aarti."

"No aarti can remove that kind of thing."

The car turned onto their street as Ravi expertly navigated around a large pothole in the middle that had accumulated rainwater from the past week.

As they drove the last few blocks, Neela thought of Mohan in Thanjavur, doing what he wanted at last. It was odd, but she found herself glad, imagining him taking lessons and becoming a musician. In the past two months, so many people had done terrible things, they had been entirely untrustworthy, and yet they had redeemed themselves in one way or another. And though she wasn't sure why, it felt as if a great crisis had been averted.

"I asked you before, I'll ask you again," Lalitha Patti said. "Do you regret giving away the veena?"

Neela shook her head. "That veena was cursed, after all," she said softly. "Not because it vanished—maybe it never did. It was because everyone wanted it so badly. For different reasons, but the wanting was the same. That *wanting* was the curse."

They pulled into the driveway.

"What about you?" Neela asked. "Do you miss the veena?"

It was Lalitha Patti's turn to shake her head. "No, I have everything I need already."

EPILOGUE

From the time Neela got back to Arlington, two things changed almost at once. The first was that Neela and Matt started walking home together from school most days, stopping at Winthrop to talk for a few minutes before going their separate ways. When Matt found out what had happened in India, he was impressed. "I told you the credit card trick would work," he said. "Or, that is, the baseball card trick."

The other change was that Neela and Lynne became friends. At first, Lynne kept her distance. Then gradually they began talking at their lockers, in the lunch line, and in class. One day Lynne said, "I thought you'd be cool. That's why I tried not to talk to you."

"What?" Neela burst out laughing. "That sounds like an insult."

Lynne flushed. "Well, my grandfather was bugging me to befriend you. But then he did that awful thing, so there was no chance of being friends with you afterward."

Neela pulled at a loose thread on her shirt. "So did you ever find out what the veena is worth? Are you now insanely rich?" She couldn't help echoing her grandmother's words.

Lynne pushed her frizzy hair back. "It's funny you ask. While we were in India, Grandpa and I went to an appraiser. Just for insurance purposes," she added quickly. "Not that we would ever sell the veena, because, um, that would be wrong."

Neela nodded, waiting to hear the dollar figure. How much did a rare veena cost anyway?

"So the appraiser did a basic examination and said the veena was very old. But to do a complete examination he would have to get the varnish chemically tested, and a bunch of other things that are hugely expensive, which he couldn't do, so he'd have to send it to some place in Mumbai. He said the value of the veena also depended on a ruby that was once embedded in the face of the dragon."

"A ruby?" Neela repeated.

"You can't tell by looking, but with his tools, he detected some residue of the stone. He was familiar with the story of Parvati, and he said rumor had it that the ruby was a gift from the King of Mysore. If that's true, the stone itself would be a priceless gem today."

"Was it one of her wedding jewels?" Neela wondered, remembering Mohan's book.

"Maybe. But we don't have the ruby, and we don't know what happened to it. So Grandpa and I decided not to get the instrument appraised anymore. We weren't planning to sell the veena, and without the ruby, the original isn't fully the original anyway."

A missing ruby.

Neela stopped. "Mohan," she said out loud.

Lynne didn't understand. "What do you mean?"

"Mohan's ruby ring."

Lynne drew in her breath. "You don't think he had it all the time? And *knew*?"

There was a silence as both girls digested this possibility.

"If he has the ruby," Lynne said slowly, "he might come after the veena. He's stolen it before. He could do it again. Maybe the curse *is* true and the veena will disappear again."

Neela wondered the same things herself. But then she saw Lynne's face. "Don't worry," she said. "Mohan wanted to play the veena, and he's doing that. And he's in Thanjavur, the best place in the world for him to be. He wouldn't jeopardize all of that."

"You think so?" Lynne asked anxiously.

Neela wasn't sure about anything when it came to Mohan, but she nodded anyway.

Lynne breathed a sigh of relief. "Thanks, Neela. I feel better."

And that was when Neela decided to put Mohan and the ruby ring out of her mind for good. After all, her life had gotten so much better since the veena mystery was solved.

She had a new veena, she was playing better, and she had two new friends in her life. And even if she didn't see Pavi at their lessons, she saw her on the weekends and whenever their moms got together during the week. Besides, the problem of losing her carpool partner was soon solved.

One evening after dinner, while Sudha Auntie was over, the doorbell rang.

"More visitors—what, my company alone isn't good enough?" Sudha Auntie joked.

Mrs. Krishnan was equally surprised. "Who could it be?" she wondered. When she and Neela answered the door, they found Lynne and her grandfather on the steps.

"Hi," Lynne said. "Can we come in?"

"Sure," Neela said, shivering from the cold air outside the front door.

"My grandfather wanted us to come," Lynne started when they were inside.

"Okay," Mrs. Krishnan said politely. Since the day at the train station, Neela's mother had made up her mind not to hate them. But she hadn't made up her mind to like them just yet, either.

Hal glanced around the room, then turned to Neela. "I came because I never thanked you properly, Neela. Here I am, once a minister, and my good senses had left me. All I can say is that I'm sorry and hope you can forgive me."

"You don't have to apologize again," Neela said.

Hal shook his head. "No, you ought to know. I told you how much Veronica meant to me. But I didn't tell you how much what you did meant to me, too. It's changed our lives. Lynne and me, we're finally talking these days like we didn't before. I'm starting to understand her pain, her difficulty with living around an old-timer like me. In fact, we're finally joining the twenty-first century and getting a computer." He gave Lynne a playful pat on her back.

Lynne looked embarrassed by her grandfather. "The good news is that I'm going to learn the veena," she said to Neela. "We wondered if you have a teacher to recommend."

Neela and her mother looked at Sudha Auntie.

"Actually, we know someone with an opening, don't we?" Mrs. Krishnan asked. "What a lucky coincidence."

"If you believe in coincidences," Sudha Auntie said.

Mrs. Krishnan smiled at Neela. "I believe in luck."

Sudha Auntie took a card from her handbag and held it out to Hal. "Please call me and we'll make the proper arrangements for Lynne's veena instruction."

"Wonderful, thank you. We'll definitely be in touch." He took the card. "Sorry to intrude on you all like this. You've been a good sport, Neela." He turned as if to go, then stopped. "But since we're here, would you mind playing us something?"

"Grandpa!" Lynne said.

"It's just that neither of us know anything about playing the veena." Hal turned to Neela. "No pressure here. You can say no, if you want."

Neela wondered what to do. What if she messed up? What if she forgot some notes? If she made a mistake, her mom would know right away. Not to mention Sudha Auntie, who would probably point out to everyone exactly what Neela was doing wrong.

But before Neela could say anything, Sudha Auntie spoke. "That's an *excellent* suggestion," she said. "You'll also get to hear what my most promising pupil sounds like."

Neela was agog. *Promising?* Had Sudha Auntie actually said something nice about her for a change? Behind her teacher, Mrs. Krishnan was smiling and shrugging as if to say, Yes, it's been known to happen.

"Let me get my veena," Neela said.

It took a few minutes to tune. The sound of the strings being adjusted filled the room, and carried all the way upstairs, where Sree had nearly fallen asleep. But when he and Mr. Krishnan heard it, they crept down to listen. On the couch, the others waited patiently as the tuning continued, up and down, until all the strings were correct.

Neela cleared her throat. "I'm going to play a *keerthana*. Do you know what that is?"

Lynne and Hal shook their heads.

"A keerthana is a kind of song," Sudha Auntie explained. "After you learn your scales and elementary songs, you start to learn keerthanas. This is the first one I'm teaching Neela."

With that, Neela began. The new veena had taken time to get used to, but she soon found it a far more powerful instrument than her grandmother's. Her hands shook slightly, then steadied as she played on, taking advantage of the sound. The keerthana she was learning was filled with long, lilting melodic lines, each of them like a small mountain to climb until she reached the summit, breathless and ready for the next valley to cross. She was conscious of Sree and her father on the stairs, and her mother, Sudha Auntie, Lynne, and Hal, sitting around her. But this time the few mistakes she made didn't faze her, and she even stopped counting them. Her notes grew bolder as her keerthana sailed in the air and washed over everyone in the room, the honey-toned instrument rocking slightly while Neela played.

AUTHOR'S NOTE

Several years ago, I was on the phone with my niece, when I realized I had forgotten to send her a birthday present. So I said, "I'm writing a story. About you." Right then, while she was on the phone, I wrote the first page. She likes mysteries, so I made the story a mystery, about her instrument getting stolen in a church, and . . . you might guess where this is going. That first page, which I read to Neela on the phone, followed by a second and third, was the beginning of what would eventually become *Vanished*.

I should point out that my niece, Neela, bears little resemblance to the Neela that ended up in my book. The funny thing about real life is that it doesn't always translate into good fiction. As writers, we might borrow bits and pieces from our lives. But most of the time, we have to make things up.

When I first began, I wrote about a veena because that was what my niece played. Later, I thought of changing it to a violin. As a violinist, I know the mechanics of playing the instrument. But I didn't want to write about a violin. I wanted to write about something I didn't know. And I didn't know much about veenas. I had to learn everything from scratch. By observing, researching, and asking a lot of questions, I was able to get closer to the truth of what it might be like to play this ancient and stately instrument.

The veena comes from South India and is part of a musical tradition known as Carnatic music. In the novel, when Neela talks about *ragam* (scale), *thalam* (beat), or *keerthana* (a musical composition), these are terms used frequently in Carnatic music. The veena is also one of India's oldest instruments, dating back to the eleventh century, or even earlier. Some historians suggest that a stringed lute instrument described in the *Vedas*, a body of religious Hindu texts composed around 1500 B.C., is, in fact, the veena.

Made from jackwood, a full-size veena can range in size from four to six feet, and can weigh from ten to twelve pounds. The instrument is positioned on the floor, partly against the player's lap, and is played by plucking its strings. The veena has no counterpart in Western music, but in terms of sheer size, the double bass might be a musical friend for the portly veena.

Like the veena in the story, all veenas have a peg box decorated with the head of an animal, which can be made from wood or papier-mâché. The animal can also have other details, like ivory (a material whose trade has been banned in many parts of the world, including the United States), gemstones, and intricate carving. Generally, the animal is thought to ward off bad luck, kind of like a lucky rabbit's foot. More often than not, the animal on the peg box is a dragon.

Dragons have always occupied a special place in my heart. In high school, I was fascinated by the tale of King Arthur and the knights of the Round Table. Like Lynne, I often doodled in my notebook, drawing knights in armor, ladies with special powers, and dragons—many dragons. When the dragon in my novel began to take on a greater role, I did more research and stumbled upon the wyvern.

Described as a winged creature with two clawed feet, a beaky nose, and a spiked tail, the mythological wyvern is placed in the category of serpent in some countries, and dragon in others. Wyverns often appeared on crests, coat-of-arms, and other forms of heraldry in the Middle Ages. Today, you can spot them on the logos of colleges and other institutions.

To me, the wyvern was perfect for the *maya veena*. With its distinct features, the wyvern was instantly recognizable, describable, and a tad mysterious. And once I brought the veena and wyvern together, I discovered other synergies, too.

In medieval England, the wyvern was seen as a symbol of valor, and also as a harbinger of disease. In Indian art, the veena is often shown with Saraswati, the Hindu goddess of wisdom. But it is also described as the instrument of Ravana, the demon king from India's epic story *The Ramayana*. With the veena and the wyvern both encompassing good and evil associations, it seemed only natural that they should come together as the *maya veena*, a beautiful instrument that attracted people with the best and worst intentions alike.

Even so, *Vanished* isn't just a story about the balance between good and evil, but also how we can sometimes overlook the very things that we love. Because you might wonder how Neela could lose such a big and beloved instrument in the first place. As it turns out, musicians have had a long history of misplacing their instruments. The famous cellist Yo-Yo Ma accidentally left his Stradivarius cello, worth an estimated $2.5 million, in the back of a New York City taxicab. Lucky for him, he was later reunited with his missing cello. Was it circumstance, bad luck, or just one of the perils of being a world-class performer? We might never really know.

FOR MORE ON DRAGONS . . .

To read more about wyverns, other kinds of dragons, and heraldry, here are some books to look at. Most of them are for young people, with the exception of the last title by Arthur Fox-Davies.

Dragons: A Natural History, Karl P.N. Shuker, Simon & Schuster, 1995

Dragonology, The Complete Book of Dragons, Ernest Drake, Candlewick Press, 2003

Bestiary: An Illuminated Alphabet of Medieval Beasts, Jonathan Hunt, Simon & Schuster, 1998

A Complete Guide to Heraldry, Arthur Fox-Davies, Adamant Media Corporation, 2006

FOR MORE ON VEENAS . . .

To learn more about veenas and Carnatic music, visit the New England School of Carnatic Music's Web page: www.nescm.com. Durga Krishnan, the school's founder, is a graduate of the Carnatic Music College of Madras, India, and a certified teacher of Carnatic music. She has lectured at several institutions on the history and development of the veena and Carnatic music.

Better yet, attend a music festival! Music festivals and concerts play an important part in the tradition of Carnatic music, by providing a meeting ground for artists and music lovers. Two major music festivals in the United States include:

- The LearnQuest Music Conference. Hosted by LearnQuest Academy of Music, this is a five-day music festival that offers a chance to hear performances on the veena and a variety of other classical Indian instruments. The LearnQuest Music Conference is held annually in Boston. For more information, visit the LearnQuest Academy of Music Web site: www.learnquest.org.

- The Cleveland Thyagaraja Aradhana. This is a ten-day music festival held annually in Cleveland, Ohio. It's the largest Indian classical music festival outside of India, and provides a wide variety in instrumental and vocal performances. For more information, visit www.aradhana.org.

ACKNOWLEDGMENTS

Publishing a book is the result of perseverance, luck, and most of all, the generosity of those who have guided a writer in the right direction.

I give special thanks to my agent, Steven Malk, who has been with *Vanished* from its inception. In my writing world, I can't think of another person whose judgment I trust more, whose sincerity and unflagging support has helped me in too many ways to count.

I'm also indebted to my editor extraordinaire, Abby Ranger, whose insight, humor, and striving for excellence has made me a better reader, a better writer, and a better person, too.

Thanks to Namrata Tripathi and the rest of the folks at Disney•Hyperion for making *Vanished* a reality.

Thank you to my family: Keerthana, Meera, and Suresh. You are the floor, walls, and roof in my life, holding me up and keeping me safe. Thank you for your love and understanding, for hearing my crazy ideas, for being excited about all the things large and small that happened to my book, and for eating some very strange concoctions for dinner when I was under a deadline.

Thank you to my parents, Geetha and B.R. Ramaprian, and to my brother, Sumanth, who have been the strongest and most enduring advocates in my life. I could not have succeeded in my endeavor to be a writer without your strength of character and your love for me.

Thanks to Neela, Srinidhi, Sumanth, and Bhuvana, for being my good-natured guinea pigs. The time I spent with you was not only one of my happiest, but has provided endless material for my fiction. Thanks for lending me your eyes and your ears, and for reading through the original gobbledygook of my first drafts.

Thank you to Pavitra and Bharat for lending me your names and for being part of the fun.

My sincerest gratitude to Durga Krishnan (no relation to Neela Krishnan!) who generously shared with me her knowledge on the history, mechanics, and other details regarding the veena. As a scholar, musician, and teacher, she answered all my questions with complete thoroughness, kindness, and humility.

I must also thank Mr. A.V. Kashinath for his expertise on the history and craft of veena-making. Like Mohan, Mr.

Kashinath travels frequently from Bangalore, India, to the United States to tune and repair veenas. From him I was able to deduce what a turn-of-the-century veena might look like.

A heap of thanks to Blair Hickson Riley, Gloria Koster, Ian Freedman, Abby Crews, Carol Frank, Howard Whitehouse, Liz Basecu, Amy Spitzley, and Kelly Fineman for reading early drafts.

And where would I be today without the generous support of the online community of children's writers? Special kudos to my writing friends from LiveJournal, and to the Elevensies and Tenners. Thank you for sharing your writing lives with me. You are priceless.

Thanks also to SCBWI for introducing me to the nuts and bolts of children's literature. I had no clue about what I was doing until I got onto their discussion board and attended their conferences.

Thank you to all my friends over the years, especially Elizabeth Luchangco-Yamaguchi, Midori Im, and Neena Dhuri for their support, and to Clare Seaton, who gave me *A Wrinkle In Time* and the gift of letter-writing.

Last of all, thank you to Sasha Ericksen, for your loyalty and your wisdom, and for sleeping out in the Quad with me during sign-ups. I wouldn't have taken that fiction-writing class if it weren't for you. As always, thanks for being my first reader in everything—and I don't mean just books.